To Jackie
Enjoy!
Tonya S Hyche

Just for You

Book 1
Just for You Trilogy

Tonya Sharp Hyche

Novels by
Tonya Sharp Hyche

Swept Away
Breathless
Intersection of Lies
Glass Shadow
Faded Memories (2014)

The Just for You Trilogy
Just for You
Fearless
Painted Fear

All titles available on Kindle
tonyasharphycheauthor.com
2011 © Tonya Hyche
All rights reserved.

ISBN: 1463742568
ISBN-13: 9781463742560

Library of Congress Control Number: 2011912871
CreateSpace Independent Publishing Platform
North Charleston, South Carolina

In memory of my grandfather, 'Gramps' Pat Sharp. Your kindness and loving, gentle heart touched so many lives. You will be missed greatly.

Prologue

Robby Singleton left his last class of the day at eight o'clock and headed home on foot. The walk from campus normally took about ten minutes, but tonight a few students had lingered outside the building to discuss football. Robby waved good-bye to his friends and glanced at the time. He was in no hurry since Becky was still in class. As his mind filled with thoughts of his girlfriend, a smile formed on his lips. Becky and Robby would be all alone tonight since his roommate Derrick was out of town.

Becky Norris was technically a third roommate since she spent all her nights with Robby. On paper, Becky lived with a classmate just a building over in the same apartment complex. Occasionally, Becky would return home just enough to appease her visiting parents. Robby thought the arrangement worked well. His parents didn't approve of him living with a girl before marriage.

As Robby walked along the pathway, he noticed some areas were darker than normal. Stopping, he looked around until he saw the reason—a burned-out streetlight—and quickly made a mental note to call someone. Becky made this same walk, and he didn't like the idea of her making it alone and in the dark. Tonight, though, she would be walking home with Jamie, her pretend roommate, so he wasn't so worried. Both girls were in the nursing program, and on Wednesday nights their lab ended late.

Robby continued on down the path for another minute or so when he felt his cell phone vibrate in his pocket. Stopping for a moment, he pulled it out and read the text.

Got out early. Leaving class now.

A big smile spread across Robby's face. He thought, *Becky is going to be in a good mood tonight. Maybe I'll get lucky.*

Robby picked up his pace. He wanted to get home to shower and download his assignment from class before she got there. Placing his phone back in his pocket, he then slipped his backpack over his other shoulder and began to jog the rest of the way home.

When Robby was five minutes from home the path took a curve and began to run alongside a main road. Suddenly, he stopped when a dark SUV pulled up beside him. From inside the vehicle, a voice said, "You look like you're in a hurry. Want a ride?"

Robby recognized who it was and said, "Nah, I just live over there."

"You sure? It's no problem."

Thinking of Becky he changed his mind. "Sure, why not."

As Becky and Jamie walked along the path, neither one noticing that the streetlight was out, Becky explained how to approach the homework they'd just been given at the end of class.

Jamie rolled her eyes and sighed heavily. "I'm so tired. We work so hard already, and then they go and throw another assignment our way, to complete in just three days!"

"I hear you. At least we have the weekend."

Jamie stopped for a second and then quickly met Becky's pace again. "I thought you and Robby were going to Houston to visit his parents."

Becky shook her head. "No, his dad got called away on a business trip. We're gonna try another weekend."

Jamie nodded and then asked Becky in a teasing voice, "So, do you think he will pop the question once we graduate?"

With a shrug, Becky answered, "I sorta hope not."

Jamie stopped again and exclaimed, "What! Why?"

"I don't know. I guess I'm just not ready. I kind of want to get a job first and work for a while."

"I don't understand. He has plenty of money to support both of you, with or without your salary."

Becky giggled. "Yes, and I look forward to spending it one day."

"I think I know what you mean." Jamie caught Becky's hand and gave it a squeeze. "We've worked so hard to become nurses. It's gonna be so exciting when we get that first job!"

"Exactly! I'm afraid if I rush into marriage there'll be pressure from his parents for us to start a family right away."

"Did Robby's mom ever work?"

"Nope, I think she only went to SMU to snag a rich husband."

Jamie laughed. "Don't let Robby hear you say that!"

"No kidding! His mom can do no wrong." Glancing around, Becky took in her surroundings. "This pathway is a little creepy," she said softly. "Come on, we're almost home."

Jamie nodded, and both girls crossed the last street and headed toward the driveway that led to their apartment. Becky said good-bye to Jamie and then made her way over to building B. After climbing the stairs to the third floor, Becky hurried down the hall and opened the door to apartment B32.

Becky hated coming home to a dark apartment, and both Robby and his roommate Derrick knew that. "Hello?" she called, turning on a light and then closing and locking the door behind her. She placed her books on the kitchen table and made her way around the apartment. On the notepad by the phone, Derrick had left a message saying that he wouldn't be home until tomorrow afternoon, but there was no word from Robby. Remembering how tired he had been this morning, Becky decided to go and check the bedroom in case he had decided to lie down.

She made her way toward the hallway turning lights on as she went. When she was just a few steps away from the bedroom door, she called out, "Robby?"

There was no answer.

At the doorway to their bedroom, Becky peered inside. Seeing Robby's sleeping form there in the semidarkness, she felt relieved and smiled. "Wake up, sleepyhead," she said softly, her fingers resting on the light switch while she waited for him to stir.

"Robby?" she said, a bit more firmly this time. Again, there was no response.

Turning the light on, she glanced around the room and then let out a scream that would have woken the dead. Robby was lying in bed with blood splattered all over the sheets and walls of their bedroom. He was dead. Becky turned and stumbled over her feet, falling to the floor. *Oh my God! Oh my God! No! Not Robby, no!* The hallway began to spin and Becky closed her eyes and balled her fist.

Suddenly Becky feared for her own life and she opened her eyes. A voice was screaming in her head, *Move! You've got to get out of here!* Becky immediately realized the danger she was in. She pushed off the worn carpet with shaky hands and wobbled toward the front door. With each step Becky tried to yell for help but her throat tightened and no sound emerged.

Rounding a corner, she saw the front door. She told herself she was going to make it. She reached for the door just as she heard a noise. Quickly she struggled with the dead bolt as the sound became louder. The door was swung open and Becky came face to face with her neighbor, Jackie. Realizing it had been Jackie banging on the door from the outside, not the killer, relief washed over Becky.

"What the hell Becky! What's going on?"

The image of bright red blood and Robby's dead eyes staring at Becky came roaring back. She began shaking uncontrollably as her mouth parted to respond. Then, Becky closed her eyes as her mind faded to a sea of darkness.

Chapter 1

Monday, September 27th
Five days later

"Lindy, your hubby's on line two."

Dr. Lindy Ashley had just finished writing her last notes on her latest case file when Erin, her secretary, buzzed in. "Erin, he's my ex-husband now, remember?"

"Sorry, I'm still trying to break that habit."

Lindy rolled her eyes and placed her pen down on the file and then pressed two. "Hello, George. What can I do for you?"

"Hi, Lindy. Sorry to call you at work, but I wanted to stop by around six o'clock to pick up Parker and keep him through the weekend."

"George, we decided Parker stays with me. All this running back and forth is confusing the shit out of him."

"I know, Lindy. It's just that I didn't realize how much I would miss the little fellow."

"Well, George, have you thought about getting your own little fellow?"

"What? This coming from you, Miss Sensitivity."

"Yeah, Parker stays with me, and no, you can't come pick him up."

"Lindy, please, I just can't go out and replace him."

Lindy sat back in her brown leather chair and closed her eyes. George was still carrying on with the speakerphone on full blast. Slowly she opened her eyes and scanned her desk until she found the photo of her and Parker at the beach. George had snapped the shot just as Parker jumped up and caught the Frisbee. Parker was six in the photo, but, according to the lifespan of Jack Russells, he had several more good years ahead of him. Silently she asked herself, *Am I being fair?*

Erin popped in the doorway and broke her train of thought. "Sorry to interrupt, but your four o'clock appointment is here."

"Thanks, Erin. Give me two minutes and send him in."

George suddenly sounded louder. "Am I on speakerphone? You know I hate when you do that, Lindy."

"Well, apparently there are other things you hate about me or you wouldn't have left our marriage *and* our dog to begin with."

Silence followed.

Fifteen seconds passed and then Lindy finally spoke. "Okay, you can come and pick up Parker Saturday morning around ten o'clock. But this is the last time, so say your good-byes."

"Can I assume you still run at eight o'clock with him?"

"What is your point?"

"If Parker runs with you, he's not gonna run again with me."

Flabbergasted, Lindy quickly sat forward and said, "Enough, George! Take it or leave it. I have to go now."

As she reached for the end button, she barely caught the last words "take it" before the line went dead. Lindy pushed back from her cherry wood desk and stood up, straightening out her black pencil skirt. She then walked over to her private bathroom and took a quick look in the mirror. Glancing at her lips, she noticed they needed another coat. She continued watching in the mirror as she reapplied her signature pink shade and moved her lips up and down. Satisfied, she left the bathroom and closed the door behind her. She had just enough time to grab a new folder and notepad before her new patient arrived.

As the door opened, her breath caught in her throat. Stunned, she looked down at her folder and read the name. "Agent Matthew Blake? Hi, I'm Dr. Ashley. Please come in and have a seat."

Agent Blake walked forward, shook her hand, and took a seat on the brown leather couch as directed. Erin appeared in the doorway behind him and, smiling big and mouthing the word "G-O-R-G-E-O-U-S," closed the door to Lindy's office.

Composing herself, Lindy walked around the sofa and took a seat across from him in her pale yellow chair. She was about to ask a question when he spoke.

"Look, you know why I'm here, and I know why I'm here. This is not the first time I've shot a man. Let's have our talk and then you can bill the agency your astronomical fee, and then, I'm out of here."

Lindy tilted her head and paused before responding. "Actually, Agent Blake, I have no idea why you are here."

Matthew frowned. "The agency didn't send you any paperwork?"

"No, I only have your name and the paper you filled out when you arrived."

Matthew leaned forward and spoke, gesturing vigorously with his hands. "Well, shit! Okay, Doc, here's the drill. In my line of work, you shoot someone dead and they send you off for a—"

"Excuse me, Agent Blake. I know the drill. I have counseled many lawmen over the years."

"Great, so let's—"

"Excuse me again, Agent Blake." She paused and smiled. "Before we begin, I want to be very clear with you that I will not sign off on any document until I've had a chance to talk, listen, and discuss the issue at hand."

Matthew looked at her with a hard stare and a scowl. She smiled back and then set her folder down on the coffee table between them.

Looking at her closely for the first time, he realized she wasn't some knucklehead shrink. She was self-confident, polished, and very easy on the eyes. Her appearance was different as well. She wasn't wearing a white coat or jacket. Instead she wore silk, and her arms were exposed for full view. She wore her jet-black hair down, and it fell across her blue blouse. His eyes continued to flow down her body and met her long legs. They were crossed at an angle, and her black skirt left her lovely thighs partially exposed. Slowly his eyes left her and took in the room. It wasn't black and white. The room had color, charm, and style. He took a second look at the walls and asked, "Are your walls painted pink?"

Lindy sat back and smiled again. "The color is called rose petal."

Blake nodded as if all made sense now.

"Agent Blake, do you mind if I call you Matthew and you call me Lindy?"

Matthew swore her blue eyes were twinkling back at him as she spoke. He only could nod, as he was mesmerized and quickly falling under some kind of weird spell.

She sat back up and re-crossed her shapely legs. "Matthew, tell me what happened the day you pulled the trigger that ended a life."

An hour later, Matthew was behind the wheel of his shiny black '69 Chevy Camaro and speeding down Interstate 20 to the FBI field office in Dallas. Cars, trees, and buildings were all flying by as his thoughts continued to reflect on his session with Dr. Lindy Ashley. He asked aloud, "How the hell did she get me to talk about my mother?"

As Matthew tried to sort through the hour-long session and pick away at when and how it all began, he looked at himself in the rearview mirror and thought, *What the hell? I look exhausted.* Without glancing down, he hit a button on the radio and it switched to an '80s rock station. AC/DC's "Back in Black" was playing, and he immediately felt a sense of relief as he sang and pounded the steering wheel to the beat. By time the song ended, he thought he had broken free of her spell until he came to the crashing realization that he had another appointment with her later in the week.

"Damn her!"

Matthew turned down the radio, took out his cell phone, and called the office. On the second ring, someone picked up, and he said, "Blake here. I'm just checking in. I'm about twenty minutes out."

A female voice on the other end said, "Hi, Matthew, it's Janet. You have a meeting at six o'clock with the boss man. I'll let him know you'll be here."

"Yeah, thanks, Janet."

Before he could hang up, Janet asked, "So, how did your appointment with Dr. Ashley go?"

"I went, and that's all you need to know."

"Touché!" Janet retorted.

"Yeah, well, it's only the fourth time I've been sent," and then Matthew ended the call.

As he continued on down the interstate, Matthew thought about what he had said to Janet. *Was it the fourth or fifth time he'd had to draw his gun and end a life? Oh well.* The latest victim, Ned Fry, would be one he would never lose sleep over in a million years. Ned was a child abductor, and Matthew was forced to use his gun when Ned held a seven-year-old boy hostage during a shoot-out last week.

Slowly Matthew's thoughts wandered back to Lindy Ashley. *What was it about her?* He remembered the way she tilted her head with her red nails holding a pen to her painted lips. She was downright sexy as she crossed her legs and talked with her hands. She had asked questions, and Matthew had responded to all of them like a pistol-whipped puppy dog.

Matthew was a little frightened by Lindy. No one had had that effect on him since Cynthia was alive.

Cynthia…with the thought of her name, memories came crashing back inside his head. He could still see Craz Numez with his bulking arms wrapped around her neck just as if it was yesterday instead of four years ago. Matthew spoke aloud, "Burn in hell, Craz!" and then he leaned forward and cranked the radio back up.

Singing along with Bon Jovi, Matthew shook his head and tried to knock loose the cobwebs as he exited the interstate in search of a new diversion.

Chapter 2

Erin popped her head into Dr. Lindy Ashley's office and then stepped quickly inside, closing the door behind her.

Looking up, Lindy saw her secretary and laid her pen down on top of agent Matthew Blake's file. The look on Erin's face warned her of what was coming.

"Oh my God, Agent Blake is stunning! Is he coming back?"

Lindy mentally counted to three and then spoke. "Yes, he's coming back later this week. So, you noticed as well that he was nice to look at."

Beaming, Erin continued, "He's not married, and he's thirty, just a year older than you."

Lindy allowed herself to crack a smile. "Erin, if you weren't my baby sister, I would've fired your ass four years ago when I started this practice."

Erin plopped down on the leather sofa and smiled. "Yeah right, your social life would be a complete disaster without me."

Lindy couldn't deny that. Outside of work, Erin took care of everything, from dry cleaning and hair appointments to bills.

Erin continued. "Matthew Blake looked like the real deal, not like some men who try to pass off as cowboys."

"Where does he live?"

Erin's face lit up. "I knew you would like him. He lives on the south side of Dallas with his own ranch and horses."

Lindy tilted her head. "Now how did you find out he had horses?"

Erin smiled back, batting her lashes playfully. "That was the easy part. I just asked."

"What else did you ask?"

"Oh, just the usual stuff. So what's his story? Don't tell me he's messed up like all the others."

"Hey, they're not *all* messed up," Lindy said loudly. "Besides, what goes on in here is confidential. You know better than to ask me."

Erin frowned. "Well, either way, I can't wait to see him walk through my door again."

Just then, the front door buzzer sounded, and Erin jumped up from the sofa. "I'll see who it is and get rid of them. I know you have that speaking engagement tonight."

Lindy called out, "Thanks," and turned her attention back to Matthew Blake's file. Looking over her notes, she felt satisfied she had everything. In the margin she sketched a horse and a cowboy hat. Smiling at her artwork, she closed the file again and said, "Until next time, Matthew."

Chapter 3

Erin stood behind her desk pleading with the patient. "Please remain calm, Mr. Barry. Dr. Ashley has a speaking engagement tonight that she must attend. I'll be happy to fit you in first thing in the morning."

Shaking his acne-scarred face side to side, he shouted, "No, I can't wait! Please, I must see her now. I'll only take five minutes, promise."

Erin was torn but held her ground. "I'm sorry, Mr. Barry, it's just not possible. She probably has already packed up and—"

Clay Barry didn't back down or away. Instead, he charged down the hallway past Erin's desk in search of Dr. Ashley.
Erin quickly buzzed Lindy. "Clay Barry just stormed past me! He's coming toward you. I'm calling security!"

Lindy had only enough time to stand up and face the doorway before the heavyset, six-foot-two carpenter barged into her office. Remaining calm, Lindy asked, "Hello, Clay. How may I help you?"

The forty-seven-year-old bald man with a large tattoo on his left shoulder started crying. Lindy motioned for Clay to have a seat and then walked toward the hallway to greet a frantic Erin. Lindy spoke softly. "All is fine. Call off the guard." Then she closed her door to a shocked Erin.

Turning her attention back to Clay, she said, "Before we begin, I must tell you I have limited time. I'm scheduled to speak at the university tonight, and I have a lot of people counting on me."

Clay shook his head. "I'm sorry, Doc. I just had to see you and I didn't think."

Lindy sat down in her chair. "It's okay Clay, but remember, you have to keep in mind the rules and procedures we've agreed to abide by if we're going to work together." Lindy thought to herself, *I've never been afraid of Clay Barry until now. I hope like hell he has enough going on inside that crazy head of his not to notice my fear.* Lindy forced a smile and continued, "Did something happen at work today that troubled you?"

Clay wiped his eyes. "Yes, I had to go back inside a lady's house three times after the job just to make sure I didn't forget anything."

"Okay, so let's figure out what happened earlier today that triggered your OCD."

As he talked about his day, Clay finally relaxed enough to grin. Lindy listened for about two minutes and then said, "There you go! That right there is the source of your stress. Now tomorrow morning, I want to see you at seven-thirty sharp, and we're going to talk and focus on your threshold level for stress." Lindy didn't wait for an answer as she stood up and extended her hand.

Hesitating only slightly, Clay stood as well. "Thanks, Doc. I will see you bright and early tomorrow morning."

With a confident nod, Lindy walked from her office to the reception area with Clay in tow. Erin stood up from her desk as Lindy walked toward her. Erin wasn't smiling, and she showed no signs of being polite toward Clay. Ignoring Erin, Lindy stopped at the front door and then turned around to face Clay once again. "Good-bye now, Clay. I'll see you tomorrow."

Clay kept his eyes focused on Lindy and never once turned around to look at Erin. He spoke quietly. "Thank you, Doc, and, um, I'm sorry about earlier and—"

Lindy smiled back. "You are forgiven, Clay. It's in the past. Now, I'll see you tomorrow morning."

Clay smiled again and then walked out the door. Lindy continued to watch him as he walked away, and then quickly shut the door and locked it. Lindy turned around to face Erin, who was standing there with her hands on her hips. Lindy immediately said, "Erin, pencil in Clay for seven-thirty tomorrow morning, and we'll discuss this at seven fifteen because I've got to go or I'm going to be late!"

Erin stuck out her tongue and then bent over and grabbed a briefcase. "Here's your notes," she said. "I packed up for you earlier today. Now go, and yes, we'll discuss this at seven fifteen."

Lindy reached for her briefcase. "When did you pack for me?"

Erin just shook her head. "When you went for coffee this afternoon."

Lindy turned away but yelled over her shoulder, "I love you, Erin!"

Chapter 4

Luckily for Lindy, traffic was moving quite well for 5:45 p.m. on a Monday. Both her practice and the university were located in Arlington about fifteen miles apart. Now, she was just two red lights away from the Dunn Building, where she would speak tonight at a Psychology 401 class.

Her good friend, Professor Joshua Dobbs, had invited her to speak on a topic for six consecutive weeks. The class met on Monday and Wednesday nights and was an hour long. She was only asked to fill the first thirty minutes, therefore leaving her no time to be late. She had been nervous last week, it being her first night, but had felt better about tonight until her incident with Clay Barry. Now she felt rushed and nervous all over again.

Turning left into the parking lot behind the Dunn Building, she had to wait as three students walked in front of her. She patiently waited and then waved. She recognized one of the young ladies from last week. The girl stopped and then turned around and waited on Lindy to park. Once Lindy turned off the engine, she made her way over to Lindy's car.

Lindy opened her car door, and the young lady said, "Hello, Dr. Ashley. It's good to see you again."

"Thank you, I'm glad to be back."

The girl continued, "My name is Candice. I'm third-year, studying psychology."

Lindy grabbed her briefcase and closed her car door before responding, "Hi, Candice, it's nice to meet you. I see you came back. Does that mean I didn't bore you to tears?"

"Not at all! I found your lecture on sociopaths quite interesting."

Lindy started walking toward the lecture hall, and Candice fell in beside her. After another few steps, Candice turned around. "I'll be done at seven o'clock, and I'll meet you here."

The young man smiled, waved and then continued walking in the opposite direction. "That's Jaycee, my boyfriend," Candice said. "He's all worried about me since there was an attack on a student last week."

Lindy thought back to the news report given on Channel Nine and responded, "He's a good boyfriend."

Lindy was about to ask a question when she spotted Professor Dobbs standing in the doorway holding the door open for her and Candice to enter.

"Good evening, Professor," she said as she approached.

"Hello, Dr. Ashley. How are you this evening?"

"I'm well. Busy day at the office as usual."

Candice spoke up. "I bet there's never a dull day with your line of work."

Lindy smiled and responded truthfully. "Never."

Professor Dobbs said, "Candice, if you'll excuse us, I need to have a word with the doctor before class."

Candice frowned and nodded. "Sure, I understand."

Lindy looked at her friend and asked, "What? Am I missing something?"

Joshua motioned for Lindy to follow him down the hallway. Once inside his office, Joshua shut the door. "The student that was murdered last week was in this class."

"Oh, Joshua, I had no idea."

"Yeah. His name was Robby Singleton, a really good kid."

Lindy didn't say anything and let Joshua continue.

"Robby was killed shortly after this class last Wednesday."

"I see. What do you need me to do?"

"Well, my plan is to address the class first and then ask for any questions or comments. I really am lost here. Do you have any suggestions?"

"Oh this is tough. Just go slow and let their questions guide you. These poor kids. I'll do my best though to help with any questions."

"Good. We'll just see how this thing plays out. I'm sorry that I didn't notify you earlier so you could adjust. I only got back into town this afternoon and heard the news."

She thought of Joshua's sick mom in Ohio and didn't expect him to explain any further. "It's okay. We'll adjust. So how's your mom? Did she have a good week?"

Joshua shook his head and looked down for a moment and then looked back up to meet Lindy's eyes. "No, she's in a lot of pain."

"I'm sorry, Joshua. Just so you know, I'll be on standby for as long as you need me this semester."

Joshua reached out and squeezed Lindy's hand. "Thanks, Lindy. You're a good friend."

"Come on, let's do this," Lindy said. She opened up the office door, and Joshua followed out behind her.

Entering the lecture hall, Lindy was shocked to see the large turnout compared to last week. Most of the students were standing around in small clusters talking and made no move to go to their seats as she and the professor entered. Making her way to the front, Lindy heard Robby's name spoken five times. Lindy continued to look around as she opened her briefcase and then took out her notes. Scanning faces, very few students looked familiar. Then, out of the corner of her eye, she caught someone waving. It was Candice. Lindy smiled back and then turned around to see if Joshua was ready.

Professor Joshua Dobbs attached his microphone to his collar and began to speak. "Good evening, class. Please find your seats and we'll begin."

Taking his cue, Lindy picked up her microphone and attached it to her blue silk blouse. By the time she had everything ready, the class was dead calm. Looking around, Lindy smiled at the faces and then walked over behind the second podium with her notes.

Joshua began, "Class, I was saddened to hear of the news about your fellow classmate, Robby Singleton." No one spoke, so he continued. "Robby was a great leader and student and a pure joy to be around. He'll be missed very much on this campus. Also, please be mindful of your surroundings and pay close attention to your friends. As you're all aware, grief has many forms, and there's no set time for the healing process."

Lindy continued to look out in the audience as Joshua spoke. Some students had tears in their eyes, and others didn't make eye contact. Lindy was introduced once again, and she was able to answer about two of the questions. Most questions were aimed at Joshua since he was their teacher and she was just a guest.

Joshua must have noticed his students' body language as well because, after a few more questions were asked, he decided to cut the night short. The last student walked out at 6:35, and Lindy found herself alone again with Joshua.

"I think that went well," said Lindy.

Joshua looked tired as he spoke. "Yeah, I hope so."

Lindy walked over and gave him a hug. "I think we should call it a night. You need some sleep."

"I know. You're right. I just need to finish up some things here first."

Lindy walked back over to her briefcase and placed her unused notes inside. "Okay then, I'll give you a call tomorrow around lunch."

"That sounds great. Let me walk you out."

Lindy picked up her briefcase and followed Joshua up the stairs and through the hallway to the exit. Standing at the door, Lindy noticed how old her good friend Joshua appeared. She guessed he was approaching sixty, but he looked older from the stress of the last few weeks with his mom.

Lindy stopped. "I'm good. I can see my car from here."

"Are you sure?"

Turning and facing Joshua, she said, "Yes, now don't stay too late. Work will always be here tomorrow."

"I promise."

Lindy gave Joshua a peck on the cheek and then headed to her vehicle. As soon as she backed out of her parking space, Joshua turned around and went back inside the building.

Driving down Cherry Lane, Lindy noticed larger groups of students walking down the sidewalks. No one seemed to be walking alone tonight. As a precaution, Lindy hit the lock button with her free hand and then pulled her cell phone out of the glove box and placed it on her lap. When she pulled up to the first red light, she touched the screen and checked her messages. There were none.

At the sound of a horn, Lindy jumped and looked up. The light was green. As she pressed the accelerator to move along, a young lady suddenly darted in front of her vehicle. Lindy barely had enough time to stop. Lindy commented aloud, "It looks like some people aren't afraid to be alone tonight."

Chapter 5

Matthew Blake was sitting at a large oval desk with three other FBI agents and his boss, Fred Copeland. They were all discussing the last page of a detailed outline of the shooting events involving Ned Fry from the previous week. Matthew glanced at his watch and thought, *Nine fifteen... time to call it a night.* "Well, I don't see any changes here," he said. "Looks great to me."

Copeland looked up from his page and removed his glasses. He also glanced down at his watch and said, "Me neither. Let's look at this one more time tomorrow before we all sign off."

Matthew's partner, Steve Toowey, groaned slightly. "If you say so, but I'm ready to sign now."

Copeland said, "Yeah, I say so. Let's meet back here in the morning at nine o'clock, and then we'll have this thing signed and wrapped up before lunch."

Steve started to protest but stopped when Matthew kicked him under the table.

Matthew spoke. "So what did Marcia's doctor say today? Has the baby's due date changed?"

"No," Copeland responded, "baby girl is right on schedule and should be here right around the thirty-first. Marcia's a little worried though. She doesn't want a baby born on Halloween."

Steve chimed in, "Since this's Marcia's third child, she'll probably have her a day or two early."

"And what do you know about babies, Toowey?" Copeland asked.

Steve pouted. "Hey! I have twins, remember? That makes me the all-knowing daddy."

Copeland got up from his chair and headed toward the door but was immediately greeted by Janet.

"Sorry, boss," she said, "but I'm afraid you guys aren't going home."

Copeland frowned. "What you got?"

"Central University Police in Arlington just called. They have another victim."

Copeland moaned. "Ahhhh damn! Just what I need, a serial killer on the loose right after we finished the last case."

Matthew spoke next. "Well, let's not jump to conclusions. They might be completely unrelated."

"Doubtful." Copeland paused and then continued. "The biggest cases in my career have all happened around the births of my children."

Steve said, "Give us the facts, Janet."

Janet looked down at her notes and read, "Victim's name is Jaycee Brown, age twenty-one and fourth-year sports medicine major. Vic was found in a grassy area off a sidewalk on Porter Lane by a dog owner named William Burns."

No one interrupted, so Janet continued. "Arlington Police have roped off the area, and their ME said it appears the victim has been stabbed with the same type knife as last week's victim, Robby Singleton."

Matthew spoke first. "Looks like you could be right, boss. We better move quickly before the crime scene gets too disturbed."

Copeland said, "Toowey and Blake, you come with me. Everyone else, go home."

One by one all the agents grabbed their stuff and headed out the door while Janet called out, "I'll keep you posted if anything else comes through."

No one responded, so Matthew turned around and said, "Thanks, Janet."

Janet winked and smiled back.

After stepping outside the building and rounding a corner, Steve said, "Janet has a crush on you."

"What? No!"

Steve Toowey nodded his head and continued walking toward the parking lot with Matthew right beside him.

As the men walked, it was easy to see that Steve and Matthew were complete opposites. Steve had sandy blond wavy hair and blue eyes, and dressed in khakis and polo shirts, while Matthew wore his dark brown hair short and was most comfortable in jeans, T-shirts, and boots. Both men continued on to Matthew's '69 Camaro without another word spoken about Janet.

Steve was older than Matthew by ten years and had twin daughters who were age twelve. Both girls lived with his ex in Houston, but Steve had them every other weekend and on holidays. Steve grew up in Houston and attended Rice University on a baseball scholarship. After a torn shoulder his third year, it was time to get serious about another profession.

Unlike Steve, Matthew attended the University of Texas in Austin and majored in criminology from the age of eighteen. Once he graduated, he immediately got a job with the FBI and had been happy and content with his profession for the last seven years. Several big cases had fallen his way, but never before had he worked a case involving a serial killer.

Steve said, "You been listening to the '80s station again?"

Matthew smiled. "Yeah, you sorta got me hooked."

Steve laughed and then said, "So tell me about that psych evaluation you had today."

Matthew hesitated briefly and then decided to spill it. "It was different this time."

Steve looked over toward Matthew. "How so?"

"Well, for starters, Dr. Lindy Ashley is a knockout."

"Really! So, are you saying I should've been the one to pull the trigger on that nutcase Ned Fry?"

"Yep, but you didn't."

"So, is she married?" asked Steve.

Matthew thought back to the moment he searched for a ring and remembered her painted nails wrapped around a pen as she made notes during their session. Finally Matthew said, "No. I'll see her again later this week."

"Another appointment?"

"Yeah, I know. I was asking myself that same question earlier today."

"So whose idea was that?"

Matthew didn't honestly know. It just sorta happened. To appease Steve, he said, "I want to ask her out, so I thought what the hell? The agency frowns on just one session anyway, so I signed up for another."

Steve was going to comment but was interrupted by his cell phone ringing. It was his ex, Karen. Looking at the time, he said, "It's a little late for her to be calling."

Sounding a little alarmed, Steve answered, "Hi, Karen. Is everything okay with you and the girls?"

"We're fine. I just wanted to remind you about the girls' recital this Saturday night at seven o'clock. Are you going to be able to make it?"

Steve answered back immediately, "I've had it written down on my calendar for two months now. I'll be there."

"Okay then. I'll see you there."

"Hey, are the girls asleep?" Steve asked.

"Yes, for about an hour now."

"Okay. In the morning, tell them I love 'em," Steve replied.

"I will. Good-bye now," Karen said before she hung up the phone.

Steve put his phone away and said to Matthew, "Regardless of this case, I'm in Houston Saturday night at seven o'clock."

Matthew smiled and just said, "Right."

Chapter 6

Dr. Lindy Ashley lived in a townhouse community on Lenox Street in Dallas called The Palms. The townhouse had everything Lindy wanted for this phase of her life. The place had two bedrooms, a study, and two full baths. The kitchen was well designed with lots of counter space for cooking. Also, the living room opened up to a large porch that overlooked a four-acre man-made lake. She was not responsible for any lawn care and had the full use of a gym, Olympic-size swimming pool, and media room with library. The best part of The Palms was that it was brand new and allowed dogs.

It was after nine o'clock and Lindy was deep in thought while soaking in her garden tub sipping red wine. Parker was stretched out on the purple bath mat below with his chin rested on his front paws. He was watching Lindy's every move and patiently waiting to call it a night.

Lindy had moved to The Palms three months ago, after her two-year marriage with George had failed. Before, Lindy had lived in George's $4.2 million home in South Park, the most affluent area of Dallas. George Williams III came from money, and it also helped that he had a thriving plastic surgery business located in South Park. George made a good living off of making women beautiful. The money Lindy brought in was hardly noticeable compared to his paychecks.

Lindy should have noticed from hello that George was from a different universe. Lindy attended SMU on a scholarship, and George never even applied for one. They were introduced to each other during their fifth year of school. George and Lindy dated all through medical school and then married a year after. Looking back, Lindy wished she would have said no three years and fourteen days ago when George had popped the question on a hot night while dining at South Park's country club. She just wasn't molded right to be Mrs. George Williams III, and no amount of time or education was ever going to change that.

Lindy took the last sip and then gently placed her glass along the edge of the tub. "Did you have a long day, Parker?"

At the sound of his name, Parker's ears shot up, and he titled his head to the side.

"Well, I had a long and interesting day."

Again, Parker looked back with silence.

Lindy sat up, released the plug, and slowly stood as the water began to drain from the tub. Water dripped on Parker as she stepped out and leaned over to grab a bath towel hanging on a hook. The dog stood up, shook, and took off toward the bedroom. Ignoring Parker, Lindy looked ahead at her body in the mirrored wall that was opposite the tub and began to slowly dry off.

Turning around, she looked at the bruise on the back of her left thigh. It was now finally fading into the green phase. The skirt she had worn today had barely covered it. *Soon I won't have to worry about it anymore*, Lindy thought. *It should be gone in a few more days*. Turning back around, Lindy walked toward the mirror. She peered into her blue eyes and asked aloud, "What's next, Dr. Ashley?"

At that moment the doorbell chimed, and Parker ran into the hallway from the master bedroom barking. A little spooked, Lindy grabbed the housecoat hanging behind the door and quickly threw it on. Glancing at the clock on her nightstand, she thought, *Nine forty-five is too late for a visitor.*

Lindy walked toward her dresser and grabbed her phone. There were no missed calls and no new messages. The only person that would show up at this time of night without calling was Erin. Placing her phone down, Lindy yelled out, "Parker, stop barking! I'm coming!"

Lindy hurried down the hallway and went straight to the front door. She peered into the peephole.

No one was there.

Lindy immediately thought of the tall iron gates surrounding George's neighborhood that kept uninvited guests out. She'd always thought it was overkill, especially when ordering takeout and having friends over. It was always such a pain to call the front gate every time one had a visitor. Now Lindy missed that service and began to question why The Palms wasn't gated.

After rechecking the locks, she picked up Parker and walked away toward the living room. Rounding the couch, she froze. Something was standing on her patio table. Cautiously, Lindy moved toward the french doors that led to the back porch with a barking Parker in her arms.

With each step came the growing realization that sitting atop of the glass patio table was a vase holding about a dozen yellow roses. To the left, lying beside the vase, was a small box wrapped in blue paper.

Looking around, Lindy saw no one.

Quickly, she checked the locks on the double door and was only slightly relieved when she found them secured. Some nights she had completely forgotten to lock the door after letting Parker out to do his business before bed. Tonight, she was thankful she hadn't forgotten.

Lindy held on tight to Parker as he continued to gaze out the glass door and growl. Petting him with her free hand, she moved toward the light plate on the wall and then flipped the switch.

When she saw that her iron gate was open, Lindy jumped. There were no locks on any of the townhouses' backyard gates. *Why would there be?* She thought. They are only waist high. The sole purpose of the gates was to keep children out of the lake, not privacy.

Lindy contemplated what to do. She had the entire backyard and porch in view. Finally she thought, *I can easily open the door and grab the card on the flowers and then get back in safely and lock the door before anyone has time to grab me.*

Lindy continued to stare at the flowers and box and waited for another two minutes. Parker was no longer growling or barking, but he kept a constant visual on the backyard. "Okay, Parker, we're gonna open the door and see what the card says." Parker looked up at Lindy with blank eyes.

Holding the dog tight, Lindy slowly unbolted the door and pulled it open. Before making another move, she looked intently over at the wrought iron gate. No one was running toward her, so she hastily took three steps toward the table and grabbed the card and then quickly stepped back inside the house. Parker let out a little yelp as Lindy tossed him to the side so she could use both hands to bolt the door.

Taking a deep breath, Lindy bent over and petted the dog before grabbing the card that she had also thrown on the floor in her haste to lock the door. As she stood to read it, the front door chime rang once more, and her heart almost flew out of her chest.

Immediately Parker took off toward the front door barking madly. With shaky legs, Lindy slowly forced herself within two feet of the front door. It took every ounce of willpower she had to make herself move forward and look out of the peephole. There on the other side of the door stood Erin, her baby sister. Relief washed over Lindy as she flung the door open, reached out and grabbed Erin, and snatched her inside.

Erin stumbled and said, "Sis, what are you doing?" as Lindy quickly locked the front door. "Oh my God! You're white as a ghost! What in the world's going on?"

Chapter 7

Agents Matthew Blake and Steve Toowey carefully followed their boss, Fred Copeland, down a path and into the bushes along Porter Lane. All three men wore protective footies, gloves and faces that showed no emotion. Matthew looked up and thought, *The weather's cooperating. No chance of rain tonight.*

Copeland, age forty-two, was an impressive man that stood six foot three inches. Well liked among both his colleagues and the staffs of the Arlington and Ft. Worth/Dallas police departments, he was fair and didn't pass judgment—two things that gave him the respect needed to run and operate the Dallas FBI field office.

Jacob Knight, of Central University of Arlington's police force, saw Copeland and his agents approaching and stopped talking with the local medical examiner and her staff. Knight walked over to Copeland and said, "Good to see you again, Copeland. Unfortunately it has to involve a murder."

"Yeah. Knight, I would like you to meet agents Matthew Blake and Steve Toowey. They'll be officially in charge of this case if the evidence does correctly suggest we have a serial killer on the loose."

Knight frowned and then commented, "I hope the ME is wrong with her initial assessment. But I wouldn't count on it."

At the sound of her name, Candy Johnson approached the men and said, "Welcome, boys, glad you could join us tonight."

Everyone was acquainted with medical examiner Dr. Johnson. She had been the ME for Arlington for over ten years now and had a very good reputation with her assessment and work. No handshakes were given tonight, not with all the protective gear and preserving the crime scene.

Knight looked around the area that was roped off and began to explain the details to the agents. "The victim is Jaycee Brown, age twenty-one. It appears the young man was walking along this path that follows Porter Lane when he was attacked. So far the only information we have is from his girlfriend, Candice Lowery, also a student that attends the university."

Dr. Johnson said, "Candice has been sedated and taken to Hope General, where she'll meet up with her parents as well as the parents of the deceased. Both kids grew up in Dallas, and their parents still live and work in the city."

Knight continued, "According to Candice, Jaycee was at her dorm until he left around eight fifteen. He takes this same path each night from Candice's dorm to his dorm."

"Jaycee was walking along and then probably stopped of his own free will. There's no blood or sign of a struggle near the path or highway," commented Dr. Johnson.

Knight motioned with his hands the direction they needed to walk so as to not disturb the crime scene. As all followed behind, Matthew noticed small spatters of blood among the weeds and grass that were marked with yellow numbers. With each additional step he made, the amount of blood increased and the grass and weeds looked more trampled and disturbed. With different numbers, a footprint was marked, as were a book and a backpack.

Matthew listened as Dr. Johnson explained, "Footprint is from the victim. There are no other clear footprints present, but everything will be tested."

Matthew's eyes continued to scan the ground until he caught a glimpse of the body up ahead. It was lying on the ground in an awkward position covered by a blood-stained white sheet. Around the victim stood many trees and small bushes, all sprayed with what appeared to be the victim's blood.

Dr. Johnson said, "Kimberly, please lift the sheet for the agents to view."

Kimberly stopped writing and knelt down beside the victim. Matthew gasped and Steve mumbled as the sheet was carefully pulled back. No one spoke for a few moments as they all digested the sight of what was left of Jaycee Brown.

The killer or killers had slashed his face so many times he was no longer recognizable. The only reason they were able to identify the body was by a wallet holding his campus identification card and the clothing he was seen wearing when he left Candice's dorm.

Copeland was the first to speak. "My God! Did his girlfriend see him like this?"

Dr. Johnson's face changed color and then she spoke softly. "Yeah. It's too small of a campus. Once the dog owner stumbled across the victim, all hell broke loose."

"By the time we got here, word had already gotten to Candice. She only lives five hundred feet away, in that building over there," explained Knight.

All agents looked at where Knight was pointing and could clearly see how quickly things would have gotten out of hand once the victim was discovered.

Knight said, "We got lucky. Even though many students and local traffic were alerted of the crime, the crime scene remains largely intact. Thanks partly to the older man who found him. Heck, once people saw the victim, they all knew he was dead. Hell, nobody wanted to get any closer."

"Yeah, I imagine. So, how's this body similar to last week's victim?" asked Copeland.

Dr. Johnson knelt down and carefully touched Jaycee's right arm. "Look at this mark here. It's a single puncture wound that appears to be the same type, size, and shape as that made by the instrument used on Singleton's body."

Matthew knelt beside her for a closer look and asked, "Do you think the wounds were made by the same person, or is it possible there might be more than one killer?"

Candy took a deep breath and then stated, "It appears to be one killer. According to Jaycee's license, he is six one. Judging the entry wounds, I would predict he or she stands around five ten."

Knight quickly asked, "She?"

Matthew stood up and answered. "It's possible. Women been known to have enough rage to destroy the opposite sex in this way. Plus, both victims were male."

Steve added, "Whoever committed this crime was angry. There's a lot of rage built up, and once the initial stabbing begins, there's no end in sight until the body is mutilated beyond recognition."

Dr. Johnson nodded and pulled the sheet back over the body. Standing up she said, "I agree. When we get him back to my lab, hopefully we'll find something lodged under his nails. Who knows, we might get lucky."

Everyone stopped talking at the sound of a helicopter approaching. It didn't take long before the lights found them and bright light filtered down on the crime scene and law enforcers.

Knight groaned. "Shit! The media is getting out of control now."

Copeland shielded his eyes from the blinding lights and asked, "Has any of your men talked to them yet?"

"Hell no! They know better. My men are keeping them fifty feet back from the tape."

Dr. Johnson interrupted. "Gentlemen, I feel strongly about these two murders being connected. But- I'm not officially stating that as fact, not yet. I need time to get our latest victim to the lab and compare the specifics with Singleton's notes."

Copeland smiled. Dr. Candy Johnson had brains, and she was not about to be the one to falsely scare the general public before facts were examined.

Knight gestured up above. "Okay, but something gotta be stated, and soon, or people will start jumping to their own damn conclusions. You think this is chaos now? Wait till news spreads that we might have a serial killer on the loose!"

Copeland tried to calm Knight. "We'll talk to the media and keep it simple."

Matthew turned toward the ME and asked, "When is the earliest you can meet tomorrow with an update?"

"I'll start tonight and call you in the morning around seven to let you know where I stand."

"Thanks." Matthew walked over and handed her a card from his wallet.

Dr. Johnson smiled at Matthew and then went back to work on Jaycee.

Copeland said to Knight, "Go ahead and send my office everything on Singleton, and we'll plan on meeting tomorrow afternoon."

"Sure thing." Knight pointed to the noise in the distance. "Good luck with that media," and he turned around and headed back toward the ME.

Copeland stepped closer to Matthew and Steve and said, "Pick a number between one and ten."

Both agents knew the drill, and Matthew replied, "Two," and Steve sighed, "Seven."

"Agent Blake, go talk to the media," Copeland instructed, never revealing his number. "I'm going home now and will see both of you around nine in the morning to finish that statement."

As Copeland walked off, Steve remarked, "I knew we should've signed off on that Ned Fry case."

Matthew just smiled at his partner. "Yep."

As both agents made their way over, the media immediately started getting their film crews ready. Matthew commented, "I think Copeland cheats with that number game."

"I think you're right. He's scared I'll piss someone off. Besides, you're better with the media."

"Whatever, but you're coming with me. Your shirt's ironed, and I'm wearing a T-shirt."

Steve rolled his eyes. "Nothing new there," and followed Matthew over and stood by his side as Matthew began to address the media.

Chapter 8

Lindy and Erin were sitting on the couch and staring at the card that was originally attached to the flowers. The card read, "Just for you. Thank you."

There was no signature and no other clues to reveal the sender's identity. The box and flowers both remained outside, and neither sister was going back out there to get them. Erin was just as spooked as Lindy. "I think we should call the police," she said finally.

"What? Why?"

"Whoever sent these was trespassing."

"Erin, the police have enough to deal with. Besides, I would be embarrassed to say, 'Someone left me flowers with no name.'"

"Yeah, but you have all those crazy people you see every day, like Clay Barry."

"Clay Barry was a little out of control today," Lindy agreed, "but I refuse to discuss him or anyone else tonight."

Erin didn't look surprised. Lindy had a switch in her brain that she turned off when she left work each day, and Erin knew it. When she had stated earlier that they would discuss Clay at seven fifteen in the morning, she had meant it. "Well, I'm staying with you tonight, just to be on the safe side."

Lindy looked at Erin's bag on the floor and then at Erin with eyebrows raised. "Somehow I think that was the plan before you got here."

Erin smiled. "Busted. I got in a fight with Leroy."

Lindy didn't say a word. She knew less was better when it came to Erin's loser boyfriend. Besides, Erin would tell her everything and then come to her own conclusions regardless of what advice Lindy gave her.

Erin was younger by seven years. At age eighteen, she had started working for Lindy as a secretary, and now she was twenty-two and without any education other than a high school diploma. Erin was beautiful with her long, wavy blond hair and dark green eyes. She was taller than Lindy by at least two inches, placing her at five ten. Erin's past was a little darker than Lindy's. At age twelve, Erin started modeling, and at sixteen, things started getting out of control.

Following an arrest over drugs, their parents, Roger and Gail Ashley, had kicked Erin out of the house. Lindy had taken it upon herself to take care of Erin at the same time she was starting medical school. It wasn't easy, but Lindy felt there was no other choice.

Lindy and Erin to this day had zero contact with their parents as a result of Erin's little crisis. For the last five and a half years, Erin had been drug free and living a very happy and normal life. With the money she'd saved from modeling, Erin was able to afford her own small three-bedroom home on the east side of Arlington. Too bad she had allowed Leroy to occasionally stay over. Now, whenever there was a fight, Erin left and Leroy either stayed or went back to his small apartment five miles away.

Erin shifted on the couch and faced Lindy. "I think it's time to move on from Leroy. I'm going to call him in the morning and tell him to come get his stuff while I'm at work."

Lindy couldn't help herself. She had to comment. "Tell him to leave the key on the kitchen counter on his way out."

Erin met her eyes and then smiled. "Yeah, good idea."

Parker began to growl again and jumped off the couch and ran toward the back door that led to the porch. Lindy jumped up and followed Parker with Erin two steps behind her. "Parker, what do you see?" Lindy almost whispered.

"You know he can sense someone without seeing them."

Lindy didn't respond and reached down and grabbed Parker into her arms. Parker stopped barking and started licking Lindy in the face. "Parker, that's enough!" Lindy gave him an affectionate hug and then sat him back on the floor. Turning away from the door, Lindy walked toward the kitchen. "Do you want a glass of wine?"

"Yeah, sure, but can you bring it to me? I'm going to go take a hot bath in your garden tub."

Lindy nodded in response, and Erin walked away. In the kitchen, Lindy refilled her glass from earlier and took a sip. After pouring a glass for Erin, she left the kitchen and stopped in the living room to turn on the news. On Channel Nine, the ten o'clock news was just about to end. Lindy sat on the couch and listened to the last five minutes of broadcast. There was live footage being shown from a helicopter looking down on an area of Central University. Lindy continued to watch as the video ended and a young brunette in the news station began to speak.

"It appears there's been another body found at Central University of Arlington. Information is slow coming in, but we'll update you with the facts as soon as we get them. Please stay turned to Channel Nine for the latest news and events. I'm Stacy Bryan. Good night, everyone."

Lindy could hear Erin calling for her wine, so she got up and turned off the TV. Taking two steps, she stopped and stared at the front door. Taking a few more steps, she could clearly see that it was locked and secure. Hesitating only briefly, she continued forward until her eye brushed up against the peephole.

Nothing.

The sidewalk leading to her front porch was empty, and no strange cars loomed about. Parker barked, and Lindy jumped and hit her head. "Damn it!" Parker looked up and tilted his head and then barked again. "Come on, you," Lindy said. "Let's go to bed."

At hearing the word "bed," Parker left Lindy and sprinted toward the bedroom. As Lindy followed behind, she heard Parker leap onto her bed just as Erin called out once more.

In a tired voice, Lindy said, "I'm coming!"

Chapter 9

Agents Matthew Blake and Steve Toowey were seated at the same large table looking over the same detailed events from the Ned Fry case as yesterday. Finally, Copeland said the words both agents had been dying to hear for the last two hours. "Okay, boys, let's sign off and pack Ned Fry away for good."

Eagerly Matthew picked up his pen and signed his name where indicated and then passed it over for his partner to do the same. Copeland hit the buzzer on the desk and explained, "Janet, we're done. It's all yours."

A minute later Janet walked in and immediately scanned the room until she met Matthew's eyes. She smiled at him and said, "Great, I'll wrap this up."

Copeland asked, "So how much paperwork came in on the Jaycee Brown case?"

Janet smiled. "It came through about five minutes ago and still printing. I'll bring it in as soon as it's done. Also, there's been countless calls coming in from media and private sector over concerns about a serial killer."

"Damn media," groaned Copeland and then added, "Thanks, Janet." Janet winked at Matthew and left the room.

Steve caught the wink and looked over at Matthew and smiled. Matthew ignored the mental jab. "I'm going to check in with the medical examiner. I called earlier, but she said she needed more time."

No one spoke as Matthew pulled out Dr. Candy Johnson's card and dialed her number. On the fourth ring, a voice replied, "Dr. Johnson speaking."

"Hi, Doc. Agent Blake again. Got anything now?"

"Yes. In a nutshell, we're looking at one killer, right-handed, height around five nine to five eleven. Also, the victim's stab wounds are very similar to the Singleton case."

Matthew frowned. "How sure are you that it's the same killer?"

Candy Johnson took a deep breath. "I'm ninety-seven percent sure the victim was stabbed by the same weapon as Singleton."

"Thanks, Doc. Let me know if there's anything new or if something changes."

"Sure will. Agent Blake?"

"Yes?"

"Catch this killer and soon. The stab wounds with the Singleton boy were ugly. With Brown, the stabbing was even more intense."

Matthew replied, "I'll do my best," and hung up the phone.

When Matthew finished reporting the ME's details to Steve and Copeland, Janet walked in with three stacks of papers and handed one to each agent. She looked straight at Matthew and asked, "Would anyone like more coffee?"

Steve was the only one who answered yes, and Janet left the room once again. Copeland flipped through the paperwork and then stood up with it. "I've got somewhere else to be. Let's meet back here at one o'clock and put together a statement on what we got and make it available for the media at two. Until then, nothing leaves this office."

Both agents nodded their heads in agreement and then Copeland left the room. Matthew hit the buzzer. "Janet, please tell my team to plan for a meeting in ten minutes."

"Will do. So far we have room A150 set up with the usual board with a map of Central University. Also we have pics of both deceased and class schedules."

"Great. Go ahead and print out a copy of whatever they got so far on friends, family, and current girlfriends and ex-girlfriends."

"Okay. Anything else?"

"Alert the media that a statement will be issued at two o'clock. Thanks... and yeah, go ahead and order lunch for the team."

"Already taken care of."

Matthew thought about Janet for a brief moment. She was an amazing assistant. She had been with the Dallas FBI field office for about three years now, and no one could recall how they had managed without her. With a sincere voice, Matthew said, "Thanks, Janet" and released the button and looked toward his partner, who was still seated, and asked, "What were your first thoughts about this case?"

Steve picked up his pen and rolled it between his fingers as he contemplated the question. "My first thought... random violence by some wacko with serious problems."

Matthew raised his eyebrows. "And second?"

"A crime of passion, both set off by a jilted lover or girlfriend."

Matthew didn't respond and began to look through the paperwork on Robby Singleton. After a few more minutes of reading, Matthew spoke. "Robby came from a wealthy family in Houston and had a steady girlfriend, Becky, for eighteen months. Many friends predicted they would get married."

"Yeah, I see that." Steve flipped over to Jaycee's file and said, "Candice Lowery is the current girlfriend for the last two months."

Matthew responded, "Doctors reported that she was so shaken up from seeing his body that she went into shock."

Steve closed the document. "Let's go see what the team has put together." As Steve walked toward the door, he paused and asked, "What was your initial thought?"

Matthew got up with his papers and walked over to join him. "I think it's a woman that those young boys grossly misjudged."

Chapter 10

Dr. Lindy Ashley was sitting in her pale yellow chair and writing on her notepad as her patient of two years, Luke James, was talking with his eyes closed. "I have a girlfriend now. Her name is Jennifer Bailey."

Lindy continued to gaze at the good-looking and fit twenty-five-year-old student. He technically wasn't classified as a full-time student because he could only handle two classes at a time. Luke lived with his grandmother and visited Lindy once a week because of psychological problems stemming from an abusive childhood.

"How did you meet her?" Lindy asked.

Luke opened his brown eyes and said, "At school."

"Great! Does she have a major?"

Luke started laughing. "Yeah, she wants to be a shrink."

Lindy smiled back. "Have you told her about me?"

Luke stopped laughing. "No. She doesn't know I'm screwed up."

Lindy placed her pen and notepad down in her lap and responded, "Luke, you've made a lot of good choices over the last year."

Luke ran his fingers through his sandy brown hair and responded angrily, "Yeah, well it doesn't change the fact that I raped my nine-year-old sister!"

Lindy patiently waited for more verbal banter before responding. After another minute had passed without any more comments, Lindy said, "Your father's in jail for his abuse toward his children. You're not in jail because you were a product of his abuse."

Luke was looking down, popping his fingers and avoiding eye contact. With a caring voice, Lindy asked, "Luke, please look at me."

Luke looked into Lindy's eyes. "I know. You've told me a hundred times that I gotta forgive myself and that I've the power to change who I'm to be and be the father I want to be one day."

Lindy smiled back. "I think it's been sixty-two times, not one hundred."

Luke's face took on a sweet, boyish grin and Lindy knew it was safe to continue. She asked, "So, have you brought Jennifer home to meet your grandma?"

Luke shook his head no.

"Why not?"

"It's too personal. I'm not ready to bring her home and introduce her to my world."

Lindy didn't push. "You'll know when the time is right. Just listen to your heart and trust what it's telling you."

Luke didn't respond.

"When do you see her again?"

Luke looked down at his watch and then replied, "Tonight. We're going to a movie."

"Awesome. I hope you have a great time."

"Yeah, well, if you don't mind, I want to cut this appointment short. Um, I want to go by and get some new jeans and get a haircut."

Lindy glanced at her watch and saw that it was one forty-five. "I'm okay with that. We covered a lot today, and I'm very pleased to see you looking happy and excited about a date."

Luke blushed and then stood up to shake Lindy's extended hand.

Lindy called out, "Good-bye," as Luke turned and opened the door to leave.

Lindy gathered up her notes and walked over to her desk. As she began to jot down ideas for her next session with Luke, she thought, *Poor kid. You still have a long way to go, but I'm definitely beginning to see progress.* In her notes, Lindy wrote down "Jennifer Bailey" and added "date with movie, not met grandma yet."

Satisfied there was nothing more to add, Lindy closed Luke's file and slipped it in the file cabinet in the far corner of her office. Just as she turned, Erin appeared in her doorway holding a cappuccino and a clipboard. Lindy smiled and said, "Thanks, sis. You read my mind."

"I generally do. Besides, I figured you were near a crashing point after last night's ordeal."

"Yes, I am."

Erin leaned against the leather couch. "Luke looked really good when he left today. Did ya'll have a good session?"

"Yes, we did. I'm glad you were able to pick up on his happiness as well. Sometimes I think I want to see them happy and misread their body language."

Erin looked down at the clipboard she was holding and said, "Your next appointment is with Carry Summerlin at two-thirty." She continued to chatter as she walked over to the file cabinet, pulled out Summerlin's folder, and brought it over to Lindy. "We need to turn on the TV. They have a special report at two on some incident that happened at Central University last night."

Lindy listened but didn't look up, as she was reading her notes on Carry from last week. Erin went ahead and turned the TV on and immediately flipped to Channel Nine. It was just one fifty, so she hit the mute button and then took a seat in Lindy's pale yellow chair. Lindy continued to read about Carry and never once looked up until she heard the sound come on the TV. Lindy placed her pen down and stood up and stretched. Grabbing her coffee, she walked over and stood by Erin as Channel Nine began to show a video feed live from the FBI Office in downtown Dallas.

Erin yelled, "There's Agent Blake!"

Lindy took a step closer. "Wow, it sure is."

Both ladies continued to listen as the events unfolded in front of them live on TV.

"Agent Blake, what can you tell us about the victims."

"Both young men were good kids, well-liked by their family and friends, strong and fit, excellent students, and both will be missed greatly among the Central University staff and students."

Another reporter yelled out, "Agent Blake, what precautions should students take while on campus?"

"Students should take the same precautions they take every day. Don't walk alone at night, take a phone with you everywhere, tell your friends where you're going and when you plan to return, and don't ever get into a car or go anywhere with a stranger."

Matthew signaled to a tall young reported near the front who had his hand raised. The reporter then asked, "The media has dubbed the serial killer 'The Night Killer.' Do you think he'll strike during daylight hours?"

Matthew replied, "First, we don't know if it's a he or she, and just because the attacks have happened at night doesn't mean one should be less cautious during the daytime."

A flood of shouts and questions were fired away by the media over the hint of a woman serial killer. Agent Blake raised his hand for all to quiet down so he could speak. "A woman serial killer is unlikely, but we're not ruling it out."

"What makes you think it could be a woman?" asked Stacy Bryan with Channel Nine News.

Agent Blake looked toward the beautiful and talented Ms. Bryan and answered, "The killer stands between five nine and five eleven, and there were multiple stab wounds that would fit the profile of a crime of passion."

Again Stacy Bryan spoke. "I don't understand. Both victims had a steady girlfriend. Are you suggesting they were involved with the same woman at some point in their past?"

"No, it doesn't have to be an ex-girlfriend or lover. It could be a woman that both men knew who has issues with men and their state of happiness."

Another reporter jumped in the conversation. "So, Agent Blake, are all the women who knew the victims on campus suspects?"

Very calmly Blake said, "The facts are one, it appears we have a serial killer. Two, the killer is between five nine and five eleven. Three, the killer may be male or female. Four, the victims probably knew their killer. Five, both attacks happened at night with no witnesses coming forward. Now, thank you for coming today, and I want to again remind everyone to be cautious of their surroundings and to please call the emergency number we set up if you have any knowledge of these crimes that'll help the authorities apprehend the killer. Again, thank you."

Reporters yelled out questions and statements as Agent Blake walked away from the podium and through a back door that led away from the

media room. The camera turned back toward Stacy Bryan, and she commented, "That report was given by Agent Matthew Blake, who's the lead
investigator of The Night Killer. Please stay tuned to Channel Nine for
any breaking news updates throughout the rest of the day, and we'll have
more tonight on the six o'clock news. I'm Stacy Bryan with Channel
Nine. See you tonight."

Erin looked over at Lindy with wide eyes. "Holy shit, sis! You were there
last night!"

Lindy calmly said, "The first victim was a student of Joshua Dobbs. He
was there last Wednesday, when I gave my first lecture. He died that
night."

"What about the second victim? Was he a student as well?"

Lindy shrugged. "I have no idea. When I talked to Joshua at lunch, he
didn't say anything. I'm assuming he doesn't know. He's been so down
with his mom, he probably hasn't even turned on the TV today."

"I don't like this, Lindy. Especially since you were on campus both times
this happened."

Lindy was about to respond when the door buzzer went off in the front
office. Erin jumped up and said, "That's probably Carry and her mom,"
and then walked out and left her alone.

Lindy went back to her desk and sat down to review Carry's file one more
time. She had about five more minutes before Erin would send her back.
Scanning over the information, Lindy punched a button and said, "Erin,
I'm going to try and get in touch with Joshua. Send Carry back at two
thirty-five."

Chapter 11

Agents Matthew Blake and Steve Toowey were back in room A150 with their team combing over the facts and trying to connect some imaginary dots between Robby Singleton and Jaycee Brown. Don Grey, an analysis specialist, had produced nothing so far on their class schedules. The students had different majors; Robby was studying business, and Jaycee, sports medicine. They had different classes and only shared two buildings for two of their classes. The classes were on different days and at different times. Matthew looked at both schedules again and found nothing to add.

"Both of their girlfriends have different majors as well. Robby's girlfriend, Becky, is in the nursing program, and Jaycee's girlfriend, Candice, is studying psychology" said Steve.

Matthew put the schedules down. "Back up. Compare Candice's schedule to Robby's."

Steve pulled Candice's class schedule and placed it beside Robby's. "Candice is in her third year studying psychology, and it appears they have a class together, PSY 401."

Matthew asked, "Why was Robby in a four hundred–level psychology class with a major in business?"

"I don't know, but look. Their class is on Monday and Wednesday nights."

Matthew said, "I'm willing to bet Jaycee was with Candice last night at or near the Dunn Building."

One of the team members, Pamela Meadows, spoke from the opposite side of the table, "I'm on it. I think Candice was released today from the hospital. I'll call her parents' house first."

Steve said, "That makes sense. After last week's unsolved murder, students would be on edge and probably wouldn't want to go anywhere alone."

Don Grey was over at the board updating the list of friends that had been discovered in the last couple of hours. "Bingo, boys!" he stated loudly. Grabbing his notepad, he walked over to Matthew and Steve. "Just made a connection between Becky and Jaycee."

Matthew spun around and asked, "How?"

Don responded, "Becky's roommate and best friend, Jamie, used to date Jaycee before he met Candice."

Steve replied, "Good. Find out how long and why they broke up."

"On it now," Don said.

Pamela hung up the desk phone and walked over to report what she found out from Candice. "I found Candice at her parent's home in Dallas. She said Jaycee walked her to class and met her again after class, and they returned together back to her dorm."

Matthew walked over to the map and added a clip to show Jaycee at the Dunn Building before and after class. "Who's the teacher?" he asked.

Pamela looked at a paper and then said, "Name is Professor Joshua Dobbs."

Matthew suggested, "Okay, Pamela, why don't you check out the good professor, and I'll go see Becky's roommate, Jamie."

Steve said, "I'll keep digging here with Don."

Matthew looked at his watch. It was four o'clock. "Let's meet back here at seven." Steve and the others agreed, and Matthew grabbed the info sheet on Jamie and left the room.

Chapter 12

Erin looked nervously across the reception area at Lindy's last patient of the day, Rhett Dobby. She did not like him. The twenty-eight-year-old electrician, whose body was covered with tattoos and piercings, had spent time in jail when he was a juvenile for starting fires throughout old warehouses on the south side of Arlington. Last week he had openly shared with her why he was there: "To please my new wife. She thinks I'm still fascinated by fire."

If one covered up Rhett's arms and dressed him up without the face piercings, he might easily be taken for a successful businessman. Rhett was good-looking, but the way he dressed and talked warned people to stay the hell away.

Erin could tell he was getting agitated. He kept looking at his watch and randomly turning the pages in the magazine without reading. The display on her computer screen read 4:02 p.m. Lindy had said to hold him two or three extra minutes before sending him back, and Erin had agreed without asking questions. She knew Lindy had her hands full with Carry Summerlin. One could just look at that girl and know she would be coming back to see the doctor for a very long time.

Finally, Erin stood up in her cowboy boots and khaki shirtdress with belted waist and said, "Mr. Dobby, Dr. Ashley will see you now. Please follow me."

Erin grabbed the updated file and led Rhett down the hall toward Lindy's office. Once they reached the door, Erin turned around to stare at Rhett. He smiled back and said, "You got a nice ass."

Erin didn't comment. She just opened the door and said, "Dr. Ashley, Rhett is here for his appointment. I'll be out front if you need anything," and then closed the door behind her.

Lindy took a look at Rhett Dobby and tried not to frown. Erin had just given her a code when she stated, "I'll be out front if you need anything." The statement meant that Rhett had made an inappropriate comment or something along those lines that offended Erin.

"Hello again, Rhett. Please take a seat and we'll begin."

Lindy picked up the file that Erin had laid on the side table and scanned it. Nothing looked alarming, so she set it aside and took a seat across from Rhett. "How was work today?"

"Good," he responded. "I survived, and I didn't burn anything to the ground."

This is going to be fun, Lindy thought as she picked up her pen and notepad and began to dig around in his warped head.

Chapter 13

Matthew Blake pulled his Camaro into the apartment complex where Robby Singleton's body had been found almost a week ago. It didn't take long for him to spot apartment B32, on the third floor with yellow tape draped across the door. As he got out of his car and walked toward the building, Matthew spotted teddy bears, flowers, ribbons, and cards placed along the railing outside of Robby's room. Students around campus had turned the outside of his apartment into a memorial.

Matthew turned away from the building in search of apartment C29. He didn't have to look long because it stood, identical in shape and size, just one building over from Robby's. Finding the staircase, Matthew began to make his way up to the second floor in search of Jamie Conrad, Becky's best friend and roommate.

Walking along the breezeway on the second floor, Matthew could still see apartment B32 across the small courtyard that separated the buildings. *This is convenient*, he thought.

Matthew stopped when he found C29 and knocked on the door. As he waited for a response, he made a mental note of his surroundings. To his left, he could see a patch of woods across the street with a sidewalk. From this elevated view, it appeared the sidewalk led to Central University, where most of the kids in this complex attended college.

At the sound of a dead bolt being unlocked, Matthew turned back around to face C29. From behind a cracked door with the chain securely latched in place, a tall, fair-complexioned redhead stared back with dark green eyes.

In a not-so-steady voice, she said, "Yes?"

Matthew held up his FBI badge. "Hello, my name is Agent Matthew Blake. I'm with the Dallas FBI division. Are you Jamie Conrad?"

The girl responded, "May I have a closer look at your badge, please."

"Sure." Matthew smiled and placed his badge in the girl's outstretched hand.

A moment passed and she said, "Just a moment," and then she shut the door. Matthew could hear the clatter of the chain being released and then she opened the door back up. "I'm Jamie Conrad. Sorry about that. I've had a lot of press people coming around pretending to be someone else."

Matthew frowned. "I'm sorry. May I come in? I would like to ask you some questions."

There was a slight hesitation before she opened the door all the way and motioned for him to enter. Matthew walked in and then turned around to watch Jamie bolt and latch the door behind them. Immediately he noticed that she was wearing flip-flops and stood just an inch short of his five-eleven height.

Jamie was dressed in something from Victoria's Secret's Pink Collection, and she wasn't wearing any makeup. Her tank was white with the words 'Want to hang out?' written in pink sequins. Her pink cotton shorts were rolled over at the waist and had the Pink logo spelled out on the back over her cute little ass. Jamie's red hair was pulled back into a ponytail, and her eyes gave the impression that she hadn't gotten much sleep the night before.

Matthew asked, "How's Becky doing?"

"Not good. We both feel like we're walking around in a nightmare begging to wake up."

"How long have you known Becky?"

"We met our freshman year. We're in the nursing program together."

Matthew asked, "And how long have you known Robby?"

Jamie tensed a little and then said, "I dated Robby first, during my sophomore year."

"Why did ya'll break up?"

With a shrug, Jamie walked over to the refrigerator and pulled out a soda. "He met Becky, and the rest is history." She opened the can and took a swig. Suddenly realizing her manners, she said, "Would you like one?"

Matthew shook his head no and continued on. "Let me get this straight. Becky broke you and Robby up?"

Jamie took another drink and then set the can on the counter. "Robby and I were too different. I think I was the first to notice how well he got along with Becky and how much they had in common."

"So you broke up with Robby and said go for Becky."

Jamie smiled. "Not exactly. He broke up with me and asked Becky out the very next weekend."

"Did she accept the date?"

"No. But I asked her to meet me at the Pork N Ribs joint on campus, and then I called and told Robby to show up instead of me."

"Wow, so did you not like Robby, since you let him go and gave your best friend the green light?"

Jamie took another sip. "Robby was not my first boyfriend or my first love. There's lots of guys out there, you know? Besides, it was just my second year in college. Things weren't clicking between us, and I was fine with moving on."

"How long went by before you went out on another date?"

"The same night I set them up." Jamie laughed and motioned for Matthew to follow her into the living room. As she settled on the leather couch, Matthew took a look around and noticed how clean the apartment was and how nice the furniture looked. He chose to sit across from her on the recliner.

Jamie leaned back and pulled her legs in under her. "I saw your press conference on the news today."

Matthew didn't respond and just waited for her to continue.

"I'm a little over five nine, and I dated Robby and Jaycee. Does that make me a suspect?"

Matthew looked hard at Jamie and tried to read her body language. She was really exotic looking with her high cheekbones and red, spirally hair. "Has anyone ever told you that you could pass for a young Nicole Kidman?" Matthew asked.

"Yes, a hundred times. But I'm going to be a nurse, not a brain surgeon like her role in the movie 'Days of Thunder.'"

He said, "Yeah. You know, I think she was like twenty-two when they cast her for that role. Doesn't it take like ten years before one can operate on the brain?"

Jamie said, "I've said the same thing before!" and she picked up her soda and took another drink.

When she was done, Matthew put on his serious face and asked the hard question. "Where were you last night around eight fifteen?"

Jamie frowned. "I was home alone."

"And last Wednesday night around eight-thirty?"

Her eyes twinkled back at him. "You already know the answer to that."

Matthew smiled back and said, "You were in class with Becky, correct?"

Jamie nodded.

Next, Matthew asked, "What can you tell me about your relationship with Jaycee?"

Jamie leaned forward and, slipping her legs out from under her, sat up straight. She continued to make eye contact with Matthew as she crossed her arms and then placed one hand under her chin. Finally she said, "Jaycee and I went out about five times before we called it quits."

"Why did you call it quits?"

Jamie narrowed her eyes. "Between you and me?"

Matthew went with it. "Okay, between you and me."

"He was terrible in bed."

Matthew tried to read her body language once again and came up empty. Either she was telling the truth or she was one hell of a liar. Matthew said, "Jamie, I have to be honest with you. At this point I'm more concerned about your safety than suspecting you of murder."

Jamie's face drained of color. "Are you saying I'm in danger?"

"I don't mean to frighten you, but you did know and date both victims."

Jamie shook her head and leaned back in the sofa with a much more relaxed demeanor. "Yeah, well, so did Becky and Candice."

Chapter 14

Parker took the snack from the man on the other side of the fence. The person was nice. He got a pat on the head as well as a snack. Moments later, Parker felt tired. Parker left the nice person and slowly walked over to the edge of the back porch and lay down. Parker continued to gaze sleepily at the person on the other side of the gate until his eyes slowly closed and he couldn't fight the sleepiness anymore.

With the dog out of the way, the man opened the wrought iron gate and made his way over to the back porch. Still lying on the table beside the yellow roses was the blue box. He quickly placed it in his pocket and then pulled out a key to the door.

The french door opened and then closed quietly as the man entered the house. Taking a look around, he noticed how nice and clean the place was. He walked over to the sofa, picked up an orange and brown throw pillow, and brought it to his nose. He couldn't smell her! Angrily, he threw the pillow back on the sofa.

The man continued on toward Lindy's bedroom. Once inside, he closed the door behind him and began pulling his clothing off as he made his way over to the king-size bed. He grabbed the blue and brown pillows and threw them to the floor before pulling the comforter down. The man stood there naked and just looked at the uncovered bed. As he closed his eyes, he tried to visualize Lindy lying there waiting on him. Having a hard time picturing his fantasy, he turned away from the bed, went to her dresser, and opened up the drawers one at a time until he found her silky panties and bras. A matching purple set caught his eye, and he carried the garments back over to the bed and sat down, placing them on his lap.

That was much better.

Chapter 15

Lindy had just finished her last notes on Rhett Dobby when Erin walked in. "Rhett Dobby is a jerk. He really creeps me out!"

Lindy said, "What did he say to you?"

"Told me I had a nice ass."

Lindy smiled. "Sorry. But hey, at least he didn't say you had a fat ass."

"Lindy, that's not funny! He's a—"

"Sorry! I know. He's a male chauvinist pig."

Erin pouted. "Why can't you just refuse to see him again?"

"Well, I did tell him to bring his new wife to the next session. So, he'll either cancel or bring her along. Either way will be better than today. Here—" She finished the statement by holding out Rhett's file.

Erin grabbed it and shoved it into the file cabinet with all the others. "I wish when I left this place, I can just turn it all off like you do."

Lindy replied, "Well, I have to or I would go crazy."

Erin looked down and fidgeted slightly. "Do you want to go out tonight and grab something to eat...maybe see a movie?"

Lindy thought about the question. *Erin didn't want to go home to an empty house now that she had broken things off with Leroy.* "Sounds great. But we'll need to go back to my place and check on Parker first."

Erin's mood immediately brightened, and a big grin spread across her face. "Let me grab my purse, and I'll turn everything off up front and lock up."

As Lindy reached for her bag, her private line started ringing. "Hello, Dr. Lindy Ashley speaking."

There was only silence.

Hmm, that's odd, Lindy thought. *Not many people have my private number.* She pulled the phone base closer and looked at the screen. It read, "Unlisted number."

"Hello? Is anyone there?"

Again, silence. A cold chill ran down her back and Lindy thought of saying more but just hung up instead. Erin popped back in and said, "Who was on the phone?"

"No one. Just a wrong number."

"Oh, okay. You ready to go?"

With bags and keys in hand, the girls left Lindy's office through the private door in the back, which opened up to another hallway on the opposite side of the building. The girls only had to take a few steps before they were on the elevator and headed down to the parking garage located under the building.

The elevator went from the fourth floor to the basement without stopping. The doors opened up to a well-lit parking garage with a security guard in sight. As they stepped out, the guard turned and looked their way.

"Evening, ladies. How your day go?"

Erin smiled at Davey. "Good. How's things down here?"

"Pretty boring day, which is a good thing."

"See you tomorrow, Davey," Lindy said as she walked over to her vehicle and hit the unlock button. She thought she caught Erin wave at him as she opened up the passenger door and got in. Once out of the parking garage, Erin commented, "I think Davey is good-looking. Do you think so?"

Lindy smiled. She'd seen correctly. "Yes, I think he's handsome. But I thought he was married."

Erin shrugged her shoulders. "I'll ask him tomorrow."

Lindy took her eyes off the road and looked at Erin. "Erin, he's twice your age!"

Erin tilted her head and pondered. "You really think he's in his forties?"

Lindy focused back on the traffic in front of her and just nodded her head.

"I'll ask him tomorrow," Erin said, "but I think you're wrong. Mid-thirties at the oldest."

Lindy was about to say something, but Erin's phone began to ring. Digging around in her purse, she finally found it after the fourth ring. "Hello?"

"Hi, babe, are you on your way home?"

With an exasperated look on her face, Erin said, "No, Leroy, I have plans tonight. Did you leave the key on my counter as I asked?"

Lindy heard only silence for several moments and then Erin finally said, "No, Leroy. Sorry, but it's over. Please erase my number and leave my key, and lock the door behind you."

Again more silence and then Erin hung up the phone after a very loud, "Well, up yours too!"

Lindy spoke next in a calm voice. "Erin, why don't we drop by your place first and pick up your key and some clothes. You can stay with me again tonight."

Erin was quiet for a moment and then said, "Thanks, Lindy. You're so good to me." Lindy reached out and patted Erin's hand. "I think I'll call a locksmith tomorrow and have them come by and change the locks."

Lindy was so relieved to hear Erin say that. Lindy had often wondered how many keys had been given out over the last few years and just how safe Erin really was staying alone. Erin quickly shattered Lindy's safety net by saying, "I hope we don't find anymore gifts at your house when we get there."

Lindy nervously said, "No one would dare come around my back porch with Parker outside."

The man left Lindy's bedroom and then headed into the bathroom and opened the shower door. Stepping in, he looked at his watch. It was a little after five. He was cutting it close but couldn't help the temptation building inside. He turned on the cold water only and then picked up her bottle of shampoo and began to wash.

Ten minutes later he was drying off with the purple bath towel that had hung on a hook nearby. The man smiled as he realized Lindy had used it last and it was not a fresh towel.

Chapter 16

Lindy pulled into Erin's empty driveway and said, "Good, it looks like Leroy left."

Erin stepped from the car and walked up the driveway that bordered her neat and tidy yard with her keys in hand. Lindy followed and stood by her side as she opened the front door. Though it was still light out, the interior of the house was semi dark. Erin flipped the light switch to her right, and, at first glance, everything looked fine. She took a few steps forward, and Lindy followed, shutting the door behind them. Erin turned down the hallway and was immediately hit with a nauseating smell. "What the hell is that smell?"

Entering the kitchen, they could instantly see what was producing the horrible odor. There, lying on the counter, was a pile of what appeared to be dog shit with a key sticking out of it.

Lindy said, "Oh, now that's a mature statement."

Frustrated, Erin went to the pantry, grabbed a plastic shopping bag, and scooped up the contents. She quickly tied the top of the bag in a knot and then carried it out the back door to the garbage can.

Lindy already had the Clorox bleach wipes out and was wiping down the counter when Erin returned. "I got this," Lindy said. "Go get some clothes and let's get out of here and have some fun."

"Thanks, Lindy. I sure know how to pick 'em."

Lindy didn't comment as Erin made her way down the hallway toward the master bedroom. Lindy finished up and then headed out the back door with the wipes to find the trash can. When Lindy opened the lid and threw them inside she heard Erin screaming at the top of her lungs.

Quickly Lindy ran back inside the house and toward the bedroom as fast as her legs could take her. When she got there, Erin was standing in the middle of the bedroom screaming, "Look what that asshole did! I'm going to kill him!"

Lindy looked around and immediately noticed Leroy's handiwork. He had apparently written 'bitch' on her walls with his urine. Lindy walked over and gently placed a hand on Erin's elbow. "Erin, let's just go. I'll call my housecleaner to come and clean tomorrow. Okay?"

Erin slowly turned away from the wall and looked at Lindy with tears in her eyes. "I'm so stupid! How can I have such horrible intuition about men?"

Lindy took a step closer and hugged Erin. "Don't say that," she said softly. "There's nothing wrong with having such a warm and trusting heart."

Erin slowly pulled away and sniffled. "I'll just wear some of your things. Let's just go."

Lindy looked one more time around the room and then followed Erin out of the house. Both were silent for the next twenty minutes as they drove toward Lindy's townhouse. Lindy had turned on her favorite country CD for them to listen to, and both were happy just to listen and watch the traffic and houses go by.

Lindy knew better than to talk about Leroy or give advice. Erin needed time to work through it all on her own. Over the years, Lindy had learned that Erin would approach her when she wanted to talk or needed advice. Until then, Lindy would have to wait patiently while her sister struggled with another of life's mishaps that seemed to always float her way.

It was dark now as Lindy finally turned into her driveway and waited for the garage door to roll back revealing the near-empty interior. Slowly Lindy moved forward in the car until she was safely inside the house and then pressed the garage button once more. Both girls stepped out and made their way over to the unlocked door that led to the kitchen. Once inside, she placed her keys and purse on the counter and went directly to the back door to let Parker in. When she didn't see him, she said, "That's odd. Normally he can hear the garage door and usually sits by the back door waiting." Lindy turned on the porch light. There in the corner of the porch lay the sleeping dog.

Erin walked over and said, "Did Parker not get enough sleep last night with all the commotion?"

Lindy looked at the flowers still sitting on the patio table and noticed that something was missing. "Where's the box?"

Erin looked over Lindy's shoulder. "I have no idea. Do you think Parker jumped on the chair and got it?"

Lindy quickly unlocked the door and called for Parker. He didn't move. Lindy walked over and bent down in her navy skirt and gently nudged the dog. "Parker, it's time to get up."

Parker slowly opened his eyes and then got up and stretched out his front legs and then his back legs. He looked up at Lindy and began licking her face. As if a switch had been turned on, Parker began jumping around and then took off into the house once he saw the door wide open.

Lindy just said, "Crazy dog!"

Once inside, Erin closed the door behind them and locked it. "Why don't we order in and pick a chick flick from your collection to watch instead of going back out?"

Lindy nodded. "Sounds perfect. What do you want to eat? I'll go find a takeout menu."

"Mexican sounds great."

Within ten minutes, dinner was called in and Lindy was making frozen margaritas. Pulling two teal blue margarita glasses from the cabinet, she placed them top down in some salt and then flipped them back over. After pouring the frozen concoction into the glasses, she topped them off with a straw. Handing Erin a glass, Lindy said, "I'm going to go put on a T and some shorts. Do you want a set?"

Erin nodded her head and followed Lindy into her bedroom with Parker a couple of steps behind. At the sight of Lindy's clean, tidy bedroom with the bed all made up, Erin said, "Sorry I didn't make my bed this morning."

Lindy smiled. "That's fine. You'll get another chance tomorrow."

Erin smiled back and then opened up a dresser drawer and removed a pink tank with matching pink and blue stripped boxer shorts. "This works for me." She immediately stripped down to her black thong underwear and her near-perfect body and pulled on the shorts and the tank. Afterward, she bent down and picked up her bra and dress and tossed them on the chair located in the corner of the room.

Lindy walked into the master bath and immediately said, "That's odd. The shower is still wet from this morning."

She walked over to the closet and opened it with her margarita glass still in her hand. Taking another sip, she set it aside on the built-in dresser and began to unzip her navy skirt. As her skirt hit the ground, Erin asked, "Where did you get that ugly bruise?"

Lindy continued taking off her white silk blouse with navy flowers on it and said, "I fell last week getting out of the tub."

Erin looked over at the garden tub. "Sis, be careful next time! That could have been really bad."

Lindy turned around and looked at the bruise in the mirror. "It was!"

Erin went over to the bathroom counter and began to brush her long blond hair, pulling it back into a ponytail. By the time she finished,

Lindy had already changed and was headed back to the living room. Erin yelled out, "Let's watch 'The Holiday' with Cameron Diaz."

"Works for me. Dig it out of the cabinet. I'm going to set the plates and let Parker out one more time."

Lindy opened up the french doors again, and Parker zoomed by headed for his favorite grassy corner. Soon he was finished and back in the house, but Lindy continued to watch the backyard.

Erin walked up behind her and said, "What is it?"

"I just wonder what Parker did with that box."

"Who knows," Erin said, looking around. "It was windy today. Maybe it could've blown into the lake."

"Maybe."

As Lindy and Erin turned away from the door, the front doorbell rang, and they both jumped. Erin said, "I'm sure it's just our food. You lock this door while I go check."

"Use the peephole!" Lindy shouted after her as she closed and locked the door.

From the front door, Erin turned around and smiled. "It's delivery." She opened the door to a young Hispanic teenager holding two bags. He took one look at Erin and immediately his eyes ran up and down her body. His face turned a bright shade of pink as he realized Erin noticed him staring. Lindy walked up from behind and, handing him two twenties, said, "Keep the change."

"Awe, thank you, miss," he said as Lindy closed and locked the door.

"That's funny," Erin commented. "Parker didn't even bark."

Lindy looked down at Parker, wagging his tail and following on Erin's heels as she carried the bags of food into the kitchen. *What is going on with him?* She wondered. Shrugging her shoulders, she quickly pushed aside any further thought about the matter and went into the kitchen to eat.

Across the street sat a man in a dark vehicle. He was holding a pair of binoculars as the laptop sitting in his lap played his newest video. Placing the binoculars to the side, he finished watching the scene unfold in the master bedroom and then master bath. He said aloud with a wicked smile, "This is a sweet treat. I got both of the Ashley girls tonight."

Chapter 17

Matthew arrived back at the Dallas headquarters at six-thirty sharp, thirty minutes before his planned meeting with the team. Since he was wearing part of his fast-food burger, he decided to go to his office first and grab a fresh T-shirt. As Matthew rounded the corner, he nearly collided with Janet.

"Hi, Matthew. I would ask if you had dinner, but that looks a little obvious."

"Yeah, well, eating and driving in Dallas sometimes doesn't go together."

Janet smiled and said, "I have a couple of messages here for you."

Matthew grabbed the papers and started sorting through them as he walked into his office. He didn't expect to find anything urgent; any calls about the case went straight to A150 and someone took the call. On the fourth message, Matthew stopped.

Just a reminder: next session with Dr. Lindy Ashley on Wednesday, Sept. 29, at 4:00 p.m.

Matthew placed the messages on his desk and pulled his T-shirt over his head. Opening the last drawer of his file cabinet, he took out a gray T-shirt, ripped off the tags, and quickly put it on.

Rolling his chair back, Matthew took a seat and then flipped through the rest of the messages. When he was done, he went back to Dr. Ashley's message. Drumming his fingers lightly on the desktop, he thought, *Another appointment coming up. I really did want to ask her out. Damn! Too bad the timing is just all wrong.*

Steve interrupted his thoughts when he poked his head in and said, "Hey, have you eaten?"

Matthew put the message down. "Yep, fast food."

Steve frowned. "Too bad. I have leftover seafood pasta."

"How are things here? Anything new?"

Steve said, "We have more data on the kids...and a lot of useless calls coming in. How about you?"

Matthew thought for a moment about his meeting with Jamie Conrad. "Yeah, I got in touch with Jamie and asked a series of questions. Basically, Central University is like one big soap opera where everyone knows and dates everyone."

"I know what you mean. More info keeps coming in, and nearly everyone has a tie with someone."

Matthew stood up. "Let's go check in."

The men walked out of Matthew's office, and Steve waved to Janet as they passed by her. With thoughts of Dr. Lindy Ashley on his mind, Matthew never even gave her a glance.

When Steve and Matthew entered A150, Don and Pamela stopped what they were doing and came over to greet them. Pamela began filling them in first. "I met with Professor Dobbs. He says he was on his way to the airport when Robby Singleton was killed. It appears his mom is dying in Ohio. Anyway, he stated he returned just in time for Monday's class and stayed in the Dunn Building till nine o'clock the night Jaycee Brown was killed."

Matthew asked, "Have you been able to confirm what he said yet?"

Pamela glanced at her notes. "He checked in DFW at nine twenty-nine for the ten o'clock flight to Ohio last Wednesday night. I wasn't able to find any teacher or cleaning staff to confirm Monday night's late office hours though."

Matthew thought, *Killing Robby Singleton and making it to DFW airport by nine-thirty check-in is doable but unlikely.*

Steve held up a photo. "Looking at the crime scene pictures of Robby's apartment, it's hard to imagine the killer going straight to an airport and getting on a plane. He would have to change and possibly get a shower."

Matthew said, "I agree, but I don't want to overlook him. How tall is the professor?"

"Joshua Dobbs is five eleven," responded Pamela.

Matthew shook his head. "Too close to rule him out just yet."

Don asked, "What can you tell us about Jamie Conrad?"

A vision of the red-haired beauty sitting on her couch flashed through his mind. Her laugh, her smile, her carefree attitude on life intrigued Matthew. After a moment he answered, "Her height is right, and she knows and dated both victims, but if I'm reading her body language correctly, I don't think she killed them."

Don nodded. "She was counted present in class Wednesday night, along with Becky. Did she have an alibi for last night?"

Another flash of Jamie entered his mind and he remembered her comment 'I was home alone' so he answered, "No."

Pamela picked up her pen and made a note. "I will talk with her professor tomorrow and find out if there were any breaks with Wednesday night's class."

"Even so, she didn't have a vehicle. She walked to and from class with Becky," added Steve.

Matthew instructed, "Yeah, but still check on that, Pamela."

No one made any more comments concerning Jamie, so Matthew continued. "According to Jamie, Becky and Candice both dated Robby and Jaycee."

"Wow! These girls sure get around," exclaimed Pamela.

Don remarked, "Yeah, they do. Great. Gonna be a fun night."

After a couple of hours of answering phones and gathering more personal information on both of the victims, Matthew looked at his watch. "Okay, guys, it's ten o'clock. Let's let the night team handle the phones and call it a night."

Steve got up from behind a computer and stretched. "Yeah, I'm losing concentration."

"Let's meet back here in the morning at six. I'll get breakfast brought in" continued Matthew.

Pamela placed her notes down and shoved her chair back from the table. "Fine, but no doughnuts!"

Don patted his waist. "What's wrong with doughnuts?"

She smiled, "Calories!"

Matthew tossed some papers in his backpack and walked out to Janet's desk. "The night team can take the calls now."

Janet stood up. "It's about time! Some days I feel like I live here."

Matthew said, "Yeah, well, I don't see that changing anytime soon."

Janet asked, "What time do you want breakfast brought in?"

Once again Janet read his mind. "I was just about to ask. How does six-thirty sound?"

"Fine, I will call it in from home and pick it up on my way here."

"Thanks. Oh, and Pamela requested something healthy."

"No problem. I'll get a combo of things to carry ya'll over till noon."

Matthew noticed she was all ready to go with her purse slung over her shoulder. He asked, "Are you ready? I'll walk you to your car."

Janet's face lit up. "Thanks, Matthew."

Miles away, the one the media dubbed "The Night Killer" was restless. The next victim had already been chosen, and now the only thing left to do was wait. Tossing and turning now for an hour, sleep just wouldn't come.

Getting up, the killer left the bedroom and went into the kitchen. Opening the cabinet, the Night Killer took down a glass and a bottle of whiskey. A double shot was poured and then quickly tossed down. A burning sensation immediately filled the back of the killer's throat as the smooth liquid made its way down. Satisfied, the killer placed the bottle of whiskey back into the cabinet and returned to bed. Sleep would come now, and the countdown would begin very soon.

Chapter 18

Dr. Lindy Ashley took the day's schedule from Erin and walked toward her office. Erin yelled out behind her, "Hey, look at your last appointment of the day."

Lindy didn't have to look; she already knew her four o'clock appointment was Agent Matthew Blake. After standing around in her closet for fifteen minutes and trying on at least a dozen outfits this morning, she finally admitted to herself that she was excited to see him.

Lindy looked over her outfit now as she entered her office. She had chosen dark red cowboy boots and a navy denim dress that was sleeveless and had a silver zipper along the length of the front that stopped just above her chest.

Setting the schedule on her desk, she gave it a glance as she readjusted the silver belt that hung loosely on her hips. "First up today we have Jimmy Thorn, at eight o'clock," she said softly to herself. According to her watch, she had about twenty minutes before he was scheduled to arrive—plenty of time to look over his file and refresh her memory.

Jimmy was a depressed sixty-year-old man who had been married for the last thirty-five years to his wife, Patricia. Together, they had four kids, and two grandchildren from their oldest son. Jimmy worked full time as an accountant while Patricia stayed at home since her retirement two years ago.

As she read over her notes from their last meeting, Erin walked in and began to pull the rest of the files for the day. Turning around she said, "I got a call from Ms. Summerlin earlier. Carry had a bad night and wants to see you again today."

Lindy picked up her schedule and glanced over the names and times. "Where did you fit her in?"

"Three-thirty to four. I figured you didn't need much prep time for Agent Blake."

Lindy continued to analyze the times and then after a moment said, "You made a good choice, Erin."

Erin smiled really big and then went back to pulling files. After about two more, she turned around again and said, "I forgot to ask you yesterday, what did Professor Dobbs say when you called?"

"Shit!" Lindy said "Nothing. I got his voice mail and said I would call back after work."

"Well, that was my fault. You got caught up in my melodramatic life."

Without further comment, Lindy picked up her private line and dialed Joshua's number, and Erin left her office.

On the third ring, he said, "Hello?"

"Hi, Joshua, it's Lindy. Sorry I didn't get back with you last night."

"Fine, fine, Lindy. I will see you tonight though, correct?"

"Yes. I will be there around five-thirty."

"Good. I guess you heard there was another murder Monday night?"

"I did. Was he one of your students as well?"

"No, no. Thank goodness, though, because an FBI woman came by yesterday and questioned me. I'm afraid it wouldn't look good for me if I lost two students."

"Joshua, what are you talking about? Did she suspect you?"

"Well no, at least I hope not. Besides, I was on my way to the airport last Wednesday night when Robby was killed."

Lindy asked, "Did you tell her about me?"

Joshua paused for a moment and then said, "No, I never mentioned you. Anyway, I think tonight will be a full class."

For a few seconds, Lindy thought about what he said. "I guess you're right. More students are going to be interested in my lecture on sociopaths now that it appears we have a serial killer on the loose."

"Yeah, I would expect a lot of questions."

Just then Erin popped her head in and said quietly, "Jimmy Thorn is here."

Lindy nodded and held up two fingers.

"Hey, Joshua, I have to go now. We'll talk more when I get there."

"Okay, Lindy. Have a good day, and I'll see you tonight."

Lindy stood up to greet Jimmy as he made his way in. Immediately she noticed that he had continued to put on weight. "Please, Jimmy, have a seat."

Jimmy walked around to the front of the sofa and sat down while Lindy placed her notepad on the coffee table and took a seat in the yellow chair. Lindy asked, "Jimmy, I want you to think back on the last week and come up with five things or events that made you smile."

Jimmy sat back some and closed his eyes. After about one minute, a smile spread across his face and he spoke.

Erin was behind her desk scheduling an appointment when Clay Barry waltzed in. She briefly made eye contact with him and motioned for him to have a seat while she finished up the call. Clay sat down in the chair nearest her desk and began flipping through a magazine while he waited.

Finally Erin said, "Hello, Mr. Barry. Can I get you some coffee or water while you wait? You do know you are thirty minutes early, right?"

Clay glanced at his watch. Looking a little embarrassed, he nodded. "I was already in the neighborhood. But I'm good, thank you."

Erin said, "Okay. Just let me know if you change your mind."

Erin was the first to break eye contact, looking away and punching a few keys on her computer keyboard. She struggled to concentrate as Clay continued to fidget and stare at her. Feeling self-conscious, she re-crossed her legs and smoothed out her black skirt. The blue knit top she wore today was Lindy's, and it fit a little tight across her chest. The skirt, also Lindy's, was a perfect fit in the waist but a little short due to the height difference.

Erin tried to brush aside any insecure feelings and concentrate on her computer screen. It appeared to be working until the phone rang and she jumped, knocking over the last of her coffee.

Clay Barry immediately sprang up and, grabbing the box of Kleenex beside him, rushed over to help Erin with the coffee. "Thanks," she said as she pulled three tissues out and started cleaning up the mess while also reaching to answer the phone.

"Dr. Ashley's office, Erin speaking. How may I help you?"

On the other end a male voice said, "Hi, Erin, Agent Blake."

Erin felt herself smile but then immediately tried to correct her facial expression since Clay Barry was still standing in her space. She motioned to him that she was good and to have a seat. Awkwardly, he stepped backward until he found the couch and sat down with eyes still on Erin.

"Hello? Erin?"

Erin turned away in her swivel chair and said, "I'm sorry, Agent Blake. Yes, I'm still here."

"Well, about my appointment this afternoon…"

"Yes, it's at four o'clock."

"Well, as you probably have heard by now, I'm working the Night Killer case, and I might be too tied up to come back in today."

"I know. Lindy and I saw your interview on TV yesterday. It's all really sad and scary, especially since Lindy was on campus both nights."

Matthew sat up in his office chair and picked up his pen and asked, "What did you just say?"

Not noticing the change in the agent's voice, Erin simply stated the facts. "Lindy is a guest speaker for Professor Dobbs for the next several weeks, and his class meets on Monday and Wednesday nights."

Matthew asked, "What is her topic? Is it the same, or does it change each week?"

Erin saw this as a wonderful opportunity to get Agent Blake back into the office, so she lied. "I'm sorry. I really don't know. You'll have to ask Lindy."

"I see. Well, I tell you what, I will keep my appointment, but I can't guarantee I'll be on time or stay the entire length of the session."

Erin broke out in a big grin; her plan had worked like a charm. "I understand. We'll see you sometime then between four and five."

Clay Barry never took his eyes off Erin. Noting the way she looked and acted with the agent on the other end of the line, he felt his face turn red and his temper begin to rise up from deep down in his chest. He took a deep breath and looked away just in time to control his urge to explode.

Chapter 19

Matthew Blake spoke aloud in his empty office. "What the hell? I tried to cancel the appointment, but instead I'm going back for more?"

Shaking his head, he got up and headed back to room A150, where his partner, Steve, and the others were working. Without giving Janet so much as a glance as he passed her desk, he made his way to the conference room.

Once inside the room, Matthew loudly announced, "It appears that a Dr. Lindy Ashley was the guest speaker for Dobb's psychology class the last two sessions. Coincidence that she was on campus both nights that a murder occurred? I don't know, but we need to find out."

Pamela was the first to respond. "Professor Dobbs never mentioned a guest speaker, and I didn't think to ask."

Matthew asked, "Did you ask what they were currently studying?"

Pamela walked over to her desk and riffled through some papers until she found what she was looking for. "Dobbs gave me a handout on topics this semester. There's no mention here of a guest speaker."

Steve said, "Well, I'm not surprised. His mom is dying, and his handout probably has an asterisk at the bottom that says something about 'subject to change...'"

After reading the handout, Pamela looked up in surprise. "I'd forgotten about that since attending college, but you're right."

Matthew said, "Okay, so what are the topics stated for study?"

Pamela rattled off, "Weeks one and two, death and grievances. Week three, schizophrenia. Weeks four through six, mental illness and its effects on society. Week seven—"

Don interrupted. "Stop right there! We're currently in week five."

Matthew commented, "There's no way of knowing for sure what her lecture is about without asking. I'm scheduled to see her today at four and will ask her then."

"For now, I'll pull some background information on the doctor," Steve suggested with a wink.

Matthew caught his gesture and just smiled and shook his head. Pamela noticed it as well and asked "What?"

Steve was going to answer but stopped when Fred Copeland entered the room. "Hi, gang. How's it going in here?"

All chatter in the room stopped as everyone directed their attention to the front, where Copeland was standing. Matthew walked over to the board and, speaking loudly enough for everyone to hear, began to summarize their progress to date.

All day Erin had been eagerly checking patients in. With each appointment that passed, her excitement grew. She had decided earlier this morning that Matthew Blake was a great catch, and if Lindy wasn't going to give it a go, she would. And now, finally, the schedule was down to the last appointment before the handsome FBI agent was due to arrive. By three twenty-five, Mrs. Summerlin and daughter Carry were seated and sipping the beverages Erin had offered them while they waited for Carry's three-thirty appointment. When the light went off at Erin's desk signaling Lindy's readiness to see them, Erin nearly jumped from her chair. Reining in her excitement, she very calmly walked over to the waiting clients and said, "Dr. Ashley will see you now. Please follow me."

Carry stood up as did her mother. Erin hesitated only briefly and then decided to let Lindy handle the matter. After all, it was the parent's right to sit in on a session.

Just as they reached Lindy's office, the front door buzzer went off. Erin quickly stepped in and handed Lindy a file and then breezed back out closing the door behind her.

Back in the reception area, she found Luke James pacing back and forth. When Luke saw Erin, his boyish face registered a big grin as he gave Erin the once over in her short skirt and tight top.

"Hi, Erin. How's it going?"

Erin smiled back at Luke and said, "I'm doing well. How about yourself?"

Erin liked Luke. He was extremely good-looking and worked out all the time. She knew he was also trouble, and that was probably why she liked him.

Luke said, "I'm good. Does Lindy have a moment to see me? I need to ask her something."

Erin frowned. "Oh, I'm sorry, Luke. I just walked a patient back, and Dr. Ashley won't finish until four o'clock. Would you like to wait and I can squeeze you in for about five minutes before her next appointment?"

Luke looked at his watch and then shook his head. "No, that won't work. I have somewhere else to be at four-thirty. If you would though, maybe ask her to call me on my mobile around four?"

Erin replied, "I will be happy to. Would you like me to schedule you an appointment for tomorrow?"

Luke thought for a moment and then said, "Nah, next week is still good."

"Okay then, I'll see you next week."

Luke waved good-bye and then left. Erin watched his backside all the way out thinking, you sure look really good in a pair of jeans, Luke. Once he was gone, Erin went to the room that served as their small kitchen. Opening up the refrigerator, she took out two kiwis and a bottle of water. Finding a sharp knife and cutting board, Erin peeled and then chopped the fruit into bite-size pieces. When she was done, she cleaned up after herself and then grabbed a fork and her snack.

As Erin turned to head back to her desk, the front door buzzer went off again. Thinking it was Agent Blake, she hurried down the hallway. Rounding the last corner, Erin walked into an empty waiting room. A little confused, she looked out through the glass of the front door but saw no one. She glanced over at her desk. Nothing looked disturbed or was missing. Hmm, someone probably just had the wrong office, she reasoned. When she returned to the desk, however, Erin immediately jumped back.

On her chair sat a small box wrapped in purple paper with a white bow. There was a card attached with no name on the outside. As she reached to pick it up, the front door buzzer sounded again, and Erin jumped. Her eyes darted toward the door, but there was no one there.

Erin took a deep breath to calm herself and then decided to step outside to see what was going on. Slowly she pushed the glass door open. There was no one in the hall. Hearing an elevator bell chime, she immediately took off in that direction. As she rounded the corner in two-inch heels, Erin only caught the elevator door closing. She instantly pushed the down button, but the elevator continued on without opening back up. Frustrated, Erin turned and walked back to the office.

Erin never once noticed the stairwell door cracked and someone peering at her from behind. The person smiled and continued to watch Erin's long legs and shapely hips swing side to side as she walked away.

Chapter 20

Back inside the office, Erin took a few steps down the hallway before noticing that Lindy's door was still shut. Quietly she returned to her desk to have a look at the box, but first she grabbed the note and opened it. All it said was
"Sorry."

Erin picked up the box and placed it on the desk. She continued to stare at it as she picked up her fork and started to eat her kiwis. With each bite she was more convinced the box was from Leroy. Satisfied with her conclusion, she picked up the box and unwrapped it.

Erin held the white unmarked box for a moment before setting it back down and tossing the paper and bow in the wastebasket. Picking it back up, she flipped it over a few times and noticed all edges were taped shut. As she began to peel the tape from one edge, the front door buzzer sounded once again, and Erin reflexively threw the box to the ground.

Erin looked up and there stood Agent Matthew Blake with a concerned look on his face. Erin breathed deeply as Matthew said, "I'm sorry, Erin. I didn't mean to startle you."

Quickly she composed herself and then stood up. "No, no, I'm good." Erin glanced at the clock and saw that it was five after four. "Dr. Ashley shouldn't be long. Can I get you something to drink?"

Matthew never once took his eyes off Erin as he replied, "A cup of coffee would be great. If you don't mind."

Erin smiled. "Not at all. Take a seat and I'll be right back."

When Erin turned to walk out, she stepped right on the box, crushing it with her heel. She stopped and looked at it and decided right then and there that Leroy wasn't worth her time. She bent down and picked up the box, and into the trash it went. Erin smiled back at Agent Blake and then left to get his coffee.

When Erin returned to the waiting room with a coffee and small plate of cookies, Matthew was seated on the leather couch flipping through a magazine. She handed him the coffee and then placed the cookies on the coffee table. "I baked those earlier today. They're chocolate chip."

Matthew grabbed one and said, "Thanks."

Erin smiled again and returned to her desk. As she sat down, she heard Lindy's door open and voices down the hall. Soon another door was closed and all was quiet once again. Erin looked at the clock; it was now four ten. She picked up a file and headed toward Lindy's office.

Dr. Lindy Ashley's office had three exit doors. One was used by Lindy and Erin and was located at the very end of the hall beside the kitchen. Another one was directly in front of Lindy's office and opened up to a hallway, so patients could leave the office without bumping into anyone in the front waiting room. Both of these exits were locked from the outside and could only be opened from the inside. Erin checked the door and made sure it was completely shut and then opened Lindy's office door.

Lindy was sitting behind her desk and frantically writing in Carry's file. She never looked up as she said, "Give me one minute."

Erin took a seat in Lindy's yellow chair and waited patiently. About three minutes passed before Lindy stopped writing and closed the file. With a distraught look on her face, she glanced at Erin and said, "Is Agent Blake here?"

"Yes, but you need to call Luke James first on his mobile. He stopped by earlier, just as you started your session with Carry Summerlin." Erin handed Lindy a note that had Luke's number written on it.

"Did he say what he wanted?"

Erin shook her head. "I'll go and keep Agent Blake company. Just let me know when you're ready."

Lindy picked up her phone as Erin walked out and shut the door behind her. "I'm sure you will," Lindy said to herself.

Three unanswered rings sounded and then a message. "Hi, you've reached Luke. Leave a message."

"Hi, Luke, it's Lindy." She looked at her watch and frowned. "It's four fifteen. Sorry I missed you earlier. I will try to call again around five. Bye."

Lindy stood up with the note and Carry Summerlin's file. She walked over to her filing cabinet and filed Carry away and then pulled out the J drawer and looked for Luke's file. Finding it, she pulled it out and took it back to her desk. Opening it up, she placed the note inside and documented the time called. Closing it, she set it to the side and picked up Matthew Blake's file. It was already four twenty now and Lindy went ahead and hit the light for Erin to send him in. Lindy ran a hand through her jet-black hair and readjusted her silver belt. Picking up his file, she headed toward the door just as it opened to Erin and the agent staring back at her.

Lindy said, "Thank you, Erin. Hi, Matthew. It's good to see you again. Please come in."

Matthew responded, "Hi, Lindy. Busy day?"

Lindy waited until Erin closed the door and then motioned for Matthew to take a seat. Once both were settled, she said, "Yes, a busy day. I'm sorry to keep you waiting so long."

Matthew looked into her blue eyes and said, "No trouble. Besides, it allowed me to have a cup of coffee and some fantastic chocolate chip cookies."

Lindy couldn't help but smile. "Yes, Erin is great."

For a moment neither spoke, and they just sat looking at each other. Finally Lindy said, "I saw you on TV yesterday. It appears you've jumped right back into another big case. How's that going?"

Matthew commented, "I have. My line of work is never boring either."

"So, do you think you are ready for something so intense after the way the last case ended?"

Matthew wanted to say, *Ned Fry is a useless piece of shit, and this world is better off with him dead versus paying good taxpayer money to keep his sorry ass alive in jail and watching satellite TV.* Instead he said, "It was unfortunate that Ned Fry was killed, but the life of a young boy outweighs any lost sleep that one might have for pulling the trigger."

Lindy's eyebrows shot up and she asked quizzically, "Have you lost sleep or had nightmares?"

Shit, here we go again! Matthew thought.

For the next several minutes, some hard questions were once again asked and answered by what appeared to be a weak and vulnerable FBI agent. Gradually, Matthew's skilled, trained mind took back over, and he was able to turn the discussion around. Leaning back some on the leather couch, Matthew finally saw an opening to ask the question that had brought him to her office today in the first place.

"So, Lindy, in the course of my investigation into the deaths of the university students, I noticed you were on campus both nights. Did you know either of the victims, Robby Singleton or Jaycee Brown?"

Lindy never missed a beat as she said, "No. However, Professor Dobbs informed me that Robby was his student. I was with Professor Dobbs last Monday when we addressed the class over Robby's death."

Matthew studied her face trying to gauge her innocence. "What is your lecture about, and are you planning on attending class tonight?"

Lindy tilted her head and spoke frankly. "I plan to arrive at five-thirty. My lecture will start shortly after six and I plan to discuss the characteristics of sociopaths for about twenty to thirty minutes."

"And the remaining class time?"

She smiled and said, "Professor Dobbs will open it up for a class discussion. I will stay and answer questions till seven, when the class ends."

"I see. What was class like on Monday night?"

Lindy thought back, "The kids were visibly upset as Professor Dobbs talked about Robby, and a short discussion took place afterward."

He paused briefly and said, "I can imagine. I was told the class ended earlier than normal. Did you lecture at all on Monday night?"

"No, I really didn't talk much that night since he was the professor's student and I didn't know Robby."

Lindy looked at her watch and then back up at Matthew. "Tonight Professor Dobbs anticipates a large turnout. All this talk about a serial killer has got the kids interested in psychology."

Matthew said, "Do you plan on altering your lecture any and discussing serial killers?"

Lindy replied, "Well, at this point, I plan to go with my original notes from Monday night, but I am definitely using the current situation to gain interest from the students."

Matthew looked at his own watch and noticed it was ten till five. Lindy placed her file down on the table and said, "I have no concerns that your mental state would interfere with or inhibit you from continuing with your line of work. I'm now willing to sign off on your papers so you can focus fully on this investigation."

Matthew was a little taken aback but said, "Thank you. I would appreciate that."

Lindy smirked. "Yes, well it seems you're the one asking the questions now, so I don't see any ghost of Ned Fry interfering with your current case."

It was Matthew's turn to smile. "You know, I'm planning to attend class tonight too. Would you like to have dinner afterward?"

Matthew watched as Lindy twisted her sexy mouth as she contemplated what he asked. A few seconds passed before Lindy answered, "That would be lovely but I make it a rule not to date my patients."

He smiled. "Well, I'm not exactly one of your patients. Besides, I'd like to get your thoughts about this case."

She laughed. "Not one of my patients? I have a file on you."

"A file that will be collected today. Oh come on, I was a temporary case that was quickly dismissed. How could you possibly count me as a patient?"

Lindy rolled her pen between her fingers. She couldn't deny the attraction. She felt her face slightly blush at the thought of running around this morning trying to figure out what to wear. *Now what?*

Taking her silence as an answer, Matthew stood up with a grin. "Great! I will see you later then."

Lindy rose from her chair to walk him to the door. "Um, yes, well, we'll talk about this case and"

"Of course." He smiled. A beautiful smile that tugged at her heart.

She continued, "I won't have your papers ready till tomorrow."

"That's fine."

Lindy opened her office door and jumped backward into Matthew. Standing just outside the door was a terrified, white-faced Erin.

"Erin, are you okay?" Lindy immediately asked.

Erin shook her head side to side and pointed down the hall. Matthew gently pushed Lindy aside and quickly made his way to the front of the office. There lying on Erin's desk was the crushed box opened up to reveal a lock of hair splattered with what appeared to be dried blood. Matthew looked around the office to make sure they were alone before saying, "Where did you get this?"

With voice shaking, Erin said, "It showed up a few minutes before you got here. I only decided to open it a minute ago."

Matthew saw the card and used a pencil from Erin's desk to gently pull it open.

"Who brought it?" Lindy asked.

"I don't know. I found it in my chair when I came back from making a snack. When I saw the card, I just thought it was from Leroy. At first I threw it away, and then I decided I would…"

"It's okay, Erin," Lindy said. "But I don't think Leroy would send that."

Matthew studied Lindy's face and then Erin's body language and asked, "Who's Leroy?"

Lindy quickly filled Matthew in about the events from the last two days. Matthew never once interrupted. He just listened and observed Lindy as she explained Leroy, the flowers, the box, and the ghost at her front door. Within minutes, phone calls were made, and a new plan was set in motion.

Chapter 21

Erin hung up her cell phone and said, "I'm meeting Tiffany for dinner, and she'll go home with me tonight."

"Excellent," Lindy said. "I just checked my voice mail. Judy cleaned your house today and dropped your key back into the mailbox."

An expression of relief spread across Erin's face but then disappeared when Matthew scowled. "It's a locked mail box," she exclaimed.

Matthew nodded and then said, "I will walk both of you to your cars. Also, I'm going to leave this with security downstairs," he pointed to the box, "and someone from the office is going to come by and pick it up for analysis."

Erin said, "Thanks, Agent Blake. Let me go get my purse and I'm out of here!"

"Please, just call me Matthew."

She replied, "Sure. I'm glad you were here today."

"So am I. This isn't your average prank."

Lindy frowned and then said, "You two go on down. I need to call a patient back."

Erin looked at Matthew and shook her head no.

Matthew smiled. "We will wait here while you finish up."

Lindy nodded and walked back to her office, shutting the door behind her. It was now five after five. She quickly opened up Luke's file and retrieved his mobile number. Taking a seat behind her desk, she punched in the numbers on her desk phone and waited as the phone on the other end rang. After a few seconds, she was again connected to his voice mail.

Lindy said, "Hi, Luke, it's Lindy again. Just trying to get in touch with you. Please call the office tomorrow if you want to set up another appointment before next week. Good-bye now."

Lindy made a note in Luke's file and then tucked it away in the cabinet for the night. With nothing else that needed her attention, she grabbed her purse and then popped into her bathroom to freshen up. Five minutes later, Lindy looked in the mirror and said to herself, "Okay, Matthew Blake, let's see where this goes."

It didn't take long before they were all in their vehicles and ready to leave. At five fifteen Lindy waved as Erin pulled out of the parking garage in her little yellow convertible. Looking in her rearview mirror, Lindy noticed Matthew waiting on her to pull out next. Once out on the highway, she tried to relax and focus on tonight's lecture. Once again she felt rushed, and that only added to her anxiety about tonight's class. Pulling up to a red light, Lindy took out her cell phone and dialed Joshua's number.

He answered after the second ring.

"Sorry, Joshua, but I'm just now leaving. Traffic is moving good, so I should be there around five forty-five or ten till."

"That's fine, Lindy. I'll see you when you get here."

Lindy hung up the phone and accelerated when the light turned green.

Two blocks away from the Dunn Building, a couple was sitting on a bench under an old live oak tree. The tree was one of the largest on campus, and four benches had been placed around it for students to gather under its shade. Tonight Andrew Mitt and Melody Montgomery occupied one of those benches. Melody and Andrew had been dating on and off for about a year now. Melody was in her fourth year and studying to be a school psychologist. Andrew was in medical school specializing in pediatrics and had two more years left before graduating. Currently, Andrew and Melody were a happy couple.

Melody's head was resting in Andrew's lap with her knees bent over the armrest and her long, beautiful legs dangling over the end. Andrew had one arm draped around Melody's large chest, and the other was holding a book. He was attempting to read but kept shifting and moving his arm to the side, as he was finding it extremely difficult to concentrate. Melody had her eyes closed and was smiling. Andrew's eyes traveled from her lips down to her light pink tank top that only covered three fourths of her cleavage. He paused there and watched as her chest rose and fell with each breath. She was wearing faded cutoffs that were very short, and his eyes slowly continued down to her smooth, tan legs. He thought, *God, she is beautiful! How the hell am I supposed to concentrate with her wearing that?*

Melody was beautiful, but she was also smart. Andrew was just as turned on by her mind as he was her body. She could hold her own with chess, Trivial Pursuit, or any other mind game they played. Finally Andrew placed his book down and said, "You're going to cause me to flunk out of medical school."

Melody opened her hazel eyes and then pouted her sexy lips. Andrew shook his head and smiled. "Well, I guess I can always be a nurse."

Melody laughed and wrapped her arms around him, bringing him down for a kiss. She could feel his body tensing beneath her, and, in one swift move, she sat up and straddled him.

Andrew looked around and saw that they were getting some attention, so he grabbed her by the waist and held her up into the air as he stood up. Andrew's muscles bulged under his tight Central University T-shirt as he continued to hold her. Gracefully, Melody wrapped her long legs around his waist and pulled him into her.

Melody kissed Andrew again and then slowly allowed her legs to slide down his body. Andrew continued to hold her tightly until her feet touched the ground. Melody was the first to pull away, and she said, "I've got class soon. I should go."

"Oh, I get it! It's time to cool down when you've got class."

Melody winked and said, "I'm free after class. How about you?"

Andrew had an exam scheduled for tomorrow and hesitated a bit before answering, "Okay. I'll go to the library and hit the books hard and then I'll meet up with you later."

Melody smiled and leaned in for another kiss, and Andrew hugged her tightly before letting her go. Melody bent over and picked up her backpack and then tossed her long blond hair over her shoulders and walked away. Andrew just stood there and watched. When she was about thirty yards away, she turned back around and blew him a kiss and then rounded the corner of the Brown Building.

Once she was out of sight, Andrew picked up his book and backpack and headed for the medical library.

Chapter 22

Matthew stayed in his Camaro and watched Lindy walk across the parking lot and enter the Dunn Building. Once the doors closed behind her, he pulled out his cell phone and called his partner, Steve Toowey.

Steve answered on the second ring, "Toowey."

"Hi, it's Matthew. I'm outside the Dunn Building now and have about five minutes to talk."

"Okay great. I just picked up the box, and I'm heading over to the ME's office now. Also, Officer McGinney just called. He collected the flowers from Dr. Ashley's back porch and should arrive soon at the ME's office as well."

Matthew said, "I'm not sure if any of this is related, but something just doesn't feel right."

"I agree. Look, Pamela pulled Dr. Ashley's history, and nothing stands out. She is divorced from a Dr. George Williams III for about three months now. They were married two years and have no children. Williams comes from a long line of serious money."

Matthew tried to picture Lindy married to a wealthy doctor and living in an expensive estate with all the finest jewelry and lots of fast cars. *Well, something must have gone wrong because now she lives alone*, he thought.

Steve continued, "There is nothing in the divorce that suggests abuse or infidelity. The only thing that really stands out with Dr. Ashley is her sister, Erin, who happens to be her secretary."

Matthew said, "I didn't realize they were sisters."

"Well, they are. Erin's records are sealed because she was a juvenile, but it appears she has a history of drug abuse. Erin moved in with Lindy when she was sixteen, after attending a rehab clinic."

"Are the parents dead?"

"Nope, they reside in Ft. Worth."

"Okay, thanks. I've gotta go now, but let me know if anything crucial comes up. I'll keep my phone on vibrate."

"Have fun in class," Steve teased.

Matthew looked around the grounds outside of the Dunn Building and spotted a blonde wearing short cutoff jeans and a little tank top. "Yeah, this brings back memories," he said and hung up.

Matthew tucked his phone in his pocket and opened the car door. Immediately he was approached by two young ladies wearing very little clothing. The brunette said, "Howdy, partner," and gave him the once-over. The blonde said, "I like your boots."

Matthew just smiled and said, "Thanks. Are ya'll girls headed to class?"

The blonde winked and said, "Maybe. How about you?"

Matthew was a little blown away by her forwardness considering the fact that there was a psychotic killer running around loose with a knife. Pushing the thoughts aside for now, he motioned toward the Dunn Building and said, "I'm going to Professor Dobb's psych class."

The brunette smiled and said, "I'm Jennifer Bailey. I have his class as well."

Matthew looked back at her. "Well, technically, I'm just a visitor."

The blonde took a closer look at his car and then back at his face. Suddenly she said, "Hey, I saw you on TV yesterday! You're that FBI guy."

"Yep, busted!"

"I'm Kathryn Black," she said. "I've got his class as well." With a tilt of her head, she asked, "What's your name again? I don't remember."

Matthew looked at his watch and then said, "I'm Agent Blake, and I think we need to get to class now. It's about to start."

Kathryn didn't move forward. Instead she asked, "Why are you visiting this class? Do you think the Night Killer is one of Professor Dobb's students?"

Matthew started walking toward the building. "No. I'm just here to listen to the guest lecturer tonight, Dr. Lindy Ashley."

"Oh yeah, I remember her," Jennifer said. "She didn't lecture last week though. She was just sorta here answering questions."

Kathryn replied, "Sorry, I wasn't in class the last two sessions. I don't know her."

Matthew continued the conversation as they neared the Dunn building. In a more serious tone, "Did either of you know Robby Singleton or Jaycee Brown?"

Both girls nodded their heads, and Kathryn said, "By your fourth year, you sorta know everyone that lives on campus and has the same major."

Matthew asked, "Yeah, but Robby was not a psych major. Do you know why he was taking a four hundred–level psych class during his final year?"

Jennifer answered, "A lot of students like Professor Dobbs. He's interesting."

Kathryn laughed and then added, "Yeah, and it's an easy A."

When they reached the entrance to the Dunn Building, Matthew took a good look at both of the ladies. They were young and attractive with bubbly personalities. Finally, he said bluntly, "Both of you need to be more careful. Don't be approaching strangers again like you did with me. It's not safe."

Jennifer stopped smiling, "I don't go anywhere alone, and I'm careful. Besides, I had Kathryn with me when I started talking to you."

Matthew looked over at Kathryn and thought, *She probably only weighs a little over a hundred pounds soaking wet. A lot of good she would've done.*

Running his hand over his hair, he said, "Good. But still, don't approach strangers."

Kathryn nodded her head and said, "Now that we know your name, we aren't strangers anymore."

Matthew just smiled at her young, free spirit of innocence and then turned away and walked inside the Dunn Building to find Lindy.

Dr. Lindy Ashley and Professor Joshua Dobbs were on stage in front of the lecture hall wearing microphones and standing behind podiums ready to start class when Matthew found a seat. Matthew looked around and counted the rows and seats and did the math in his head. He concluded over two hundred students were in attendance. That was a large number for a four hundred–level class.

Professor Dobbs was dressed in khakis with a dark blue, short-sleeved button-down shirt. Lindy hadn't changed and was still wearing her cowboy boots and denim dress from earlier. Both looked professional as they stood behind the podium and addressed the class.

After a very short introduction, Lindy began her lecture. Staying true to her earlier comment, she began to talk about the recent killings on campus and began to discuss common myths about serial killers. Matthew looked around, and he immediately recognized how attentive the audience was to Lindy. They were all staring straight ahead and looked as if they were hanging on her every word.

Matthew thought, *Lindy Ashley is a very captivating speaker. Huh, I don't feel so weak now after she turned me into a babbling fool in our previous sessions. If the good doctor wanted to say, 'Boo,' everyone would literally jump straight out of their seats.*

Lindy's lecture lasted around thirty minutes but only seemed like ten to anyone who was actively listening. When Professor Dobbs asked for questions, nearly half the class raised their hands.

Professor Dobbs suggested, "I will use my computer to pull a name from my attendance roll. If your name appears on the screen, please stand and speak loudly for all to hear."

In a matter of seconds, a name appeared up on the screen behind the professor and the doctor. Matthew looked around until he saw a young Asian girl stand and say, "This question is for Dr. Ashley. What is the likelihood that the Night Killer attends Central University?"

Lindy didn't immediately answer and contemplated her words carefully. Finally, she said, "In my opinion—and I stress 'in my opinion'!—the Night Killer has some connection with this school. Now that could mean he attends the college or works on the grounds or maybe just lives or works within a few miles of the campus."

Matthew smiled at her answer. Lindy looked his way, and he swore her eyes twinkled back at him. She quickly turned away because another student stood up and began to speak.

"The news media is suggesting that the Night Killer is a female. Do both of you agree?"

Lindy looked toward Joshua and signaled for him to answer.

"In my opinion, I think a female serial killer is unlikely."

The student immediately asked, "Why?"

"Frankly, because female serial killers are quite rare when looking at history and judging our society."

The young man looked toward Lindy and said, "Do you agree with Professor Dobbs?"

Lindy said, "Women serial killers are quite rare, and just because both victims were male doesn't mean I would point a finger at a female. No, I don't think the Night Killer is a female."

Matthew felt his phone vibrate in his pocket, and he looked down to see who was calling. It was Steve. Matthew quietly slid out of his seat and walked toward the exit. Opening the front door, Matthew felt glass crack beneath his feet. Looking up, he noticed a light was broken. Once darkness fell, the only light visible would be the street light in the parking lot and along the sidewalk. Pushing the thought aside, he touched his phone and said, "What you got Steve?"

"Well, besides the press breathing down my back, I'm here with the ME, and she says the lock of hair doesn't match either victim and it's not blood. But she's going to test the hair to be one hundred percent sure."

"Okay, how about Leroy Bullock? Were you able to track him down for an alibi around four o'clock?"

"Yep, Don found him around six at his home. According to Leroy, he left work at five and got home around five-thirty. Don was not able to verify this from his boss yet, but he does have the boss's number and left a message for him to return our call."

"Looks like a dead end."

Steve replied, "Not necessarily. Leroy has a record. According to Pamela, Leroy was arrested in 2009 for aggravated assault and battery."

"What happened?"

"Leroy's girlfriend changed her mind and charges were dropped."

"Great! Erin sure picked a winner."

"Yeah, I saw a picture of her. She's hot!"

Matthew grinned. "Yes she is, but too young for you."

Steve laughed. "I know. I was just stating a fact."

Silence followed and then Steve asked, "Where you going after class?"

"I'm going to grab dinner with the good doctor and then escort her home and check her residence."

"Hey, hey! I think that's a good idea."

Matthew didn't want to continue down this path, so he said, "I gotta go. Just call me if anything comes up. If not, I'll see you in the morning at seven."

"Okay later," Steve said.

Still bothered by the broken light bulb, Matthew decided to call it in to Central University. He pulled a leather card holder from his back pocket and sifted through the cards until he found the number to the university's police department. On the second ring, someone answered the phone.

"Hi, this is FBI Agent Matthew Blake, and I wanted to report a light out on the Dunn Building's front entrance."

The lady said, "Thank you. I will make a note and have someone repair it first thing tomorrow."

Matthew said, "Thanks," and hung up the phone.

Just then, students started pouring out of the Dunn Building. Matthew looked down at his phone and saw that it was seven o'clock. Class was over. Matthew stayed put and just observed the many students as they made their way down the stairs and into the parking lot or down various sidewalks leading away. A couple of students remarked about the light, but most didn't even notice. Matthew began to wonder how long the light had been broken.

The blonde he saw earlier in the short cutoff jeans and tank top departed the building with a backpack slung around her shoulders. She was talking to two guys as she walked. He watched the three as they continued down the sidewalk and then turned and disappeared behind another building. So far, it appeared the walkers were not walking alone.

Matthew turned back toward the building and began to climb the stairs in search of Lindy and the professor. When he reached out for the door, it opened up from the other side, and out popped Jennifer and Kathryn. Both girls smiled at Matthew and then Kathryn said, "Bye. See you around."

"Good night, ladies." Matthew walked in the building and down the hallway that led to the lecture hall. When he rounded the last corner, he saw Lindy surrounded by four students and engaged in a conversation. Professor Dobbs was packing his notes in his briefcase and then he slowly made his way over to the group.

Professor Dobbs said, "Students, if you will, please excuse Dr. Ashley and myself. I appreciate your attendance tonight and will see you on Monday."

The students looked a little disappointed but could take a hint. Lindy said, "Good-bye. Thanks for coming tonight."

The students continued on out the door and didn't pay Matthew any attention. Lindy took one look at him and asked, "So, how did I do with the Q and A?"

"You did fine. I had to leave toward the end though."

Joshua cleared his throat and said, "I have a plane to catch. I must be on my way now."

Lindy said, "I'm sorry, Joshua. This is FBI Agent Matthew Blake. He's the lead investigator in the murders here on campus."

Joshua shook Matthew's outstretched hand. "Nice to meet you. Lindy—"

Lindy reached out and gave Joshua a hug. "Have a safe flight, and let me know if anything changes with your mom."

Joshua nodded and said, "Thanks, dear," and then turned and walked out of the room.

Lindy looked at Matthew and said, "I need to grab my briefcase. Just a minute."

Matthew watched as she walked back to the podium and packed up. When they were on their way to Lindy's car, he said, "There's an Italian restaurant just a few blocks away called Delano. Ever been there?"

"Yes, and Italian sounds fantastic."

Matthew nodded and replied, "I'll follow you."

Matthew closed Lindy's door and then jogged over to his Camaro and jumped in. As they pulled out of the fairly empty parking lot, neither spotted the person hiding behind the tree and watching their every move.

Chapter 23

Just outside of the medical library, Melody said good night to her class-mates and climbed the stairs that led to the entrance. Once inside, the lady behind the counter politely asked, "May I help you, miss?"

"No thank you. I know just where to look."

The woman smiled and then turned back to her computer.

Andrew was a creature of habit when it came to studying. He always chose the table in the far corner, away from any distractions one might have with the front desk and help center. Melody quietly walked up behind him and brushed the base of his neck with the tips of her painted fingernails. Knowing who it was, Andrew put his pen down and reached back to grab hold of his girl. Slowly Melody made her way around and bent to give him a gentle kiss on the lips.

"How was class?" he asked as she pulled out a chair and took a seat beside him.

"Extremely interesting. Our guest speaker talked about psychopaths, sociopaths, and serial killers."

Andrew shook his head and then said, "Disturbing."

She smiled. "That was the most students I've ever seen in a psych class. I think some of them aren't even in the class but just showed up to listen."

"So what did you learn?" he asked.

"Oh, that the tall, dark, and handsome medical student I date could be a serial killer and I wouldn't even know it."

Andrew closed his notebook and said, "Great. How *do* you know who to trust around here?"

Melody touched his hand and then placed her other hand on his face. "You look tired."

"I am. Let's call it a night. Your place or mine?"

Melody smiled and said, "Yours."

Matthew and Lindy were escorted to an open table without waiting. Once they were seated, the hostess handed each one a menu and left. Soon a waiter appeared, and Matthew and Lindy settled on a bottle of red wine. Lindy asked, "So if you can drink, what are your official hours?"

"I'm always on the job, but technically I'm logged off for the day. And you? Are you on call twenty-four seven with your patients?"

Lindy surprised him when she said, "Hell no! Everything gets left at the office. When I lock up, I don't return or think about work till I arrive the next day."

Matthew sat back in his chair and gazed into her blue eyes. She looked mysterious tonight under the soft light with her olive skin and jet-black hair. He wondered, *How can she get so tuned in with her patients and then turn it all off with a tick of a clock?*

Nothing else was asked, as the waiter appeared with their glasses of wine and remaining bottle. He then took their order and left them once again.

"You're at an advantage here," Matthew said. "You know more about me than I know about you."

Lindy picked up her wine glass and took a sip and then gently placed it back down on the table. Leaning forward slightly, she asked, "What would you like to know?"

Matthew stretched out his hand and slowly pushed Lindy's hair back from the side of her face. "Everything."

Chapter 24

Luke James was walking around Central University looking for his new girlfriend, Jennifer Bailey. She was supposed to meet up with him after class and had failed to show at their designated area. Finally he decided to sit on the bench and wait some more. Another five minutes passed and still no Jennifer. He was starting to get frustrated now. He thought, *Damn, she's probably with Kathryn, and God only knows what she has talked her into.*

Luke turned his head when he heard a noise. It wasn't Jennifer. Instead, it was a small group of girls carrying backpacks. Luke stood up and approached them. "I'm waiting on Jennifer Bailey. Have ya'll seen her?"

The tallest of the three said, "Yeah, she left a while ago with her friend Kathryn."

The disappointment was clearly written all over his face as Luke came to the realization that Jennifer had stood him up. "Thanks," he said and slowly headed back to his car.

Ten buildings away from the medical library, Andrew and Melody had just opened Andrew's apartment door. Somehow between the moments they left the library and now, Andrew had caught his second wind. Looking back at Melody as he closed the door, he had no doubt in his mind the reason why.

Melody dropped her backpack on the floor and then in one swift move pulled her pink tank top over her head. Smiling back, Andrew picked Melody up and carried her to the couch.

Andrew gently laid her down and then lifted his own T-shirt up and off his hard, muscular body. Melody was wearing a hot pink lace bra, one of his favorites. He gently knelt down beside her and ran his hands over her large, full breasts. Melody closed her eyes and slightly arched her back.

Andrew looked at her exquisite body and then slid his hands down over her flat stomach, stopping at her shorts. Finding the top button, he slowly began undoing them. When the task was completed, he slipped her shorts down over her long, gorgeous legs. He wasn't surprised she was wearing a matching hot pink thong. She always matched her underwear, and Andrew was really turned on by that.
Andrew leaned down close to Melody's mouth and whispered, "You take my breath away."

Melody gently ran her hands through his hair and then leaned forward to kiss him on the lips. Andrew fell into her then and began to kiss her neck and work his way down toward her perfectly rounded breasts. As he kissed, his hands worked the bra clasp on her back. Slowly he pulled the straps down and pulled the bra off. Andrew continued working his way down with his mouth and began to play gently using his tongue.

It didn't take long before they were both sweating and aching for more. Andrew quickly stood up and pulled her into his waiting arms, and Melody wrapped her long legs around his hips so he could carry her to his bedroom.

Lindy stood inside her townhouse with Matthew, and they both watched and waited as the garage door glided down to the concrete and stopped. Satisfied that it was secure, Matthew shut and locked the door behind them. As they walked toward the living room, Lindy said, "I would like you to meet Parker."

Matthew didn't have to ask who Parker was because he could hear the dog scratching and whimpering at the back door.

"Just a minute, sweetie," Lindy said as she reached for the lock, but Matthew stopped her with a firm, "Stop!"

Lindy turned and looked quizzically at him. Stepping to her side, he turned on the switch beside the door that illuminated the backyard. Seeing only Parker outside, he said, "Go ahead."

As soon as the door was opened, Parker pushed forward and into Lindy's waiting arms. "I'm sorry, buddy. Mommy was gone a long time."

Parker jumped down and began to run around the room in circles and then sailed onto the couch. When Matthew took a step forward, Parker jumped down and ran circles around his legs. Matthew bent down and gave him a pat. "You're a funny little thing. Are you always this hyper?"

Lindy laughed and said, "Yeah, but walks and runs help a lot."

"When do you guys go out to exercise?"

"In the mornings we go for a two-mile run, and in the evenings we take a short walk on the trail around the lake."

Matthew walked back over to her french doors and looked out into the backyard. He could barely see the walking trail with some lamps set up along the way for lights. Matthew turned back around and said, "Why don't I go on that walk with you guys tonight."

Lindy grinned. "Great, let me change first."

Matthew and Parker both watched as Lindy left the room. While she was gone, Matthew took the opportunity to check the locks on both doors as well as the windows throughout the front of the house. When Lindy returned, she found Matthew standing by the tall windows by the front door. "What are you doing?" she asked.

"I was just checking the place for security measures."

"Did I pass?"

"Yeah, the locks on your doors and windows are of good quality. Do you ever set your alarm?"

Lindy frowned. "No, they gave me a standard code when I moved in, but I haven't called the company to come out and hook up the system for monitoring."

"Well, give them a call tomorrow. I think with your line of work, and the events from the last few days, it would be wise to have the system monitored."

"I already decided that I would after today's gift. Before, with the flowers, I really didn't think I was in danger. I just thought someone left me flowers and was too embarrassed to give his name."

Matthew looked at Lindy in her short, fitted black shorts, green sports tank, and running shoes, and thought, *You, pretty lady, could be in a lot of danger.* But he kept his thought to himself. He didn't want to scare her, he just wanted her to be more cautious of her surroundings and get the alarm system monitored. Looking down at Parker, he felt slightly relieved knowing she had a dog.

Lindy grabbed Parker's leash and the back door key and then they worked their way through the backyard and onto the walking trail. As they walked, Lindy mostly talked about her new life without her ex, George.

"I like having my independence again. I've missed that."

"Was George controlling?"

"Well, let's just say the expectations were high."

Matthew didn't interrupt or ask any more questions, so she continued explaining. "With George's family's status in the community, it kept us busy, and I always felt like I was being watched and compared to his mother and other ladies of distinction."

"You must miss the money."

Lindy stopped and faced Matthew. "Actually, I'm quite happy enjoying the simple life. Every time I walk out the door, I don't have to worry about what I look like or what I'm wearing. Just this morning I wore a stained tank top when I went running. When I lived in George's neighborhood, you would have never caught me wearing anything but designer workout labels with my hair pulled back perfectly in a ponytail."

Suddenly, Matthew leaned in and kissed Lindy on the lips. The kiss was soft and short, but it left an effect on both of them. Matthew smiled at Lindy and then started walking again. Lindy eventually met his pace and neither said another word until they were back inside her house five minutes later.

"Let me check out the place. Stay here with Parker."

Lindy obeyed and patiently waited for Matthew to do a complete walk-through of the house. After a couple of minutes passed, he walked back into the living room and said, "Everything looks good and locked up tight. I need to leave now. Will you be okay alone?"

Lindy bent down and unhooked Parker's leash. "We will be just fine. I enjoyed dinner and the walk."

Matthew's face lit up with a big smile, and he walked closer to Lindy. "I enjoyed the evening as well, and I would like to see you again, soon."

Lindy just nodded and smiled.

Matthew turned away and started for the front door, but Parker ran forward and began jumping up on his legs. Matthew bent down and said, "I will see you again soon, Parker. Take good care of Lindy while I'm gone."

Matthew stood back up as Lindy walked toward the front door. He said, "Don't forget to lock the door. Good night, Lindy."

"Good night," Lindy said and then watched him walk down her front sidewalk. She gently closed and locked her door.

Chapter 25

Melody was lying in bed beside Andrew sleeping peacefully with one arm resting on his chest. Andrew was wide awake and watching Melody as she slept. A lot was on Andrew's mind, and it was preventing him from falling asleep.

Lately he was worried that his feelings for Melody were getting in the way of medical school. He still had a long road ahead of him, and she was high maintenance and required a lot of effort on his part to keep her happy and secure. He just didn't know if he could handle the stress of trying to juggle both.

One reason their relationship had been on and off so many times was because Melody kept calling it quits when she didn't have him at her beck and call. As Andrew continued to watch her sleep and listen to her peaceful breathing, he knew in his heart that he wanted to be at her beck and call.

Andrew smiled and leaned in to kiss her on the cheek. He softly said, "I love you, Melody Montgomery, and one day I plan to marry you."

Melody moved her arm and then slowly moved her head to the side and faced Andrew. With half-opened eyes and a sleepy voice, she said, "Hi, babe, you still up?"

Andrew kissed her on the lips, and she met him with a deeper kiss. Andrew lifted the sheets and pulled her naked body close to his, and once again Melody responded.

From the kitchen, noises could be heard coming from the bedroom. Slow, silent steps carried the killer toward the source. From the short hallway, the outline of Melody's female curves could barely be seen in the dark as her body rocked back and forth. Several minutes passed as the killer continued to watch and wait for the right moment.

Exhausted, Melody collapsed on top of Andrew and then gently rolled off so Andrew could cradle her in his loving arms. Andrew kissed her neck and nuzzled his face into her golden locks. He loved the smell of her hair and always liked the fact that his pillow still held her scent long after she left. Slowly, Melody lifted Andrew's arm up and began to move toward the edge of the bed.

Andrew touched her back and said, "Hey, where're you going?"

"To get some water."

Andrew released his hand from her back when a pain sliced through his chest. Groaning out in agony he tried to catch the shiny object flashing in front of his eyes with his hands.

Hearing his cries, confused, Melody turned around just in time to see the same shiny object plunging straight toward her. She was able to move to her right as the blade caught her left shoulder and ripped its way down her arm. Melody let out a scream but was immediately hit with a heavy object that sent her sailing off the bed and into a pit of darkness.

Andrew could not move and watched in horror as the knife that punctured his chest continued moving up and down, up and down. The pain felt like acid burning his insides. Soon, the pain was too great and Andrew faded away.

The Night Killer pulled out a phone and entered a number.
A voice on the other end responded, "Hello."

"I need your help."

"Oh no, you said I was done after that kid Robby."

The Night Killer paused a moment and then finally replied, "Just get to 241 Maple Street."

Chapter 26

Matthew was home at his ranch feeding his horses when his cell phone started ringing in his pocket. Immediately he knew the call wasn't going to be good. No one would call at five-thirty in the morning unless it was important.

Matthew opened the phone and answered, "Matthew Blake."

"It's Jacob Knight with Central University. We got another one."

"Shit! Where are you?"

"I'm on campus. The address is 241 Maple Street, apartment five. Come as fast as you can."

"Yeah, I'm on my way. Be there in about twenty to thirty minutes. Just keep as many people away as possible. Oh, and stop anyone that leaves the apartment complex. Someone is bound to have heard something."

"Will do," Knight said and hung up the phone.

Matthew looked at Fred and Ethel and said, "Sorry, guys, I've got to go, but I promise I'll call Danny to come ride both of you and give you snacks." Matthew finished throwing the last handful of hay and then took off running toward the house.

Lindy and Parker were on the last stretch before returning home from their run. Lindy's arms and legs were aching as she made the last few steps. Seeing her home, she began to slow to a fast walk. This was her cool down, walking the last fifty feet to her backyard.

Lindy let go of Parker's leash, and he immediately ran ahead of her when she opened the gate. He went straight to his water bowl and began to drink up. When he was done, Lindy removed the leash from his collar and gave him a rub on his back. "Good job, Parker. Rest up now."

Lindy removed her key from her pocket and let herself into the house and glanced at the clock. She had about forty-five minutes before she had to leave for work. As she made her way to the master bath, she began stripping. By the time she got to her shower, she only had to remove her running shorts.

Stepping into the shower, Lindy quickly adjusted the water temperature and began to wash. While rubbing down her legs and arms, she noticed two new bruises and stepped out from under the water to inspect. As she looked closely at each one, anxiety nearly overtook her. Taking a deep breath, Lindy turned the hot water up and stepped back under the hot spray. She closed her eyes and hoped the water would help soothe her aching joints and muscles.

Matthew turned on Maple Street and immediately saw the commotion up ahead. News vans with reporters were lined up on the opposite side of the street waiting for the latest information that could verify that the Night Killer had struck again. Matthew parked his Camaro and stepped out, ignoring all the shouts and questions from the media. It didn't take long to get past the yellow tape and find Jacob Knight talking to Matthew's partner, Steve Toowey.

Steve saw him coming and said, "Looks like the same artwork in there. Here, take this. You'll need it."

Matthew grabbed the protective gear and began to put it on. As he was suiting up, the medical examiner, Candy Johnson, approached him. "Hi, Matthew. Sorry to see you again so soon. Are ya'll making any headway with your investigation?"

Matthew walked closer to Candy and said, "Obviously not enough to prevent another attack."

Dr. Candy Johnson led the way inside the apartment and then said, "The victim is Andrew Mitt, a medical student, age twenty-four. Time of death, sometime between eleven last night and two this morning."

"How did we find him so early?"

"Apparently Andrew and his neighbor, Gabe West, who lives two doors down, work out every morning at five. When Andrew failed to show by five after, Gabe used the key Andrew keeps under the mat and let himself in."

Candy reached the master bedroom and then turned around and said, "Brace yourself. It's worse than before."

Matthew was about to ask how that could be, but he stopped short when he saw the amount of blood on the bed and floor.

Candy said, "The killer stabbed him so many times that the head has been severed."

Timidly, Matthew stepped forward and saw what was left of Andrew. The room seemed to tilt then, and Matthew said, "Shit! What kind of monster are we dealing with?"

Candy touched Matthew's arm and then led him out of the room. "Are you okay?" she said. "You don't look so good."

Matthew felt the room start spinning, and he reached out to grab Candy for support. Quickly she pulled something from her pocket and held it up to his nose. It worked, because Matthew got hold of himself and was able to walk out of the apartment of his own free will. When he was nearing the front door, though, something on the floor by the couch caught his eye. Matthew stopped and turned toward the living room.

Candy said, "What?"

Pointing at the pink tank top on the floor, "That looks familiar," and Matthew began to rack his brain to try and figure out why.

Candy said, "There's also a pair of denim shorts off to the other side; both belong to a female."

"That's it! I saw that girl going to Professor Dobb's class last night. She was wearing those clothes."

"Are you sure?"

Matthew carefully picked up the tank with his gloves on and took a closer look. "Yeah, I remember the sequin logo across her very large chest."

"These are the only items found, so I guess she left in her underwear or wore something of Andrew's."

"Is there any evidence of another victim?"

Candy shook her head and looked at Matthew's pale face. "I'm sorry, Matthew. It's just too hard to tell. We'll have to wait until the blood is tested."

Matthew closed his eyes and placed his hands on the sides of his head. Candy took another step toward him and said quietly, "I know this sucks. I will call you as soon as I have something. I promise."

Matthew opened his eyes and stared into her big brown eyes. She looked tired and scared. Matthew dropped his hands from his head and then reached out and touched her shoulder. "I know you will. Thanks."

Matthew pulled back his hand and slowly turned around and walked out of the apartment in search of his partner. Finding Steve a few feet away, Matthew asked, "Any clues about a girlfriend with long blond hair? We need to get her name ASAP. She could be in danger."

Steve pointed ahead and said, "Gabe gave us a list of people to call. A girlfriend was listed."

Matthew walked toward Gabe's apartment, and Steve followed. "Matthew, what you got?"

"The clothes lying on the floor by the couch were worn by a blonde attending Dobb's class last night."

Steve had a weird look on his face. "And you remember that how?"

Matthew stopped at Gabe's door and turned to face Steve. "You would've remembered her too, trust me."

An officer saw the two agents and opened up the door. "He's in his room lying down."

Matthew and Steve made their way through the apartment toward Gabe's room. When they peered in, they found Gabe sitting on his bed looking intently at a beach poster on the wall.

Matthew said, "Gabe, I'm sorry to bother you. I'm Agent Blake, and you met Agent Toowey earlier."

Gabe nodded his head in acknowledgment.

Matthew continued, "I know this is hard, but could you describe Andrew's girlfriend."

Steve looked at his notepad and said, "Melody Montgomery."

Gabe slowly peeled his eyes off the poster and turned his head toward Matthew. "Did you see Andrew?"

Matthew nodded his head yes and took a seat on the bed beside Gabe. "I know this is difficult, but I'm worried about Andrew's girlfriend. She could be in danger."

Gabe said, "Melody? Oh no, don't say that. I already lost Andrew."

Matthew asked, "What does she look like?"

In a quivering voice, "She...she is beautiful and sweet."

"Does she have long blond hair and olive skin?"

Gabe jumped back. "What are you saying? Did something happen to her?"

"We don't know. We're trying to find her. So far she's not answering her phone, and someone's checking out her place as we speak."

Gabe grabbed his phone off the nightstand, pressed a few buttons, and placed it next to his face. A few seconds passed and Gabe said, "Melody, it's Gabe. Where are you? Please call me when you get this!"

Gabe lowered his phone and turned to the agents with a distraught look on his face. "Find her. Don't let that monster do that to her!"

Matthew asked, "Do you have a photo of her?"

Gabe picked up his phone and scrolled around some and then handed it to Matthew and Steve.

Matthew looked at the beautiful smiling girl and winced. "I saw her last night at class. Does she ever stay the night at Andrew's place?"

Gabe nodded his head. "Yeah, about two or three times a week."

Steve handed the phone back and asked, "Did you happen to see either of them last night?"

"No, I was out with my girlfriend, Mandy. I did talk to him. He called sometime last night and had a question about our test that we have today. Oh shit, I can't go, I can't do this!"

In a gentle voice, Steve replied, "You don't have to. Your professor has already been contacted. He wants you to call him, though. He cares and he's worried about you."

"What the hell's going on? Why did this have to happen to Andrew? He was such a good person. He didn't deserve this!" Shouted Gabe.

Matthew placed a hand on his shoulder. "You're right, and we're going to do everything possible to catch who did this."

A moment passed and then Matthew continued, "Can you look at your phone and see when he called you last night?"

Gabe scrolled through his phone again and showed it to the agents.

Steve wrote down '6:15 p.m.' in his notepad.

"Did he tell you his plans for the night?" asked Matthew.

"I was with Mandy at dinner, so I didn't talk long. I just answered his question and quickly hung up. Now I'll never get to talk to him again." Tears began to roll down Gabe's face. Quickly he stood up and walked over to the far corner of the room and punched as hard as he could at the punching bag hanging from the ceiling.

Matthew was about to say something but stopped when a young, petite brunette came running in the room and yelled out, "Gabe, tell me it's not true!"

Gabe turned around and embraced her. "Oh, Mandy, it was horrible!" He started to weep uncontrollably on her shoulder.

Matthew and Steve turned and left them to grieve in private. When they got out of the apartment, Matthew spoke quietly, "Let's get to Melody's place. We've got to find her."

Chapter 27

Melody slowly opened her eyes and tried to turn her head a little to look around. The only light in the room was coming in through a small window with a closed blind.

Melody swallowed. She hurt all over. And she was so thirsty. She tried to sit up, but something held her back. Confused, she looked at her arm and saw that it was wrapped in a bandage. And it was tied down!

Panic immediately set in as Melody came to the crashing realization that she was tied up on a bed in a strange room. She tried to pull her legs in and then looked down to see that her ankles had been tied to a bedpost. She was stretched out on a bed and wearing only her hot pink underwear. Melody screamed out, "Help! Andrew! Someone!"

No voice answered her cry.

Melody closed her eyes and tried to think past the pain in her head. It was so strong that it was clouding her thoughts. She tried to remember what had happened and how she had gotten like this, but she couldn't. Turning her head back toward her arm, she stared at the bandage that wrapped from her shoulder down and began to cry as she slowly remembered the shiny object crashing down on her last night.

She mumbled softly, "Andrew? Oh my God!" Her thoughts were hazy, but she remembered an image of Andrew holding his chest and whimpering her name. "No, no. Andrew, where are you?" Tears continued to fall as Melody faded out again from the pain throbbing in her head.

Lindy Ashley walked into her office and was immediately greeted by a happy and upbeat Erin. "Hi, Erin. You look happy."

"I am. You, on the other hand, look like shit."

Lindy frowned and said, "Thanks!"

"Well, your red dress is nice. It shows off your amazing figure, but everything else needs work."

Erin walked over with her makeup bag in hand. "Stand still. I'm just going to smear this stuff under your eyes. Did you stay out all night with Matthew or what?"

"No, I just didn't sleep well."

Erin said, "I'm sorry. I should have stayed with you again last night."

"No, I'm fine. I just think it was the wine that kept me up, that's all. So how was your night out with Tiffany?"

Erin's face lit up. "Fantastic. We went into downtown Ft. Worth. We started out at the bar in Rio's and met two guys that ended up taking us to dinner across the street at Franklin's"

"Wow, so are these guys local?"

In a disappointed voice, she said, "No, they were here on business from Houston. But Charlie did give me his card and told me to call him if I was ever in town."

"And the other guy?" Lindy asked.

"Well, John was married, so Tiffany refused his card."

Lindy said sarcastically, "How noble of Tiffany."

Erin finished with Lindy's face and said, "Here, come sit down and let me pull your hair up."

Lindy didn't feel like fighting, so she just did as she was told. Erin handed her the day's appointment list to look at as she pulled out her brush and clip and began to transform Lindy's appearance. Ten minutes later, Lindy stood up and walked over to the mirror behind the navy sofa. "Wow, thanks, Erin."

Erin smiled. "Anytime."

Lindy looked at the time and said, "I need to get busy. My first appointment arrives in twenty minutes."

"Okay, your first appointment is a new patient. I started a file with her name on it and laid it on your desk with the others."

"Thanks, Erin. I'll let you know when I'm ready."

Lindy made a stop in the kitchen to grab a banana and then settled in at her desk. She picked up the new folder and read the name: 'Amber Fritz, age 33.' Lindy closed the file and tried to remember if she had ever heard that name before. No memory stood out, so she just assumed she didn't know her.

Lindy picked up the banana and began to peel it when suddenly a sharp pain radiated along her right side. She closed her eyes and took deep breaths, and soon the pain was gone. Thinking little of it, Lindy finished peeling and then ate her banana. As she took the last bite, Erin buzzed in and said, "George is on line one."

"Thanks, Erin."

Lindy picked up the phone and pressed line one.

"Hello, George."

"Hi, Lindy. I have to go out of town this weekend, so I won't be able to come by and pick up Parker."

"Okay, thanks for letting me know. Bye now."

"Wait! Lindy? Lindy?"

"Yes."

"How are you doing? I mean, is everything good?"

Lindy decided to keep it simple. "All is good here. The practice is busy, which is good, and I really have settled in well at The Palms."

"I miss you, Lindy, and I still think about you a lot."
An awkward moment passed and then George continued. "Do you want to get together sometime next week, just for coffee or a drink?"

Lindy didn't hesitate at all. "No, I don't think that would be a good idea. It's best if we continue to go our separate ways."

"Okay, I understand. Bye, Lindy."

"Good-bye, George."

Lindy hung up the phone and thought, *How odd? Does he really miss me?* Picking up the file for her new patient, she buzzed Erin to send her in. A few short moments passed and then Erin entered with Amber Fritz, a stylish blonde.

Lindy walked over and extended her hand. "Hello, Ms. Fritz, I'm Dr. Lindy Ashley. Please come in and take a seat."

Dressed in a baby blue pant suit, the beautiful young woman looked around the room first and then looked over Lindy before finally walking forward and taking a seat. As soon as she sat down, she stated, "I'm dating George."

Chapter 28

This is not how Lindy pictured starting her day. The lady sitting across from her was dating her ex-husband and had made the appointment only to size up her competition. Very politely Lindy said, "Ms. Fritz, I'm really not sure why you're here. George and I are divorced."

"Yes, but you're still in contact with him."

Lindy was about to say something but realized the woman probably overheard Erin announce George's call. So, instead, she just patiently waited for more.

"I know George talked to you. He said he keeps in contact with you only because of some dog."

Lindy smiled. "The dog's name is Parker."

Amber had an annoyed look on her face. "I don't care if the dog is named Snoopy! I would rather George move on without any baggage from you."

Lindy stood up and said, "You need to be talking to George, not me. Now if you'll excuse me, I came in today to work, not to discuss my ex-husband."

Amber stood up and said, "Well, you have seen me now, and you know George has moved on with a new girlfriend. Whatever there was between you two is over and done with. You are in the past."

Lindy restrained herself from exploding and calmly walked over and opened the door. "Please leave now, Ms. Fritz, and don't ever make another appointment with me."

Amber looked down the hall and saw Erin coming her way.

Looking back at Lindy she stated, "No, I don't anticipate hearing or seeing you ever again." The woman opened the side exit door, took two steps, and turned around. "Oh, here is three hundred. That should do for your time."

Lindy was about to protest, but Erin quickly seized the money and said, "Thank you. Good-bye now." With the lady gone and the door shut behind her, Erin turned around and said, "What was that all about?"

Lindy just frowned. "A bitch wanting to inform me that George has moved on, with her."

Erin's mouth dropped open. "What? Oh, she isn't going to get away with this!" Erin opened the door and started to move after her.

Quickly Lindy seized her arm. "No, you come back in here and shut the door, please."

Erin did as she was told and said, "I'm sorry, sis. I had no idea the nature of her appointment. She was extremely vague on the phone and wouldn't divulge anything in the waiting room."

"It's okay. What I would really like for you to do is go and buy yourself a pair of expensive shoes with that money."

Erin laughed. "No problem."

Lindy smirked. "Can you believe that really just happened?"

Erin shook her head no. "I'm so glad I fixed you up this morning. She had nothing on you."

Lindy responded, "Yeah, me too."

The front door buzzer went off, and both girls looked toward the waiting area. Erin said, "I hope it isn't another ghost." Lindy followed Erin down the hallway and they found Matthew Blake standing in the waiting room with a very solemn look on his face.

Lindy stepped forward and said, "Hello, Matthew."

"Good morning, ladies. I was nearby, so I decided to drop by and pick up my release papers and check on things here."

Erin grabbed an envelope from her desk and handed it to Matthew. "Any word on that box?"

Matthew answered, "It doesn't appear that it has anything to do with the brutal attacks on campus, and it wasn't blood on the hair."

Lindy said, "Somehow I don't feel relieved."

Matthew looked at her and then to Erin. "Yeah, it doesn't change the fact that someone left you flowers and then walked into your office in broad daylight to leave another gift."

Lindy took another step toward Matthew. "There's something else you're not saying."

"There was another murder last night on campus. It should be all over the news by now."

Lindy softly said, "Oh, Matthew, I'm so sorry. Who was it?"

"Name is withheld for now, but he was a medical student."

Erin said, "Three dead in just one week. This is really bad and scary."

Matthew looked at Erin and said, "Have you heard from Leroy again?"

"No. Why?"

"Did you know that his last girlfriend had him arrested for aggravated assault and battery?"

Erin's eyes got really big and she took a gulp of air. "No, I had no idea."

"Well, the girlfriend ended up dropping the charges. I would stay clear of him, Erin, and have your locks changed."

"Don't worry, Leroy is yesterday news. And I changed my locks last night around midnight. Did you know those guys work twenty-four seven?"

Lindy said, "Midnight?"

"Yeah, I just thought why wait another day. Tiffany and I weren't really tired anyway, so we just went ahead and made the call and had them come out."

Matthew turned toward Lindy. "No surprises at your house last night? Nothing unusual?"

Lindy shook her head no. Matthew said, "Thanks for the papers then. I really need to go now, but call if either of you need me."

Erin smiled, and Lindy said, "Thanks. I'll walk you to the elevator."

Lindy and Matthew walked out the front door and then Matthew said, "Keep an eye on Erin. I wouldn't leave her alone. In fact, I think it's better if neither of you are alone for a while until all of this is sorted out."

Lindy said, "We'll stay together. Thanks again for coming by."

Matthew pressed the elevator button, and the door immediately opened. Matthew leaned in and gave Lindy a quick kiss on the lips and said, "I'll call you later, if that's okay."

Lindy smiled and said, "Yes," and then Matthew disappeared behind the elevator doors. Lindy turned around and started walking back to her office but stopped when she heard a noise from behind. Turning around, she saw the stairwell door cracked behind her a few feet away. Instinct told Lindy to turn around and keep walking as fast as possible. Rounding the corner, she glanced back and didn't see anyone following her. By the time she reached her office door, her heart was pounding so hard she thought she could hear it.

Erin was behind her desk and talking on the phone. When she saw Lindy come in, she said, "Please hold," and hung the phone up.

"Luke James is on line two and really wants to talk to you."

"I'll take it. Just give me one minute." She sprinted down the hall in her two-inch black pumps.

Settling in her chair, Lindy picked up the phone and said, "Dr. Lindy Ashley speaking."

"Hi, Lindy, it's Luke. I'm in trouble."

"Luke, where are you?"

"I'm driving around with nowhere to go."

"Okay, why don't you come on in and see me. I have time to talk."

"I'm about twenty minutes away. Will you still be free?"

Lindy thought of Amber Fritz and how forty minutes was still blocked out. "Yes, I have time. Just come on in. I'll be waiting for you."

"Thanks, Lindy."

Chapter 29

What a day this is turning out to be, Lindy thought as she got up from her desk to greet a grief-stricken Luke. "Hello, Luke. Please come on in and take a seat."

Luke hurried over to Lindy, shook her hand, and then settled on the sofa.

"First of all, we need to define trouble."

Luke just gazed back without comment.

Lindy pressed on. "Did you physically hurt someone, or are your actions going to cause bodily injury to someone now or in the future?"

Luke waited a moment while Lindy hung in limbo. Finally he said, "No."

With that, Lindy was able to smile and breathe again normally. "Okay, so tell me what's going on. Maybe it would help if you rewound some and started with your visit to my office yesterday."

Luke shook his head back and forth. "I don't know. That seems like a week ago."

"Try."

Luke took a deep breath and popped his fingers and then looked straight at Lindy. "Yesterday, Jennifer called and wanted to talk about us. You remember me telling you I had a girlfriend, right?"

"Yes. Last we talked, you were taking her to the movies."

"Right, well, the movies and date were perfect. I thought everything was good until she called yesterday and wanted to talk."

"So were you going to meet Jennifer to talk in person?"

"Yes, I was to meet her at four-thirty. That's why when I stopped by yesterday I couldn't stay."

"I see. What were you going to ask me or talk about when you stopped by?"

He let out a long breath. "I don't know really. I just had a lot of anxiety and wanted you to walk me through my emotions."

"Luke, that's great! You are learning to feel your emotions and then take responsible action. That's progress."

Luke smiled. "I guess."

"So what happened next, when you met Jennifer?"

"I met her on campus at the diner where we first met. She was late, and she had her friend Kathryn with her."

"Did Kathryn stay?"

"She would have, but I asked to talk to Jennifer in private, so she left. So now that I have her alone, I asked her what she meant by wanting to talk to me about us."

"Good, so far you are handling things well, Luke."

This time he didn't smile, "Well, she immediately said she wanted more space and wanted to be able to date other people besides me."

Lindy asked, "And you responded how?"

"Badly. I just sorta lost it."

Lindy leaned forward and said, "How?"

Luke stood up then and began to walk around behind the sofa. After another minute he finally said, "I got up and cussed her out in front of everyone at the diner. I called her a lot of names; I think 'whore' and 'slut' were tame compared to some of the other words I used."

Lindy sat back in her chair. "Did you push her or threaten her?"

Luke thought back and then shook his head. "I didn't hit her, but I can't promise I didn't say anything threatening."

He stopped pacing and sat back down. "I just had so much rage and disappointment inside of me, my chest felt like it was exploding."

"What happened next?"

"The owner walked over and stepped in front of Jennifer and said I needed to leave his place and never come back again or he was going to call the cops."

"And did you leave immediately?"

Luke looked down. "The man was tall, fat, and bald. He reminded me of my father. Looking back on it now, it was probably a good thing because he scared the shit out of me. Yeah, I left."

Lindy sat back up and said, "Luke, do you realize that you were filled with rage and were approached by someone that resembled your father and you didn't hit him!"

Luke leaned back into the sofa. "Doc, you amaze me."

Lindy asked quizzically, "How?"

"You always look for the positive, and thank God you always find something." He smiled then. "Can you imagine what would've happened if I did take a swing?"

"Yeah, I would be visiting you in a jail cell."

Luke laughed. "That's not funny."

Lindy asked, "So did Jennifer ever make any response as you were blasting away at her?"

Luke stayed quiet, and she could tell he was trying to search his memory. Finally he said, "I just don't remember."

"Okay, how about when you were outside? Did you immediately leave or stick around in the parking lot?"

Luke looked back at Lindy with a completely different expression on his face, and his brown eyes appeared darker in color. He sat up straight and held his shoulders back and calmly said, "I planned to meet her later after her psych class."

Lindy was alarmed by the change in his demeanor as well as his last statement. She carefully probed. "Where were you two planning to meet?"

"We decided we would discuss this again after class and I would meet her outside the Dunn Building at the nearby bench."

Lindy tried to steady her nerves and keep her body relaxed. "Did you meet her after class?"

Luke looked down and said, "No, she didn't show. She stood me up."

"What did you do then?"

Luke looked back up with his boyish grin and said, "I went home and went to bed."

Lindy did her best to smile. "Luke, I would like to talk with you some more about this. Are you available to come back in tomorrow?"

Luke took out his phone and appeared to be checking his messages. Another minute passed and Lindy continued to wait for a response.

Finally Luke put his phone away and said, "I have my English class at eight, but I am free afterward."

"Let me check and see what time I can fit you in." Lindy calmly walked over to her desk and buzzed Erin. "I need to see Luke tomorrow any time after ten."

Erin said, "Let me look."

As Lindy waited, she made eye contact with Luke. He smiled at her, and she returned a half smile. Erin's voice came back on the line. "We can squeeze him in at eleven-thirty; your next appointment would be at one o'clock."

"That works. Thank you, Erin."

Lindy walked over and said, "Luke, this is all the time I have today, but I can see you tomorrow morning at eleven-thirty. Will that work?"

"Yeah, if you think we need to talk again before my appointment on Monday."

Lindy just smiled. "Let's talk about this again while it's still fresh on your mind."

"Okay then," he stood up and stretched a little, "I will see you tomorrow after class." Then he turned and headed toward the door. As he turned the door handle, he looked back with different eyes and said, "Tomorrow, Doc," and then he left, closing the door behind him.

Lindy stood still and watched him leave as a cold shiver ran down her spine.

Chapter 30

Matthew arrived at the medical examiner's office at four o'clock. It had been a long day, and the location of Melody Montgomery was still unknown. The news conference earlier had been a disaster. The media was tearing them apart at the news of a third victim with no new leads.

Matthew opened Dr. Candy Johnson's door and was instantly greeted by her staff member Kimberly. "Hi, Agent Blake. Go on back. Dr. Johnson is waiting on you."

Matthew walked down the hall that led to the lab. Candy Johnson was working on some papers as Andrew Mitt's body lay upon the steel cutting table. Candy stopped writing when she saw Matthew enter, and said, "Any word on Melody Montgomery?"

"No, but her parents have given us permission to search her apartment and take some samples. Once they realized she wasn't a suspect, they became worried and gave their full cooperation to help locate her."

Candy said, "They should be worried. We need her blood type and her bedroom sheets as soon as possible."

"They are getting them now. You found something?"

"Oh yeah. The sheets we took from his apartment had traces of semen and two different blood types."

"Two?"

"Yes. When examining the sheets and mattress, Andrew's blood is mostly on the right side of the bed, where his body was found. But on the left side, a different blood type was found. This gives me the impression we have another victim, who was lying on the left side of the bed."

"Was it a lot of blood?"

"A significant amount to cause worry."

Matthew frowned. "Is there any chance the blood came from the suspect?"

Candy put down her papers and said, "Yes, the killer may have had sex with the victim, and while she was stabbing him, the victim was able to wrestle away the knife and take a strike at the killer."

Matthew said, "Yeah, and Melody ran out of the apartment naked and left her clothing behind."

"I need her data. Until then, we can only speculate."

"We're on it. Damn, we have got to find Melody."

Erin walked into Lindy's office and found her stretched out on the leather couch with her head buried in a book on multiple personalities. Quietly Erin approached her and said, "Lindy?"

Lindy stopped reading and looked up. "Any word on my four o'clock patient?"

Erin shook her head. "No, I called her house and cell number. I left a voice message on each and asked her to give us a call."

Lindy looked at her watch. It was 4:35. She said aloud, "Where are you, Melody Montgomery?"

Chapter 31

Melody woke up again. This time the room was dark. She felt a breeze and looked to her left to see where it was coming from. The window that had been covered earlier was now open, and Melody could see that it was dark outside with very little light from the moon and stars. She listened for any sound but only heard crickets.

The pain in Melody's head had subsided but not the throbbing in her shoulder and arm. Slowly she tried to move her bandaged arm but stopped when pain struck at her shoulder and worked its way down her arm like lightning. Gritting her teeth, Melody took a deep breath and told herself to breathe through the pain. Once it subsided some, Melody slowly turned and lifted her head and tried to adjust her eyes to the darkness. In the faint light, she could see her legs but could barely make out the rope that fastened her ankles to a bedpost.

A chill ran down Melody's spine as once again the truth of her situation crept in. She was tied up wearing nothing but her underwear in a strange house. Again, she thought of Andrew, and tears began to flow down her cheeks. She wanted to scream out but didn't have the energy. She felt so tired, and the more she tried to concentrate, the foggier her mind became. Melody laid her head back down and closed her eyes as darkness filled her mind once again.

Satisfied the drug had kicked in again, the Night Killer left the dark doorway and whispered, "Good night, Melody, and sweet dreams."

Lindy closed and bolted the french doors once Parker was safely inside her townhouse. Immediately she punched in the new code that the alarm company had issued her earlier this evening. A red light appeared, and Lindy knew it was set properly. Back in the kitchen, Lindy poured herself a glass of red wine from the opened bottle sitting on the counter. As she took a sip, she thought of Erin and her date tonight with Charlie.

Charlie had called Erin's cell number around five o'clock when he got out of his business meeting. The two had planned to hook up one more time for dinner before he left to go back to Houston on Friday. Lindy only slightly protested but then stopped when she realized how tired she was. With thoughts of a quiet evening alone and turning in early for bed, Lindy gave Erin her blessing and wished her lots of fun. At least this way, she knew Erin wasn't alone. Lindy smiled at the thought of Tiffany joining them again; this time Charlie was bringing an unmarried business partner.

Lindy picked up her wine glass and started toward her bedroom with Parker. It was almost nine o'clock, and she was past ready for bed. Once inside her bedroom, she closed and locked the door and then stopped short of her bed to strip down. Placing her wine glass on the nightstand, Lindy decided to just sleep in her tank top and underwear; she was too tired to change again. With a yawn, she pulled off her yoga pants and climbed into bed.

After she was settled, Parker jumped up and snuggled at Lindy's feet. Slowly sipping her wine, Lindy flipped through the local news stations but only found the standard Thursday night sitcoms on each channel. She finally settled on a rerun of I Love Lucy on TV Land and continued to drink the rest of her wine. When she finished her last sip, she picked up the remote and hit the off button. Within two minutes, Lindy was asleep.

From outside Lindy's window, a man stood watching her. Once the TV was off and the bedroom was dark, the man became frustrated that he could no longer see her. Now that the house was set with an alarm, he was going to have to come up with a different plan. Turning around, he silently made his way back to the vehicle parked down the road. Once inside, he opened up his laptop and typed in his secure password to unlock the screen. In a matter of minutes, a video was playing of Lindy pulling off her yoga pants and climbing into bed wearing only blue underwear and a fitted white tank top. Noticing a small bruise, he paused the video and frowned at the imperfection.

Matthew was heading down Interstate 20 toward his ranch. By morning, he would know more from the medical examiner. If it was Melody's blood, the decision had been made to alert the media that she was missing and could possibly be in danger. It was going to be an ugly press conference, but they needed to call on any and all resources that might help them find her.

Looking at the clock on his dashboard, Matthew decided nine twenty wasn't too late to call Dr. Lindy Ashley. Picking up his cell phone, he contemplated what to say. *Should I just state that I'm worried about her and want to check on her? Or, should I just get straight to the point and say that I want to go out again and soon?* Slowly Matthew pressed the numbers while trying to keep his eyes on the road. Soon the phone was ringing on the other end. After the third ring, his call went to her voice mail.

"You have reached the voice mail of Dr. Lindy Ashley. Please leave a message, and I'll return your call shortly."

Not knowing exactly what to say, Matthew hung up his cell phone without leaving a message.

Chapter 32

Friday, October 1st

Lindy walked into her office at seven o'clock dressed in black slacks and a sheer, white long-sleeve blouse with a white satin tank underneath. Her hair was down, but her pearl and black earrings were still very noticeable as they dangled from her earlobes. Lindy was wearing the matching necklace, and the large pearl sat right above her scooped neckline. Erin looked up from her desk as Lindy walked down the hallway.

"Hi, sis. Wow! Don't you look beautiful and well rested?"

"Thanks, Erin. How was your date with Charlie last night?"

Erin hesitated and then smiled. "Good enough that we're going out again."

From the look on Erin's face, Lindy could tell she was really excited about the upcoming date. But Lindy didn't push anything and instead just asked, "Great, when's he coming back to Ft. Worth?"

Erin twisted her lips and looked down at something on her desk. Lindy stood and patiently waited for Erin to elaborate. Finally Erin said, "Charlie changed his flight until Sunday afternoon. We decided to spend the weekend together."

Lindy forced a smile and said, "Wow, when do I get to meet him?"

"Why don't you join us tonight for drinks after work? You could call up Matthew Blake and invite him as well."

Lindy spoke immediately. "I'm sure Matthew has his hands full with this case. I don't see him having the time for drinks and dinner."

Erin shrugged her shoulders coyly and said, "You can always ask..."

Lindy walked forward to the desk and picked up the day's schedule. "I have an appointment after work at three. Where are you going tonight? I might be able to join you, with or without Matthew."

Erin looked at her questioningly. "I don't remember making you an appointment for today."

Lindy smiled as she walked away toward her office. Over her shoulder, she said, "I can make appointments all on my own sometimes."

Lindy closed her office door and took a seat at her desk. Looking over the day's appointments, Lindy thought, *Doesn't look too bad...if you don't count Luke James coming back in.* Lindy noticed his appointment time; she would have to squeeze in something quick and light for lunch before her one o'clock arrived.

Like most doctor offices, Lindy's hours on Friday's were shorter. The last appointment she would take was one o'clock. Today, that would be with an old and established patient, Sally Jenkins. *Shouldn't be any surprises with her,* Lindy thought. *I should easily be able to walk out by two-thirty.* Glancing at her watch, Lindy had about thirty-five minutes before her eight o'clock appointment, so she picked up her multiple personalities book and began to read where she left off yesterday.

Matthew Blake and Steve Toowey were going through Melody Montgomery's apartment once more to make sure nothing was missed from yesterday. Matthew was going through her closet and checking pockets while Steve went through dresser drawers looking for pictures of friends.

"Hey, Matthew, Melody has some new messages. The light is blinking on her phone."

Matthew walked over and, with his gloved hand, hit the play button, and both men stood patiently waiting through Melody's greeting. "Hi,

Melody, this is Rhonda from Campus Dry Cleaners. Your dress is ready for pickup. Thanks."

Matthew said, "Let's go by there and check the dress out. Maybe she went to a special event lately and met someone."

Several hang up calls were recorded, and finally another message began. "This is Erin from Dr. Ashley's office. You're late for your four o'clock appointment, and I was just calling to check on you. Please give us a call so we can reschedule. Thanks."

"We need to go see the doctor," Steve stated.

Matthew shook his head. "Yeah, that's three strikes. One, she was on campus all three nights. Two, she received a threatening gift. And now three, she's Melody's doctor...the same Melody who also attends the psych class where she lectured."

Steve commented, "Way too many coincidences. So, do we call first or just arrive unexpectedly?"

"I have her card. Let's call. If not, we'll end up waiting in between patients to see her. Besides, I don't think she has anything to hide."

Steve asked, "Does she have an alibi for any of the nights the victims were killed?"

Matthew didn't get offended; he simply answered with a shrug. "I left her place Wednesday night around nine forty-five. The other two nights, I never asked what she did after class."

Steve grinned. "Nine forty-five?"

"Yeah, she wanted to walk her dog, and I didn't think it was a good idea for her to go out alone. Look, I don't think she killed anyone, but it wouldn't be the first time I misjudged a woman."

Steve waved his hands in the air and responded, "You know my track record. I'm not saying anything."

Matthew took out his card case and quickly found her office number. "I'll call her. We have to ask." Soon he had Erin on the line.

"Dr. Ashley's office, Erin speaking. How may I help you?"

"Hello, Erin, it's Matthew Blake."

"Hi, Matthew. Lindy and I were just talking about you."

"Oh?"

"Yeah, we were planning on having drinks later after work."

"Well, I don't know. I'm pretty busy right now with this case."

"Yeah, that was the same comment Lindy made."

"Oh, she did, huh? Well, the reason I'm calling is because I need to see Lindy today—the sooner the better."

Erin got quiet for a moment and then finally asked, "Why, did you find out something about the box?"

"I'm sorry, Erin. I'd rather not discuss this over the phone."

"Oh sure, sorry. Um, let me see when the best time would be to fit you in today..."

Matthew waited and continued to look around Melody's apartment for any sign of a troubled mind. He thought, *Why else would she visit a psychologist?* Erin came back on the line. "Well, the best I can do is twelve-thirty to one o'clock, during her lunch break."

"What time is her last appointment?"

"We close at two on Fridays, but Lindy has to be somewhere at three today."

"I see. I'll be there at twelve-thirty then."

Erin smiled into the phone and responded, "Great, we'll see you then. Bye."

"Bye, Erin." Matthew closed his phone and looked at Steve. "We got awhile. What do you say we drive through campus and see what's going on?"

Steve replied, "Sounds like a plan."

Chapter 33

Luke James was relaxed and lying down on Lindy's leather couch. His eyes were closed as he told Lindy about meeting Jennifer, his girlfriend, for breakfast. "We met at the IHOP this morning at nine."

Lindy asked, "How did that go after Wednesday's fight?"

"Well, it took some convincing on my part, but she finally agreed to meet me."

"Luke, did you apologize for your outburst at the restaurant?"

Luke opened his eyes up and gazed at the ceiling. "Yeah, that was the only way she would agree to meet me. Trust me, I had to beg and whine for her forgiveness."

Lindy asked next, "So where does your relationship with Jennifer stand now?"

Luke took a deep breath. "She doesn't want to make any commitments, but she said she enjoys my company and likes going out with me."

"How do you feel about that?"

Luke closed his eyes again for a few moments and then opened them and spun around and sat up on the couch.

"I'm okay with that. I mean there's a lot of chicks on campus that I wouldn't mind asking out on a date."

"Girls from your class?"

"Yeah, there's this one girl named Melinda. She's super fine."

Lindy decided now was the time to start a different line of questioning to dig deeper into Luke's mind. "Luke, how are you sleeping at night?"

He stared back with a quizzical look on his face and said, "Why do you ask?"

Lindy flashed her million-dollar smile and said, "It's my job to ask questions, remember?"

Luke grinned and then said, "Okay, sure. Um, I don't know. I've been waking up a lot during the night."

Lindy sat up a little and leaned forward. "Do you have dreams?"

"Yes, I've been dreaming a lot. Sometimes I wake up and feel like my dream is still going on. Is that strange?"

"Not necessarily. Do you remember your dreams?"

Luke got quiet and then he twisted his body back around so he could lie down again. Lindy didn't interrupt his thought process and just waited for him to respond. Soon, Luke opened his eyes and began explaining his dreams.

"One dream, I woke up and felt like I was in a cabin with a girl. I looked around and saw no one. I must have gone back to sleep in the dream, but when morning came around for real, I remembered the girl and hiking in the woods as though it had happened. And I literally felt tired, like I'd walked for miles."

Lindy asked, "When was this?"

Luke thought for a moment and said, "The night I argued with Jennifer."

"What did the girl look like in your dream? Did she resemble Jennifer in any way?"

Luke smiled and shook his head. "I can't remember if she was blond, brunette, skinny, or fat. I can recall nothing about her."

"Can you describe another dream?"

"Nothing specific. I usually don't remember dreaming when I wake up, but the vague memories of a dream usually go through my mind sometime during the day."

"At what point of the day do you realize you had a dream the night before?" Lindy prodded.

"Just depends. Sometimes in the afternoon or late in the evenings before I go to bed again."

"Luke, has your grandmother ever made a comment that would imply you sometimes sleepwalk?"

"Funny you ask that. She asked me yesterday if I had left during the night before."

"And how did you respond?"

"I told her no and asked why she thought that."

Lindy asked, "And what did she say?"

"She said she woke up in the middle of the night and thought she heard the garage door. She said she never got up to check but tried listening for another sound and drifted back to sleep."

Lindy asked, "Do you ever remember a noise waking you up?"

"I don't know, I mean, maybe. I did wake up at one point because I remembered dreaming I was in a cabin. It might have been the neighbor's garage door that woke both of us up."

Lindy smiled. "It very well could've been. So, what about your eating habits. Are you eating less or more lately?"

Luke looked down at his stomach and appeared a little self-conscious. "I'm still working out, but I think I have been eating more. I mean, my clothes still fit, but I noticed a few extra pounds when I stepped on the scale this morning."

"How often do you weigh?" asked Lindy.

"Only on Fridays."

"Why Fridays?"

"I have a set workout for each week, and I just have always weighed on Fridays."

Lindy thought, *It's time to move on.* She asked, "Okay, so tell me about your plans for this weekend."

Luke sat back up on the couch before answering. "Jennifer and I never made any concrete plans."

"Do you plan to call her and ask her out or just hang out with friends this weekend?"

"I don't know. I thought about calling Bart up to catch a movie. He lives down the street and he's in my fantasy football league."

"That sounds good. Anything else planned?"

"My grandmother wants me and my sister to join her on Sunday for church and then go out for dinner afterward."

"Good. Spending quality time with both of them is healthy for you. Plus, the weather is supposed to be nice on Sunday. Maybe ya'll can spend some time outside or go to a park."

"Yeah, maybe." Luke looked at his watch and said, "Doc, I'm a little tired and hungry."

Lindy looked at her watch. It was twelve fifteen. She said, "Okay, Luke. We can stop. I'll see you again next week."

Luke stood up and shook her hand. "I think my appointment's on Monday. Do you think I need to see you again so soon?"

Lindy smiled. "It's best to keep our routine appointments. Today and yesterday's appointments were a result of something that agitated you, and we needed to work through that."

Luke nodded his head. "You're the boss. I'll see you on Monday."

"Boss? Funny. Bye, Luke."

As soon as Luke exited out the door directly across from her office, Lindy grabbed her notepad and headed to her desk. Once seated, she opened her bottom drawer and removed the book on multiple personalities. Flipping through it, she made some notes in Luke's file, frowning as she wrote. Ten minutes later, Erin appeared in the doorway. "Sorry to bother you, but you have a twelve-thirty appointment."

Lindy looked up and said, "Who?"

Erin smiled and said, "Matthew called earlier and wanted to see you as soon as possible."

Lindy jumped up and headed toward her bathroom to brush her hair and apply a fresh coat of lipstick. Erin followed her over and peered inside. "You look great, Lindy."

Lindy looked at her sister in the mirror and said, "You're biased."

"Whatever!"

Lindy brush through her hair once more and stepped out of the bathroom to find Erin lounging on the brown leather couch just as Luke had done previous. "Erin, that hasn't been cleaned today."

"Who cares, your last patient is a hunk. I can't imagine catching anything from him."

Lindy held her tongue on the subject of Luke James and instead asked, "So did Matthew say why he was coming over?"

Erin sat up from the couch and said, "He misses you and just had to come by and see you once more."

Lindy picked up a pillow and threw it at Erin. "Go man your desk and send him back when he gets here."

Chapter 34

Matthew Blake and Steve Toowey pulled into the parking garage at Lindy's office and were greeted by the security officer. After a brief conversation between the three, Matthew continued forward and parked his Camaro.

When opening his car door, Matthew received a phone call. Still sitting with the door open, he reached in his pocket and retrieved the phone.

"Agent Blake."

"Hi, it's Candy Johnson. I got something."

Matthew felt his heart rate increase and looked at Steve and said, "It's the ME," and shut his car door.

"I can talk. What do you have?"

"It doesn't look good. Melody Montgomery's DNA is all over the victim's sheets as well as her blood—type O neg, which you know is an uncommon."

Matthew said, "Shit! Were there any traces of blood found in the apartment that would indicate how the body was moved?"

"Nothing. No blood was found in the apartment other than in the bedroom."

"Good job, Dr. Johnson. Please keep me posted if anything else comes up."

"I will. Bye now."

Steve could figure out from the one-sided conversation that it was Melody's blood. He looked over to Matthew and said, "I don't think a female could pick up Melody Montgomery and carry her out of the apartment unnoticed."

Matthew agreed and then grabbed his phone again and called in to room A150. Don answered on the second ring.

"Don, the ME confirmed Melody was in bed with Andrew and it's her blood on the sheets. No other blood has been found in the apartment."

Don said, "Nothing here on her whereabouts. No one has called in."

Matthew asked, "What was found outside the window of Andrew's bedroom, anything?"

"I'm going to put you on speakerphone." Don pressed a button and then hung up the hand piece. "Pamela, get the report of the outside surroundings of Andrew Mitt's apartment."

After a short pause, Pamela began to speak. "Okay, the report suggests nothing was disturbed outside the victim's bedroom. The intruder did not come through the window or leave through the window—"

Matthew interrupted, "What about anything heavy thrown out the window or dragged along the ground?"

Pamela read on and then said, "No, nothing looks disturbed. No broken branches, and no soil markings to indicate any such activity."

Matthew hesitated and then finally said what was on everyone's mind. "Don, I need you to call Melody's parents. We need to go live with her disappearance."

Don said, "Yeah, fun. I will set up a media conference for some time after two. Will that work?"

"Yes. Steve and I are at Dr. Ashley's office now, but it shouldn't take long."

"Will do, partner," and Don hung up the phone.

Matthew turned to Steve. "How the hell did the killer carry Melody Montgomery out of the apartment without anyone noticing?"

Steve answered, "Maybe someone did and just doesn't realize it yet. Once we get the word out that Melody is missing, someone might come forward. Or—"

"Or what?"

Steve continued, "Maybe Melody killed him and cut herself to look like a victim and disappeared. We don't know why she's seeing a doctor. Maybe she is mentally unstable."

Matthew opened up his car door again and said, "No point guessing. Let's go find out."

Moments later, Matthew and Steve were standing in the elevator and going up to the fourth floor. Matthew looked at his watch; it was now twelve thirty-five. The door opened, and both agents stepped out and turned toward Lindy's office. After a couple of steps, Matthew heard a door close behind him, so he stopped and turned around. Steve had heard the noise also and was looking in the same direction as Matthew.

Both agents quickly backtracked to the door that led to the stairwell to the left of the elevator. Matthew opened up the door, and both agents peered up and down the staircase. They saw no one. Steve said, "I'll go up the next two flights, you go down, and then we'll work our way back to here."

Matthew nodded, took out his gun, and started downward as Steve started upward. At each landing Matthew paused and listened, but no sound emerged. Matthew continued down, checking each door to each floor, but saw no one.

After the last set of stairs, Matthew was back in the parking garage. He looked at his watch, and it was now twelve forty-two. Quickly walking toward the security guard, Matthew called out, "Hey, did anyone come out from the stairway?"

Davey shook his head and said, "Why, what's up?"

"I heard a noise when I exited the elevator on the fourth floor but saw no one on the way back down."

Davey said, "I'll check the tapes."

Together they walked inside his small cubical and looked at two TV monitors. Davey hit a button, and both screens started to rewind. No movement was detected in the stairwell. Matthew asked, "Why am I not on the screen?"

Davey looked confused and said, "I don't know."

Matthew looked at his watch again and said, "Find out what's wrong, and I'll be back down soon." Matthew left Davey to work and then took the elevator back up to the fourth floor. When the elevator opened up, Steve was standing in the hallway to the side. When Steve saw that it was Matthew, he relaxed his stance and said, "Nothing. You?"

"No, and something's wrong with the security camera. Davey's working on it now. Hopefully he'll have it figured out by the time we're done here. Let's go."

When the agents stepped through Lindy's office door, Erin stood up in her black fitted dress with heels and walked over to greet them. "Hello, gentlemen. You have about ten minutes before her one o'clock appointment. Come on back."

Both agents followed closely behind Erin as she led them down the hallway. Lindy's door was opened, and she looked up when she heard them approach. Laying down her salad fork, she wiped her mouth and then stood.

Matthew spoke first. "Lindy, Erin, this is my partner, Steve Toowey." Both sisters exchanged hellos and then Erin left them alone and closed the door behind her.

"Sorry we're late," Matthew continued.

Lindy smiled. "No problem. It allowed me time to eat. Please, have a seat."

Both men walked toward the leather couch, and Lindy took her usual yellow chair across from them. Matthew said, "I was at Melody Montgomery's apartment this morning and listened to the messages from her answering machine. I heard Erin's voice and realized she's a patient of yours."

With concern in her voice, Lindy said, "In her apartment? Is she in trouble? I mean, she didn't show for her four o'clock appointment yesterday."

Steve said, "Melody is the girlfriend of Andrew Mitt, the student who was murdered Wednesday night on campus."

Lindy placed a hand on her chest and then said, "Do you suspect Melody of murder?"

Steve looked at Matthew and waited for him to answer.
"Lindy, what can you tell us about Melody without a warrant and a breach of confidentiality?"

"Not much. You need a warrant."

"Did you know Melody attended Professor Dobb's class and was there the nights you lectured?"

Lindy thought for a moment and looked into Matthew's eyes. "Yes, she told me a couple of weeks ago, before I started lecturing."

Steve asked, "Did you ever make contact with her at the school?"

Lindy shook her head. "No, we never spoke. Considering the sensitivity of our relationship, we didn't want to draw attention to the fact we knew each other."

Matthew nodded and thought to himself, *that makes sense.* He then asked, "Did Andrew know she was seeing you professionally?"

Lindy sat back and placed a hand under her chin and thought about the question. Another moment passed and she said, "I would feel more comfortable having this conversation when you get that warrant."

Matthew nodded again. "We're working on it. In the meantime, can you let us know if she makes contact?"

Lindy slightly hesitated and then said, "Since you already know she's a patient, yes, I can do that. I won't be able to divulge the conversation though without a warrant."

Matthew acknowledged. "I understand. How did your and Erin's night go last night? Any surprises or anything suspicious?"

Lindy couldn't help but think of Amber, George's newest girlfriend, and her unexpected visit yesterday morning. Quickly she pushed the thought aside and said, "All fine here."

Matthew stood, followed by Steve, and said, "Good. Well, you have my card. Call me if you need me."

"Thanks." Lindy led them to the door and opened it. Motioning to the door across from hers, she said, "If you don't mind, use this door. I have a patient waiting in the other room."

Matthew glanced down the hall but saw no one. "Oh sure. Bye now."

"Bye. It was nice to meet you, Steve."

Steve replied, "Same here, and we'll let you know when we get that warrant."

Lindy nodded and closed the door behind them and then made her way to the front to greet her next patient, Sally Jenkins.

Chapter 35

Once in the elevator, Steve said, "Wow, I can see how she could cloud your judgment."

"No kidding."

"If we don't end up arresting her, do you plan to ask her out when all this is over?"

Matthew grinned. "Most definitely."

Steve and Matthew were both smiling when they entered the parking garage. Unfortunately it didn't last long when Matthew spotted Davey talking to a man behind the wheel of a security van. Looking up as the two agents approached, Davey motioned for the guy to get back out of his vehicle.

"What did you find out, Davey?" asked Matthew.

"I couldn't figure anything out, so I called Martin here from Arlington Security. Luckily, he happened to be next door, so he was able to come right over and solve the problem."

Matthew and Steve looked toward Martin and waited.
Martin finally said, "Someone has tampered with the cameras in the stairwell. Whoever it is knows what they're doing."

"Any idea how long this's been going on?" Steve asked.

Davey's face flushed red with embarrassment, and he looked down at his feet. Martin shook his head and said, "Looking at the videos, at least the last two weeks. I will know more after I've had a chance to study the tapes."

Matthew asked, "All right, so how's he doing it?"

Martin pointed to one of the cameras in the van and said, "There's an outlet right here. The person is sticking an object in there to make the video freeze so that it appears to the computer screen that no one is there."

In an exasperated voice, Steve commented, "So basically anyone can walk up and down the staircase without being detected."

Martin frowned. "Exactly. Now I'm going to install some new cameras that have a different outlet. Hopefully whoever is doing this won't notice and we'll catch him on tape snooping around."

Matthew's phone started vibrating in his pocket, and he said, "Excuse me, gentlemen." Matthew walked toward his car and answered the phone. "Matthew Blake"

"It's Don. Guess who Melody Montgomery used to date?"

Matthew looked up at the lights on the parking garage ceiling and shook his head. "Trust me, it won't surprise me."

"Robby and Jaycee" stated Don.

Matthew motioned for Steve to come on and then said into his phone, "We're on our way."

Lindy finished up with her last appointment and then walked to the front of the office to talk with Erin. When she rounded the last corner, she heard Erin on the phone talking to someone with a big grin on her face. Lindy continued to watch as Erin wrapped her long blond hair around her finger and twirled it while talking. Sensing someone there, Erin spun around in her chair and saw Lindy. She smiled and waved.

"Okay," Erin said into the phone, "I should be there in about forty-five minutes. Can't wait to see you again. Bye."

Erin hung up the phone with a big smile on her face.

"You look happy. So, where are ya'll having drinks? Let me know, and I'll do my best to swing by."

"Downtown Ft. Worth, at Aureles."

"Sounds nice. I'm going to head out now. I'll try to be there by five."

With a mischievous grin, Erin asked, "Did you ask the good-looking agent to join us?"

"No, unfortunately their visit was all business."

"Oh, what did they want?"

Lindy ran her hands through her jet-black hair and then said, "They heard your message at Melody Montgomery's apartment. It appears she's the latest victim's girlfriend, and they're trying to find her."

Erin's face drained of color. "What are you saying? Is she dead?"

Lindy was tired, and she tried to focus on her conversation with Erin. "I don't know. But if she calls in, please let me know immediately."

"Sure, Lindy. All of this is getting too weird."

Lindy just nodded her head in agreement and said, "Let's walk out together. I don't think it's a good idea for either of us to be alone."

"Well, I plan on being with Charlie all weekend. What about you?"

"I have that new security system now and Parker. I should be fine."

"I don't know," Erin said. "Why don't I plan to come over after my date?"

"Let's just see how things are going when we meet up. Are you ready to go?"

Erin grabbed her purse and then shut down her computer.
"Yep, after you."

Davey was at his cubical watching the computer screens when Lindy and Erin walked out. He stood up and walked out toward them. "Good afternoon, ladies. Nice day?"

Erin said, "Yes, just ready to start the weekend!"

Davey nodded and said, "Ya'll drive safe, and I'll see you on Monday."

Erin walked over to her yellow BMW convertible and jumped in and started out of the parking lot without any time to waste. Lindy settled in her black Jaguar and buckled up and waved to Davey as she passed him on the way out. Erin turned left, and Lindy turned right toward her appointment. After a few lights and lots of slow traffic, Lindy noticed that the black SUV behind her had been there for a while. She looked carefully in her rearview mirror and tried to see if she could recognize the driver. "I'm really getting paranoid," she said aloud. The light turned green, and Lindy hit the accelerator.

Just in case she was wrong, Lindy sped up and changed lanes. For the next mile, she continued to look back as she drove to see if the vehicle appeared again. So far, she had lost whoever it was. Lindy had to slow down again for another light and decided to check her rearview mirror again. As she glanced up, she saw the dark SUV change lanes and get right behind her once again. Lindy continued to stare and tried her best to make out the face of the driver.

The light turned green again, and immediately Lindy pulled ahead and changed lanes. Once she was safely in the right lane, she immediately turned right. Looking in her rearview mirror as she took the corner, she could see the black vehicle swerve into the other lane, but it couldn't make the turn in time. Lindy continued on down the street and took a deep breath. Even though this route would take an extra ten minutes, Lindy felt it was worth it.

Behind the wheel of the SUV, Clay Barry was cussing aloud. "How the hell did she lose me?"

For the next several miles, he drove around in circles looking for Lindy's black Jaguar to no avail. "I'm such a moron! How the hell am I gonna find her now?" A car pulled up on Clay's bumper and blew the horn for him to go through the green light. "Ahhhh blow it out your ass! I'm going!" Clay moved forward and extended his left hand out the window and gave the horn blower the finger.

Chapter 36

Jamie walked back toward Becky's bedroom and knocked on the open door. Becky never rolled over or said a word. Jamie wasn't buying that she was asleep; instead, she waltzed right in and took a seat on the edge of the bed.

Placing a hand on Becky's shoulder, she said, "The TV just announced there's breaking news on the Night Killer. In two minutes they're broadcasting live."

Becky slowly rolled over and looked at Jamie with a blank stare and sad eyes. Jamie didn't give up. "Becky, come on, get up. We'll watch it together and then I'll warm us up some leftover lasagna."

Becky blinked her eyes but didn't budge. Jamie pulled her into a sitting position and then reached out and grabbed her legs and swung them around. "Hey, stop it, Jamie!"

"No, I won't. You're alive, and it's time you start acting like it."

Jamie stood up and continued to pull Becky up into a standing position. "Becky, I'm not going to allow you to wallow in depression. You've got to fight this."

Becky was now standing on her own, and she pushed Jamie's hands off her shoulders. "I'm going!" yelled Becky.

Jamie stood by and watched as Becky stormed past her toward the living room. Jamie followed behind her without saying another word. When they reached the living room, the TV was already showing the news conference Jamie was referring to. Jamie took a seat on the couch beside Becky and picked up the remote to turn up the volume. On the screen was the agent that had stopped by to see Jamie a few days ago. Both girls watched intently.

"We have reason to believe that a Central University student named Melody Montgomery is missing and may be in serious danger. Melody is the girlfriend of the latest victim, Andrew Mitt. Melody is blond with green eyes. She stands five seven and weighs approximately one hundred and fifteen pounds. Melody was last seen at the medical library on Wednesday night around seven fifteen. We have reason to believe she went home with the victim, Andrew Mitt. Any information concerning her whereabouts or that would lead us to Melody would be greatly appreciated by her family as well as this task force. We have shown a current picture of Melody Montgomery as well as a phone number to call with any information. That's all that we have for now. Thank you."

Jamie and Becky continued to watch as news reporters yelled out unanswered questions to Agent Blake as he walked back into a building without another word spoken.

Stacy Bryan with Channel Nine news said, "Here's the picture of Melody Montgomery with a phone number to call. Please contact the authorities if you have any information that could lead to the discovery of Melody Montgomery."

Jamie picked up the remote and changed the channel to a music video network. "I'm going to warm up that lasagna now. It'll only take about five minutes."

Becky turned away from the TV and watched as Jamie went to the refrigerator and pulled out a Pyrex dish. When the food was in the microwave, Becky asked, "When was the last time you saw Melody?"

Jamie was reaching into the refrigerator for the milk when Becky asked the question. She continued on with her task, pulling down two glasses and pouring the milk. Finally she said, "I saw her on Wednesday morning in my science class."

"What do you think happened to her?"

Jamie walked over to the table and set the two glasses of milk down and then walked back over to the microwave and removed the lasagna. Once she had everything ready, Jamie said, "I don't know. Come on. Let's eat."

Becky didn't have to be persuaded. It had been almost twenty-four hours since she had last eaten, and her stomach was growling at the smell of food. Becky got up from the couch and took a seat at the table.

Jamie asked, "Have you talked to the authorities anymore about this investigation?"

Becky said, "Not since earlier this week. Why?"

Jamie swallowed a bite of lasagna and said, "No reason."

Matthew was seated at a table with Steve, Pamela, and Don in room A150. They were sorting through information on Melody and her past before she started dating Andrew.

Pamela said, "I was in a sorority in college, and we didn't get around as much as these girls do. Do you realize that Jamie, Melody, and Candice never went an entire month without getting involved intimately with another boyfriend?"

Don said, "Yep, times are definitely different."

Matthew said, "There has to be something else connecting these girls, and we're just missing it."

Pamela said, "We've checked classes, housing, high schools, gyms, clubs, and churches. Everything we can think of."

Matthew said, "What about doctors? We didn't know until today that Melody was seeing a shrink. What other doctors does she or the others see?"

Peter, one of the team members sitting at a computer desk behind them, said, "I'm on it. I'll see what I can find out."

Pamela suggested, "Start with the campus clinic. If they aren't seeing their doctors, maybe they recommend someone close to campus."

Steve said, "Melody was moved from an apartment to a vehicle more than likely. One strong man could do the job. So could two or three females."

Matthew thought for a moment and then said, "If it was a small group of females, who are they? I don't see Jamie, Candice, or Becky moving Melody."

Pamela said, "I agree. Becky and Candice were totally blown away after their boyfriends were murdered. I just don't think they were faking their heartache and grief."

Steve chuckled. "Sorry, Pamela, but we should never underestimate the acting abilities of females."

Pamela frowned. "Really? We're not that great at acting."

"Ha! You just admitted to acting yourself!" said Don from across the room.

A female tech handling the phone lines spoke up. "I agree with you, Steve. I learned at a very early age how to manipulate the opposite sex to get my way. Now, it just comes across naturally, and I don't even realize I'm doing it sometimes."

Don shook his head. "Ya'll ain't right."

Steve reached out and grabbed the paper they were working on earlier and circled four guy names. "All girls dated these guys. We need to find them and fast."

Matthew said, "You're right. Let's each take a name and split up and meet back here in two hours."

Steve stood up and said, "Be careful, guys. Any of these boys could be the one."

"Or the next victim" suggested Pamela. All nodded in agreement and then they were out the door holding a name, address, and phone number.

Chapter 37

Melody Montgomery woke up again. This time the room looked different. It was daylight, and she could see. The window that was opened before was now closed, and the blinds were slightly shut. She still felt a breeze, though, and looked up to find the fan running on medium speed above her. Melody looked back toward her shoulder. A silver stand held a pouch of liquid that was slowly draining in her left hand through an IV tube. Melody tried to move her hand, but it would barely budge.

Looking around some more, Melody felt something on her leg and looked down. There was a bag filled with yellow liquid lying beside her right leg. Her eyes followed the tube and then instantly she realized she was hooked up to a catheter and that the bag was holding her urine. Melody silently cursed. *What the hell is going on?* She wanted to scream but was too afraid of who or what would come walking through the door.

Melody took some deep breaths and tried to stay calm. Obviously someone had made a lot of effort to keep her alive. *But who, and why?* A sound came from down the hallway, and Melody lifted her head to see who it was. With each passing second, Melody could feel her heart pounding faster. Finally, an image appeared in the doorway and stood there quietly staring back at her.

The mysterious person took a few steps toward Melody and then stopped right beside her bed. Melody recognized who it was and finally got a sound out. "You? Why have you done this to me?"

The person picked up Melody's IV and began to insert a liquid through the tube. Melody's throat hurt to talk, but she pushed through anyway in a crackling voice. "Did you kill Andrew?"

After all the liquid was inserted, the person turned around and said, "All in good time, Melody. Go back to sleep now."

Melody tried to protest, but the drug was working fast. The only sound she was able to get out was "N—" before falling back under into a dark abyss.

Erin and Charlie were seated in a corner at the ritzy bar in downtown Ft. Worth. Both were in deep conversation and oblivious that anyone was watching from across the room.

Erin laughed and then tilted her head back. She ran her left hand through her long blond hair and continued to laugh as Charlie talked.

Leroy felt nauseated at the thought that Erin was able to hook up with a new guy so quickly. He thought, *What is this, the third date already?* Angrily he turned toward the bar and ordered another shot from the red-headed bartender. In a sweet voice, the redhead with a name tag reading Mitzi said, "Hey, take it easy, cowboy. Tonight's still young."

Leroy ignored her comment and downed the shot. "Pour me another."

Mitzi said, "Another five dollars, please."

Leroy pulled out a twenty and said, "Will this work?"

Mitzi took the twenty, made change, and poured another shot. Quickly she made eye contact with her boss, Jack, and gestured toward Leroy and then walked away to help another customer. When Jack made his way over to Leroy, Leroy instantly knew what was going on. "Don't worry, I'm leaving," he said. "This place is too classy and stuck up for my taste anyway."

Jack remained quiet and calm and continued to watch Leroy as he walked out of the establishment and down the sidewalk.

Two blocks away, Lindy was circling around trying to find a parking spot. She was having no luck. Finally, after making another loop, a big pickup truck pulled away from the curb and left an opening. Lindy quickly accelerated to get the spot, barely beating a sporty blue convertible coming from the opposite direction.

Once parked, Lindy pulled down her mirror and checked her face. She looked tired. Reaching in her black purse, she grabbed some lipstick and applied it. Next, she dotted under her eyes with some base and powder. Looking again, she decided that it would have to work and placed the makeup back into her purse.

Lindy stepped out of her Jag and looked around before crossing the street. The parking spot actually wasn't too far away because she could see the lights from the sign that read "Aureles." Walking down the sidewalk, she was not alone. Other couples and groups from various businesses were walking along and headed for their own after work drinks, which was very common in downtown Ft. Worth on a Friday. Lindy made it to the entrance without mishap and opened the door. Immediately she started looking around for Erin and her new fling.

Erin was talking to Charlie when she noticed him look away and take a second look at something behind her. Erin turned around and saw Lindy and waved. Turning back to Charlie, Erin said, "That gorgeous lady is my sister."

Charlie winked and said, "Beauty definitely runs in your family."

After introductions were made, Erin slid over in the booth closer to Charlie, and Lindy slid in beside her. Immediately, Jack made his way over and said, "Hi, Lindy. Haven't seen you in a while. Can I get you something from the bar?"

Lindy looked at the bar owner and said, "Hi, Jack. I'll have a Seven and Seven, please."

"No problem. I'll be right back."

Lindy looked at Charlie and smiled. She was pleasantly surprised. Charlie was wearing a business shirt and tie, and his jacket was lying over the top of the booth behind him. She asked, "So, Charlie, what brings you to Ft. Worth?"

"I'm in the oil and gas business. There was a three-day seminar on nuclear energy at the Marriott Hotel."

Lindy asked next, "How often do you make it up here from Houston?"

Charlie took a sip from his Corona and then answered, "I'm up this way about once a month, but that could change." Charlie looked at Erin and winked. Erin smiled back and then turned to Lindy and asked, "Any word from Matthew?"

Lindy tried not to frown at Erin's warped sense of reality. She instead just answered with, "No, Matthew's too busy for drinks."

Erin turned toward Charlie and explained that Matthew was heading up the Night Killer investigation as the lead FBI agent. Charlie said, "No kidding? I saw his news conference today. It was playing at the Marriott. There's some bad stuff going on at Central University."

Lindy said, "I didn't see the news conference. What's the latest?"

Charlie said, "The girlfriend of the latest victim has gone missing, and they're asking the community for help."

Erin looked at Lindy. "I hope they find Melody soon."

"Do ya'll know her?" Charlie asked.

Erin said, "Yes, she's one of our patients."

"Erin!" Lindy pinched her under the table.

Erin looked over and said, "Sorry, I know, I wasn't supposed to say that with all the confidentiality bullshit."

Jack arrived with Lindy's drink, and she immediately picked it up and took a big gulp. The whiskey stung as it slid down her throat. Putting the glass down, she looked at Jack, smiled, and nodded. He knew just how she liked her drinks.

Matthew Blake was carrying a sheet of paper with the name and address of Bart Menard. He also had Bart's phone number, but Matthew believed in the element of surprise. Looking over Bart's class schedule and place of employment, he concluded that Bart would either be home or out on a Friday night date. Folding the sheet of paper and placing it in his pocket, Matthew stepped out of his Camaro and made his way over to an apartment complex on Birch Street.

According to the research team, Bart resided in apartment 14. Looking around the complex, Matthew noticed it was nicer than what he expected to find a few blocks away from campus. Matthew searched out front and saw a dark blue 2010 Tahoe parked near apartment 14. He walked over and checked the plates to confirm it was the vehicle registered in Bart's name. Matthew got lucky. Bart must be home.

Matthew followed a footpath that led up to the building and then walked along until he reached 14. Taking one more look around, he stepped forward and knocked on the door. It didn't take long before the door was opened and a young man appeared. Matthew asked, "Are you Bart Menard?"

The man responded, "Depends on who's asking?"

Matthew couldn't help but smile as he reached into his pocket and produced his FBI badge. "FBI Agent Matthew Blake."

Bart looked down at the badge and then back up at Matthew's face.

"Hey, you're that guy on TV."

"Yep. May I come in and ask some questions?"

Bart shrugged his shoulders and responded, "I guess so. I have a date later on, though. Will this take long?"

Matthew said, "I'll try my best not to keep you long."

Bart opened the door wider and allowed Matthew to follow him in the apartment. Matthew looked around and found a messy apartment with a slight odor. A couple of pizza boxes were lying on a table, and the place smelled like dirty socks. Bart commented, "Um, the place is a little messy at the moment."

Matthew said, "Bart, I went to college as well. If the place didn't look like this, I'd be concerned."

For the first time, Bart cracked a smile. "We can sit over here on the couch." Matthew waited as Bart picked up items off the couch so they could sit down.

Matthew started easy. "So, what are you studying?"

"Finance."

Matthew smiled and said, "How much longer?"

Bart proudly said, "I finish in December, a semester early."

"Congratulations, Bart. So you said you're going out on a date. Is she majoring in finance as well?"

"No, she's studying to be a nurse."

Matthew immediately thought of Jamie and Becky. "When does she graduate?"

"Not until next May."

"I see. So does she have a name?"

Bart hesitated and then said, "Jamie Conrad."

This was news to Matthew. In their preliminary search, Bart dated all the girls but didn't say he was currently dating Jamie. Matthew asked, "How long have you dated Jamie?"

Bart thought for a moment and then said, "Well, I've known her since my freshman year. We've dated before, but nothing too serious. We decided yesterday to go out tonight."

"So you two are just friends, not steady dating?"

Bart laughed. "Let's just say Jamie and I have the same philosophy. We both like to have fun without worrying about the other wanting some commitment later."

"I met Jamie earlier this week," Matthew said.

Bart lost his smile. "Why are you here exactly?"

Matthew said, "When was the last time you saw Melody Montgomery?"

Bart's demeanor began to change some. He was getting nervous. Finally he answered, "I saw her on campus Tuesday night. A bunch of us were hanging out at the bar Smokin Hot."

"Was Andrew Mitt with her?"

Bart's nerves began to settle down some, and he answered, "Yeah, she was with him."

"How well did you know Andrew?"

"We played on a flag football league once, but we really never hung out just us two. It was always with a bigger group."

Matthew asked, "Were you and Jamie planning on going to the memorial service tonight?"

Bart's faced turned a little red with shame, and he looked down for a moment and then back up at Matthew. "No, both Jamie and I attended Robby's. We decided enough was enough." Bart shook his head. "I know that sounds terrible, but it's just too damn depressing. We both decided we needed to do something fun. It's just...we're both tired of all this drama and death."

Matthew said, "Don't apologize. No one expected this to happen when they entered college. Classmates getting murdered is not the norm."

Bart looked at Matthew with a serious face. "Are you going to stop it before it happens again?"

It was now Matthew's turn to feel a little ashamed. So far they were no closer to solving this mystery than when the second victim was found.

"I hope so, Bart."

Bart said, "I'm still a little confused why you're here to see me."

Matthew just stated the facts. "Your name was flagged because you've dated Jamie, Becky, Candice, and Melody, all the girls who have also dated the deceased."

Bart got nervous again. "Yeah, but who hasn't. I don't know who the Night Killer is or anything about why he's doing it."

Matthew asked, "Why do you think it's a he?"

Bart paused to think about the question and then answered, "I just can't picture a girl overpowering Robby, Jaycee, or Andrew."

Matthew said, "Fair assumption. Look, Bart, I don't want to alarm you, but I want you to be careful. No connections have been made as to why the victims were chosen—"

"What are you saying?" Bart interrupted. "Did you come here to warn me that I could be next?"

Matthew tried his best to read Bart's body language. The kid looked genuinely concerned and frightened. Finally Matthew said, "We're trying to find Melody. We feel her life's in danger."

Bart got up from the sofa and pulled a Coors Light out of the refrigerator. Matthew remained silent as Bart twisted the cap and then took a long sip. Bart turned around to face Matthew. "I would offer you one, but I know you would decline since you're on the job."

Matthew smiled. "Thanks anyway."

Bart took another swig and then said, "What do I need to do? Stay home tonight with Jamie? No, wait! That wouldn't do any good. Robby and Andrew were both murdered in their bedroom."

Matthew got up and laid his card down by Bart's Coors Light. "Call me if you hear from Melody or if anything or anyone looks suspicious or out of place."

Bart picked up the card and said, "Yeah, I will. And find this person soon. Graduating and getting the hell out of here can't come fast enough."

Matthew nodded and headed for the door.

Chapter 38

Lindy pulled into her garage at nine-thirty. Tonight had gone on a little longer than anticipated, and Parker was scratching at the back door insistently when she entered the house. Lindy made a beeline to let him in. As soon as she opened the back door, the dog flew by her. Lindy glanced around outside and then closed and locked the door.

Once she had reactivated the alarm system, she bent down and petted Parker. "I'm sorry, baby, that I was out so late. Forgive me."

Parker bounced up and down and then ran and jumped on the couch and then hopped back down again. Lindy rolled her eyes. Parker needed a walk, but it was too late to go out again. "Sorry, Parker. But I promise we'll go for a long run in the morning. Let's get to bed."

Lindy walked straight to her bedroom and hit the light switch. All was the same as she left it. Lindy peeled off her clothing and put on a T-shirt and matching shorts before going into the bathroom to brush her teeth. By the time she was done, Parker was already on the bed and snuggled up against a pillow.

Lindy smiled. "I'm with you, buddy; I had a long day too."

She pulled the comforter down and let out a scream when a large spider that resembled a tarantula scurried across the bed. Picking up a high heel shoe from the floor, Lindy shooed it off the bed and then crushed it on her nice, clean ivory carpet. "What the bloody hell!"

Parker remained on the bed but looked down at the carpet and growled. Lindy grabbed some toilet tissue from the bathroom and picked up what was left and then disposed of it in the toilet with a flush. Looking at the carpet, she became angry. "Shit, shit, shit!"

She left her bedroom and headed to the laundry room, which was off the kitchen. Opening a cabinet, she found the carpet cleaner and a brush and then headed back to her bedroom with the two items. After about ten minutes, all evidence of the big, creepy spider was gone. Lindy placed the cleaning supplies on her dresser and then took the comforter off the bed. Parker wasn't happy, because he had to move from his spot.

"Sorry, buddy, but we need to check it out or I'll never get to sleep."

Lindy checked under the bed and all around the room including under the dresser and chest of drawers. Finally satisfied that there were no more, Lindy picked up the comforter and jumped in bed, with Parker following behind her. Exhausted, Lindy hit the light switch beside her bed and immediately fell asleep.

Matthew was out visiting his horses at ten o'clock. It was late and he was tired. The team had met again as planned, but no one had made any new or interesting discoveries. All four guys were checked out and interviewed but no one stood out as a possible suspect. To be on the safe side, the team decided all were to be placed under surveillance. Matthew thought about Bart. The kid genuinely looked worried when he suggested he be careful. *Am I misreading him?*

Rubbing down Ethel and Fred, Matthew tried to push the case out of his mind if just for the night, he needed a break. He thought, *Maybe I'll have a clearer head tomorrow.* He continued to talk gently to his horses and promised an early walk in the morning.

"I know you've missed me, and I promised I would spend more time with you, but unfortunately we got another case. A big case at that, with no new leads."

Matthew finished up in the stable and then turned off the light. Using a flashlight, he made his way back to the ranch house. Once inside, he locked up and set his alarm system. Before heading to bed, he checked his messages to make sure he hadn't missed anything and then plugged his phone into the charger. Finally Matthew climbed into bed. Settling in with his pillow, he closed his eyes. His thoughts immediately went to Lindy Ashley.

He envisioned her at home on the couch with Parker watching old movies. Somehow he pictured Lindy liking classic movies starring Hepburn and Gable. Matthew opened his eyes back up and tried to push all thoughts of Lindy away, but it didn't work. He kept picturing her with her white silk blouse, and her removing it to reveal her white satin tank underneath. "Damn, I've got to get the doctor out of my mind!"

Matthew urged his brain to stop, but somehow this brought him around to thoughts of Cynthia. God, he missed her and wished she was still alive. Before he could stop himself, his thoughts turned to Craz Numez, her killer.

Frustrated, Matthew slung the covers off his body, jumped out of bed, and headed to his office to get on the computer.

Chapter 39

Jamie and Bart tumbled into his bed at one-thirty in the morning after a night of heavy drinking. Bart had checked the apartment thoroughly and had slid a chair in front of the door as a precaution. The only other way in was a window, and he had taken care of that earlier with a chest of drawers. Jamie had said, "Bart, seriously?" when he pushed the heavy chair in front of the front door after locking the dead bolt and hooking the chain.

Bart had tried to make light of the situation by saying, "I want you all to myself; I saw how those other guys were gawking at you tonight."

Jamie laughed and said, "Come here and kiss me!"

Bart did as he was told and began smothering Jamie with kisses.

Lindy woke up at seven-thirty to Parker licking her face. Turning her head, she said, "Okay, enough! I'm getting up now."

Lindy stepped out of bed and made her way to the living room behind Parker. Punching some numbers in a keypad, she waited for the alarm light to turn green and then opened up the french doors for Parker to run out. Lindy closed the door and locked it and then walked back to her bedroom. Fifteen minutes later, she walked out into the backyard and hooked Parker on his leash for their Saturday morning run. Opening the wrought iron gate, Lindy hit the walkway running with Parker leading the way.

Twenty minutes into the run, Lindy thought she was going to die. The aches in her joints and her left side were screaming for her to stop, but she pushed the pain away and trekked on. She was not going to let the pain win. She was a fighter. She would push herself another two miles and then reward herself with a nice hot bath when she returned.

Lindy began to daydream and allowed her mind to wander to something happy. She pictured a beach with white sand and crystal clear water. With each step she could see herself lying on the sand with small waves rolling over her feet. Soon her mind wandered to Matthew Blake. She pictured him lying beside her wearing swim trunks and holding out a frozen beverage for her to take. He was smiling at her, and they were enjoying the day together alone on an island somewhere in the Pacific. Daydreaming was helping, and the image was frozen in her mind as she continued on.

Finally, after four miles, Lindy could see her back porch, and she began to slow to a walk for her cool down. Taking a few more steps, Lindy could make out a person sitting on the wrought iron chair on her back patio. She looked around but didn't see any of her neighbors out or anyone else walking along the trail. Lindy continued on. When she was about ten yards away from her gate, she could finally make out her uninvited visitor.

Sitting back in a relaxed stance, Matthew Blake saw Lindy approaching with Parker behind her on his leash, and he stood up to greet her. "Hi, Lindy. I hope you don't mind me waiting out here."

Lindy took a deep breath and then answered, "No. How long have you been waiting?"

"About twenty minutes. I remembered you ran in the mornings, so I just decided to wait here. I hope I didn't startle you."

"No, not too bad anyway."

Matthew grinned and then bent down to unhook Parker's leash. Immediately Parker ran to his water bowl and left them alone. Matthew looked over Lindy's appearance. Her face was red, and her jet-black hair was pulled back into a ponytail under a Dallas Cowboys visor. Her toned body was sporting pink nylon shorts with a white sports bra with a sequin

Nike logo. Realizing he was staring, he finally looked away toward the french doors and said, "You probably want to go in and get some water."

Lindy smiled. "Yes, and a hot bath!"

Lindy passed by Matthew and unlocked the back door. Without waiting on Matthew, she walked straight to the refrigerator and pulled out two bottles of water. Taking a swig first, Lindy then walked back around her kitchen island to where Matthew was standing and offered him a drink.

"Thanks, Lindy." Matthew watched as she continued drinking and catching her breath. He finally said, "I guess you're wondering why I'm here so early on a Saturday morning."

Lindy put the water down on the counter and said, "Well, I have several ideas, but I'm too tired to guess right now."

Matthew walked around the counter and pulled the Cowboy visor off her head. With his other hand, he reached behind her head and gently pulled out her ponytail holder. As Lindy's hair fell down along her shoulders, Matthew softly touched her cheek with his fingers and then leaned down for a gentle kiss on her lips.

Matthew leaned back up and looked into her eyes. "I wanted to see you again, and I have a warrant for Melody Montgomery's records."

Lindy's body tensed at the sound of Melody's name. She asked, "Any news?"

Matthew shook his head. "No. I feel time is not on our side either."

Lindy picked up her water, took another long sip, and then said, "I'll shower and change, and then we can go to the office. Will you feed Parker and give him some more water?"

"Sure." Matthew pointed to the pantry and said, "Food in here?"

Lindy turned around and said over her shoulder, "Yep. Leave Parker out-side though. The TV remote is on the coffee table."

Matthew watched as Lindy took a few more steps and then disappeared down a hallway. Matthew saw Parker peering in through the glass door and said, "Just a minute, buddy."

Jamie rolled over in bed and found Bart sleeping on his stomach with his left arm hanging off the edge of the bed. Gently she moved closer and snuggled up to his naked body. Bart felt Jamie, and he slowly lifted his head and opened his eyes. "Good morning, princess!"

Jamie smiled and said, "Not good! My head hurts."

Bart laughed a little and pulled Jamie closer into a tight bear hug. It didn't last long though because Jamie kissed him on the cheek and then pulled away. Frowning, Bart said, "Where you going?"

Jamie moved off the bed and pulled Bart's T-shirt over her pale-skinned body. Turning back around, she said, "I have to pee, and I'm going to find some aspirin."

Bart sat up and said, "It's under the sink." He watched as Jamie made her way into the bathroom, and then he lay back down and closed his eyes.

Jamie decided a hot shower was needed to stop the pain radiating from her head. Turning the water on, Jamie looked for the aspirin bottle and then quickly opened it and took three pills. Pulling Bart's T-shirt back over her head, she stepped into the shower and stood under the hot water without moving for the next five minutes.

Chapter 40

Lindy arrived at her office dressed in jeans, flip-flops, and a white T-shirt—a first for her. And until today, she had never once set foot in the office on a Saturday since opening up her practice four years ago. Matthew escorted her in, turned on the lights, and cleared her office. Since discovering that the video cameras in the stairwell had been tampered with, he had decided to weigh on the side of caution.

Lindy had taken Matthew's offer for a ride and had read the warrant on the drive over. The warrant requested Melody Montgomery's files to be available to the FBI in relation to their missing person inquiry. Lindy went to her file cabinet and opened up the M drawer. With painted nails, she gently flipped through until she found Melody's folder. Pulling it out, she motioned for Matthew to sit on the couch. Lindy sat in her yellow chair and glanced through the file and then finally handed it over to Matthew. "It's all here."

Matthew took the folder and said, "Thanks."

Neither one spoke a word as Matthew began reading about Melody. Several moments passed and then Matthew closed the folder. "Three plastic surgeries and she wanted another one?"

Lindy nodded her head in acknowledgment and said, "I know, it's hard to grasp. Melody was already so beautiful."

"So, in order for her doctor to complete the fourth surgery, she had to visit you first?"

Lindy said, "Yes. Her doctor is my ex, George Williams. This isn't the first time I've seen one of his patients."

"Okay, I get that. No doctor wants to be sued for performing surgeries on someone who might be unstable." Matthew looked at the file again and then asked, "Were you going to clear her for the surgery?"

Lindy frowned. "It's not that easy. I really wanted to work with her, but the last session didn't go too well. I started digging into her childhood, and she got really defensive and uncomfortable. I was afraid if I pushed too hard she would just go to another doctor, one who didn't care about her state of mind."

Matthew asked, "And Dr. Williams does?"

Lindy smirked. "George is more concerned with covering all his bases so he doesn't get sued. But, he's one of the best, and if I ever chose to have work done, I would see him despite the fact that we're divorced."

Matthew glanced over Lindy's body and thought about what she said. Lindy followed his eyes, and her face turned pink. Finally Matthew broke the awkwardness. "You don't need anything done. You're perfect just the way you are."

Lindy smiled a little and said, "I feel the same way, but I can't guarantee I'll have the same feelings when I'm fifty."

Matthew smiled and figured he better not say anything else on that subject. After reading some more of Melody's file, he stopped and said, "She talked about Andrew Mitt a lot. Is there anything about their relationship that raised concerns?"

Lindy thought for a moment and then answered, "No, Melody never gave me the impression that Andrew was abusive physically or mentally. The real issues with Melody were with herself and trying to please family, friends, and Andrew."

Matthew continued reading and then placed the file down. "You said Dr. Williams had referred other patients. Were any of them Central University students?"

Lindy frowned and said, "I'm sorry, I can't divulge that information."

Matthew nodded his head and said, "Okay, do you have a card for Dr. Williams?"

Lindy went to her desk and came back with a card that was slightly bent. "All of those numbers were good a few months ago, but I can't guarantee it now."

Taking the card, he said, "Thanks. When was the last time you talked to him?"

"Yesterday morning. He was supposed to pick up Parker this morning and keep him for the entire weekend, but he cancelled and said he was going out of town."

"Did he tell you where he was going or when he's coming back?"

Lindy tilted her head and smiled. "No. And I really don't give a shit, so I didn't ask."

Matthew was pleased at her response and said, "Do you want to get a quick bite to eat before I go back to the office?"

Lindy nodded. "That sounds great."

Matthew handed Melody Montgomery's file back to Lindy and then watched as she tucked it away in the file cabinet.

Turning back around, Lindy said, "I'm worried about her. Even though our last session didn't go well, she gave me the impression she was coming back."

Matthew frowned and said, "Yeah, me too."

Jamie got out of the shower and wrapped up in a towel. Picking up a brush, she began to work the tangles out of her hair, and then she dried it with the hair dryer she'd found under the sink. A half hour passed before Jamie finally opened up the bathroom door. Dressed in an oversize T-shirt, she felt better now, and her headache was beginning to subside.

Jamie entered the bedroom and found Bart's bed empty. Turning, she followed the hallway that led to the kitchen and living room. Rounding the corner, she saw no one.

"Bart? Where are you?"

Jamie looked around and noticed that the furniture blocking the front door had been moved back to its usual position. Jamie walked to the kitchen counter and looked for a note. Not finding anything that would explain his disappearance, she decided to look for Bart's car. It wasn't in the parking lot.

Jamie finally realized that Bart had left. Not too concerned, she walked back to the bedroom and climbed in bed. The last thoughts as she dozed off were of Bart surprising her with breakfast.

Clay Barry was pacing back and forth in the parking lot of a sandwich shop. He thought, *Why is Lindy spending so much time with this guy? Does she like him? Surely not, he doesn't seem her type.*

Careful not to be noticed, Clay walked into the shop and found Lindy in the far corner. The guy had his back to Clay, but Lindy was in full view. Walking nonchalantly toward the counter, he ordered a milkshake. Next, he chose where to sit discreetly.

As Clay sat and sipped on his milkshake his mind began to wonder back to the first time he met the one known as the Night Killer. He was down and depressed that night sitting at a local campus bar, The Finish Line, when he struck up a conversation with the person sitting beside him at the bar. Several minutes had gone by as he spilled out his heart over his desire and need for Dr. Lindy Ashley. Somehow over the course of several shots of tequila a plan was designed to help Clay win the attention of one lovely doctor.

Clay placed down his drink and then rubbed his eyes and placed his hands on his forehead. Images of Robby Singleton flashed through his brain and the sound of his screams filled his mind. He still could not believe he had done such a thing. Closing his eyes he thought, *I've just got to stick to the plan. I only promised one kill, and in return, Lindy would come running for help and protection.*

Clay looked over at Lindy and frowned. "Why is she spending so much time with this FBI guy? This is not what's suppose to happen, damn it!" Clay looked around and noticed another couple staring at him. He suddenly realized he had spoken aloud and banged on the table with his fist. Quickly he picked up a menu and held it up to cover his red face.

Twenty-five minutes had gone by before Lindy stood up with the handsome man and headed for the exit. Quickly Clay got up and followed, leaving behind a small tip on his table. Keeping a few feet behind them, Clay got to his vehicle unnoticed. It appeared to him that Lindy was only paying attention to the FBI guy. Clay began to frown as he saw Lindy's face light up into a smile. She was laughing at something the guy said as she got into the passenger side of the nice, shiny black Camaro.

Matthew pulled out of the parking lot and headed toward Lindy's townhouse. It wasn't until after about ten minutes that Matthew said, "Don't turn around, but do you recognize the dark-colored SUV behind us?"

Lindy turned her head toward the window and then peered through the side mirror. Finally she said, "No, but I had the same type vehicle behind me yesterday. Either I was really paranoid or someone was following me."

Matthew glanced over at Lindy and said, "You never said anything. Why?"

"I don't know. I was tired when I left the office yesterday, and I didn't know if my mind was playing tricks on me."

Matthew looked forward again and then said, "Hang on!"

The Camaro swerved into another lane and took an exit off the freeway. Clay Barry's vehicle swerved but was forced to keep going due to the fast traffic behind him. Matthew said, "Sorry, but keep holding on. We're turning around and getting back on the freeway."

Lindy held on tight to the door handle as Matthew did a U-turn on two tires and skidded back toward the entrance ramp. For Lindy, time started to slow down as Matthew accelerated to over a hundred up the ramp and onto the freeway. Matthew dodged in and out of traffic for the next two miles but found no dark SUV. Lindy finally found her voice and said, "Matthew, please slow down."

Matthew glanced at Lindy and noticed her face had turned a shade green. Immediately he slowed down to regular speed and took the next exit. Finding the nearest parking lot, Matthew pulled in, and Lindy opened her car door and vomited. Matthew raked his hands over his head and mumbled. Opening the glove box, he found some napkins and then leaned over toward Lindy and said, "I'm so sorry. I didn't mean for that to happen."

Lindy took the napkins and wiped her face and blew her nose. Slowly, she leaned back in the seat and closed the door. Without speaking, Matthew continued to watch her as she laid her head back and closed her eyes. Another minute passed and Lindy opened up her eyes and said, "I'm better now. We can go."

Matthew placed his hand on hers as it was resting on her lap, and Lindy looked his way. She did her best to smile and then said, "I'm on some new medication, and it didn't agree with lunch."

Matthew replied, "Well, I'm sure my driving didn't help any. I shouldn't have done that with you in the car. That was stupid of me."

Lindy said, "Don't say anything more. I just wish we would've caught up or at least gotten a license plate number."

"Well, I got the color and make, and that's a start. Why don't you rest, and I'm going to step out and call it in. We might still get lucky."

Lindy settled back in the seat as Matthew stepped out of the vehicle and closed the door. The Camaro was still running, and Lindy leaned forward just long enough to turn the air on full blast. The cool air felt heavenly, and she closed her eyes once again and tried to breathe through the pain in her stomach and side. Feeling embarrassed, Lindy decided to pull down the visor and check her face. "My God!" she said aloud. "I look like a ghost."

Lindy leaned down to grab her purse but stopped instantly when the pain stabbed through her insides. Carefully she leaned back again. Matthew opened up the door and said, "Let's get you home. There's officers in the general area, and they're all on high alert for the SUV."

Keeping her eyes closed, Lindy nodded. Matthew put the car in reverse and headed toward the freeway once again. After several miles of driving in silence, Matthew was getting really concerned. Lindy looked pale, too pale, and she had started trembling. Matthew turned the air off and continued to observe her as she laid back with her eyes closed and her arms resting over her stomach. To him, this looked like more than just an upset stomach. Finally, after carefully contemplating his words, he asked, "Lindy, do I need to take you to a doctor instead of home?"

Lindy slowly opened her eyes and then turned her head to face Matthew. "No, home is good, but thanks."

Matthew wanted to protest, but he decided not to pry and, instead, concentrate on getting her home quickly and in one piece.

Chapter 41

Matthew pulled into Lindy's driveway and shut off the engine. Quickly he got out and went around to the passenger side. Opening the door, he held out his hand to her. She took it and then slowly stepped out of the car. Matthew bent down and grabbed her purse and handed it to her.

"Go ahead. The keys are in there somewhere."

Timidly, Matthew opened her purse and found her keys. Taking Lindy's elbow, he guided her to the front door and opened up the townhouse. Immediately they both realized something was terribly wrong. Matthew pulled out his gun and gently moved Lindy over to the corner of the foyer, away from all windows.

Lindy looked around and found her furniture shredded and her pillows sliced, their stuffing spilling out all over the room. At once Lindy thought of Parker. "Where's Parker? Oh no! I don't hear him! Parker!"

Matthew scanned the room and then looked over toward the kitchen. He saw no one. Carefully he stepped toward the french doors and looked outside through the glass. Parker was nowhere to be found, and the wrought iron gate leading to the walkway was closed. "I don't like this. I want you to go wait in the car till I have a chance to look over the entire house."

Lindy was about to protest but couldn't form the words or questions as Matthew quickly escorted her back outside and into the driver seat of his Camaro. "Lock the doors and stay inside. Here are the keys. If I don't make it out in five minutes, leave."

Lindy did as she was told and watched as Matthew took out his cell phone and made a call. She tried to read his lips through the glass but couldn't quite make out all the words. It didn't take a genius to know that he was calling for backup. Lindy had no choice but to wait and watch the time tick away on her watch.

Matthew entered the townhouse once again and started his search in the kitchen. Finding nothing disturbed in there, he checked the pantry and then opened up the garage door. Looking around Lindy's car, he found nothing else suspicious, so he closed the door. Next, he noticed the alarm pad, and a memory flashed through his mind of Lindy setting the code and the light turning red. Now with the light showing green, Matthew swore under his breath.

Slowly he made his way through the living room and then into the guest bedroom and bath. Both were clear and untouched as well. So far the only damage was the living room furniture. Matthew closed the guest bedroom door and then finally made his way to a closed door that led to the master bedroom.

Matthew had a horrible feeling in the pit of his stomach that he knew what he would find on the other side. Inhaling deeply, he pushed past the bad thoughts and slowly opened the bedroom door. Lindy's room was a disaster.

Pictures, vases, mirrors, and books had all been smashed and thrown around the room. The quilt on her king-size bed had been ripped as someone slashed a big X down the middle. Holding his gun out, Matthew carefully stepped around to the master bath and found more glass on the floor. Carefully opening the closet door, Matthew encountered clothing ripped and torn and dangling from scattered hangers. The mirror inside the closet was still intact and had a message clearly written for Lindy:

DIE SLUT

Matthew read the message and forgot all about Parker. He ran back outside to check on Lindy. Rounding the corner of the foyer, he could see her still sitting in the Camaro looking intently back at him. A sense of relief washed over him, but unfortunately it didn't last long.

Matthew held up two fingers, and Lindy nodded. He turned away with his gun still out and went through the living room to the french doors. Unlatching the bolt, he opened up the door. Instantly a rope swung down from the roof with Parker dangling on the end. Matthew caught himself on the doorframe and tried to remain in control as Parker's lifeless body continued to swing left to right. Hesitantly, Matthew reached out and stopped the rope just as he heard a piercing scream behind him.

Matthew quickly turned and found Lindy, screaming and shouting, "Parker! No! No!"

Matthew placed his gun in his waistband and ran toward Lindy. He picked her up and carried her out of the townhouse and then gently placed her on the front lawn. Lindy was crying and saying, "That wasn't real. That wasn't Parker, was it?"

Matthew knelt down on his knees and pulled her into his arms. "I'm sorry, Lindy. I'm so, so sorry."

Soon they heard sirens and then a patrol car sped down the street and came to halt as two officers jumped out and ran toward them. Matthew yelled out, "FBI Matthew Blake. Suspect appears to have left the property. Go ahead. I'm staying with her."

The older officer asked, "Does she need an ambulance?"

Matthew looked down into Lindy's eyes and thought about her episode from earlier. "Yeah, I think it would be a good idea." As the officer called in an ambulance, Lindy went limp in his arms.

Luke James sat inside his vehicle outside an apartment complex at Central University. He had arrived at eight o'clock this morning; it was now two-thirty in the afternoon, and Jennifer Bailey had not left her apartment all day. He knew she was there because he caught a glimpse of her when she let her friend Kathryn in the door around ten this morning.

What the hell are ya'll up to? He thought. Lunch had come and gone, and Luke missed it. He could hear his stomach rumbling now, and he was beyond impatient. Finally, he made the decision to go up and knock on the door.

Luke stepped out of his vehicle and checked the surroundings. Not much traffic was coming or going into the apartment complex. Looking around, he saw no one as he made his way toward unit 2, located on the ground floor. Luke first tried the doorknob and found it locked. With a huff, he knocked on the door with three hard taps.

A minute passed and Luke tried again, this time louder. No sound came back, so he paced back and forth. Suddenly, the door to unit 1 opened, and a tall blonde stuck her head out and looked around. Seeing Luke, she smiled and did a quick glance over his well-toned body. With a big smile, she said, "Hi. If you're looking for Jennifer, she's out back by the pool."

All the tension and confusion in Luke's face disappeared, and he said, "Thanks. That explains why she isn't answering. Sorry to have bothered you."

The blonde smiled again and said, "No problem. Bye now."

Luke said, "Bye," and watched as she closed the door to unit 1. Luke looked up into a bright blue sky without a single cloud. He thought, *Of course she would be out by the pool on a Saturday like this.*

Luke turned right and followed the building around to a pathway that opened up to a pool located in the center of the complex. Each apartment was designed with two doors, one in the front and one in the back overlooking the pool. Luke continued down the sidewalk and stopped when he spotted Jennifer and Kathryn lying on their stomachs in the blue lounge chairs with their tops untied from the back. Both girls were sporting a two piece, and the only piece they were wearing at the time was their bottoms.

Luke opened up the black wrought iron gate and walked toward the bathing beauties. They were not alone. Several college girls were out today sunbathing with very few guys in attendance. When Luke was about two steps away, he heard Kathryn say, "Are we still going to The Rock tonight?"

Jennifer replied, "Yeah, sounds good. I think I'm done here. I'm starting to get pink."

Jennifer reached behind her back and found the strings to her swimsuit. Luke crouched down and said, "Here, let me get that."

At the sound of his voice, Jennifer tensed and turned her head toward him, giving him a strange look. "What are you doing here, Luke?"

Luke continued tying her swimsuit and said, "There you go. I came to see you, of course."

Kathryn had already flipped over and grabbed another towel and was covering up her bare chest. She said, "Am I missing something? Because the last I heard, you guys called it quits, and this is private property."

Jennifer saw the change in Luke's facial expression and instantly began worrying. The last thing she needed was a replay of their meeting the other day. In a calm voice, Jennifer said, "Luke, Kathryn is right. Why are you here?"

Suddenly, Luke's eyes turned a soft brown, and he smiled his boyish grin. "I'm sorry. I didn't mean to frighten you by showing up. I, um, just sorta hoped we could talk again, privately. There's something I need to discuss with you."

Kathryn said, "I don't think—"

Jennifer interrupted and said, "It's okay, Kathryn. Why don't you go on back in, and I'll be right behind you in a couple of minutes?"

Kathryn gave Jennifer a disapproving look and then faced Luke. "I don't like you, and you better not hurt her."

Luke didn't say anything as Kathryn wrapped up in her towel and walked away. Luke took Kathryn's seat and looked around the pool. No one was giving them any attention. Luke turned back toward Jennifer and saw that she was sitting back in her chair with her arms crossed over her chest. She looked amazing in her purple bikini, and it was hard for Luke to concentrate. He closed his eyes and composed his thoughts. After a short moment, he opened them and looked straight at Jennifer. "I know I blew up the other day and really messed things up between us. If you give me a chance, I'd like to explain some things, and if you still decide you want nothing to do with me, I'll walk away and never come back."

Jennifer said, "I don't know, Luke. You really scared me the other day."

Luke nodded his head and said, "I know. Please just hear me out."

Jennifer looked into his pleading face and could see his pain. She thought, *It seems real, but something isn't right. Oh, why the hell did I fall for this guy? Now, here he is just showing up, unannounced and uninvited.* Her heart was telling her to stay and listen and her mind was telling her to run.

Jennifer looked around and noticed Bobby sitting a couple of chairs away. If she needed him, she would just scream. There was no doubt in her mind he would come to her rescue. Jennifer finally shook her head and looked up at the sky. "Okay, Luke, but you only have two minutes."

Luke looked down at his feet and said softly, "I didn't talk about my family because…because my dad's in jail for abusing me and my sister."

Jennifer looked at Luke's face and saw his shame. She was speechless and couldn't form the right words, so she just reached out and covered his hand with hers. Luke felt the tenderness in her touch and then continued, "I live with my grandma and sister. My mom died a few years ago. I know this is a lot to dump on you, but I just wanted you to understand that I have good days, but, every now and then, I have bad days."

Jennifer asked, "Do you see someone professionally?"

Luke didn't get defensive. "Yes. She said she's noticed progress."

Jennifer gave a half smile. "Luke, I'm glad you shared this with me, and I know it was hard. I can't promise you it will change things between us, but at least I understand you a little better now, and I thank you for caring enough about me to share."

Luke met her eyes and said, "I will leave now. You have my number. Call me if you are willing to try us again."

Jennifer didn't respond, so Luke stood up and then slowly bent down and gave Jennifer a soft kiss on her cheek. Luke felt her tense, so he quickly stood back up and left the same way he entered.

Chapter 42

Melody Montgomery woke again for the second time today. Slowly moving her head to the side, she could see that it was still daylight. She felt so tired and just wanted to go back to sleep. Something in her head kept telling her that if she did, she wouldn't wake up again. Licking her lips and taking a slow swallow, she thought about yelling out. Instead, Melody concentrated on moving her arms to see if she could break through the ropes that held her down.

With each movement of her arm, pain ripped away at her sliced and bandaged shoulder. Melody had just decided to give it one harder tug when she heard a noise at the foot of the bed. A voice said, "It's no use, Melody, but I'll set you free."

Melody looked at the strange man and asked, "Who are you?"

Clay Barry looked at Melody and thought how sad and helpless she looked. He never wanted to hurt her but things had changed and nothing was going as planned.

Oh why had he listened to the Night Killer? Lindy wasn't turning toward him for help. Instead Lindy had some FBI guy helping her. No matter how many appointments he made this past week, she never shared anything with him or asked for help.

He continued to watch Melody and soon realized she thought he was going to help her. But that all changed when he lifted the knife to cut the ropes and her body began to shiver and her lower lip trembled. In one quick motion, he sliced the rope that was holding her right arm down and said, "Hush now, don't move yet. I need to cut the other ropes."

Melody tried to speak, but her mouth was so dry and she didn't have any energy left. *Why am I so tired? I cannot even lift up my body to fight,* she thought.

Melody watched hopelessly, knowing her life was in his hands. As he cut the last rope, which held her left ankle, she stared at him. Her eyes followed him as he walked around the bed to her side. Slowly, he placed the knife down on the nightstand and then lowered his face to within inches of Melody's ear. "It's over now. I appreciate your patience, but the time has come."

Lindy woke up in a hospital bed in a private room. Quickly she scanned the entire room until her eyes met Matthew's. Suddenly, all memories of the day came flooding back, and her breath caught in her throat at the thought of Parker, so innocent and now gone. Lindy closed her eyes as a tear slid down her cheek. Matthew hurried over and wiped her tear with his hand. He spoke tenderly. "I'm sorry about Parker and sorry such evil has come to you."

Lindy opened her eyes to face Matthew and saw the pain and hurt on his face as he said, "I will get the bastard. You can count on that."

Lindy didn't respond but continued to look into his gentle and sincere eyes. She thought, *He has the most beautiful hazel eyes. He's so caring as well.* Finally she broke eye contact and leaned up on her elbows to sit up. Matthew grabbed the bed remote and said, "Here, this will help."

As soon as Lindy got situated, she spoke. "Why exactly am I here? I mean, I feel fine now."

Matthew said, "Sure about that?"

Lindy saw his expression and wondered immediately what the doctor had said to him. Tilting her head, she asked in a quiet voice, "What did the doctor tell you?"

"Nothing specific, but I know they called in a specialist."

Lindy smiled. "It's not bad. I have fibromyalgia, and it's manageable with medication."

Matthew gave a look of doubt, and Lindy continued. "I have a lot of friends here, and I'm sure they appeared overly concerned because they know me."

Just then a middle-aged man wearing a white coat entered the room holding a chart. He smiled at Lindy and said, "How's my star patient? Feeling better?"

Lindy smiled briefly and then said, "Yes, Marc, I feel better. It...it was just a really bad day."

Dr. Marc Grant looked at Matthew and frowned. "Yes, I know. Agent Blake told me all about it. I'm so sorry about Parker, Lindy."

"Thanks. It just seems so surreal. I mean, why? How could someone do this to such a loveable animal? I don't understand any of this and why I'm being targeted."

Her dear friend of ten years walked forward and then sat on the bed. "Me neither, Lindy. Look, I know you don't want to hear this, but I would like to keep you overnight. I think your body could use some rest, and the medication I gave you earlier will help with the nausea."

Matthew looked over at Lindy and said, "I told the doc about you getting sick earlier today."

Lindy looked at both men and said nothing. In a concerned voice, Marc asked, "Lindy, how long have you been feeling like this?"

"Well, for a while, but I've been handling it and managing the pain."

"I see. I think I have an idea of your managing. There's another medicine that we haven't tried."

"Yes, I know, but I'm not comfortable taking it. I will continue on with this one and give it a little longer to work with my body."

Dr. Marc Grant looked at Matthew and said, "Doctors are the worst patients."

Matthew smirked and started to respond but stopped short when Erin rushed through the door. "Lindy, oh my gosh! I can't believe this has happened. Are you hurt?"

Marc frowned at Lindy. He knew at that moment she had never confided in Erin about her illness. Lindy saw his scowl and said, "Gentlemen, if you two would excuse us, I need some alone time with my sister."

Marc squeezed Lindy's hand and said, "Of course. I will check on you in the morning. Don't hesitate to call if you need anything before then."

Lindy squeezed his hand back and said, "Thanks, Marc."

Erin waited until the doctor had gone and then she took his place at Lindy's side. Lindy leaned over to Matthew and said, "Would you stay close by? I would like to talk to you again later."

Matthew smiled and said, "I'll be right outside making some calls. Hi, Erin."

"Hi, Matthew."

Matthew looked back at both sisters and then left the room so Lindy could spill the beans on her health. Once outside the room, Matthew closed the door and spoke to the officer on guard. "I'm going to step outside and make some calls. Do you need a break before I leave?"

"No, sir, I'm good. I will not leave this spot till you get back."

"Thanks." Matthew walked down the hallway and found a quiet corridor to call his partner. Steve Toowey answered, "Hey, Matthew, you just caught me."

"What do you mean?"

"I'm about to catch the three o'clock flight to Houston. Remember, I have the girls' dance recital tonight?"

Matthew said, "Damn, sorry! I forgot."

"Hey, I'm the one sorry, but I gotta go. This job will kill your soul if you allow it."

"No, you're right, Steve. There will always be an active case. Go and try to have a normal night with your family."

"Thanks, but before I hang up, Don should have the warrant for the rest of Lindy's files by now. Good luck with that, and I'm on the first flight out at six o'clock in the morning."

"Got it. Have a safe flight."

"Yeah, thanks, man."

Matthew ended the call and pressed another button for Janet. "Hi, Janet. Forward me to the phone in A150."

"Sure, just a moment, Matthew."

"Thanks."

Matthew didn't have to wait long before he was transferred and placed on the speakerphone. "So what's the latest?"

Don responded, "It's not good, Matthew."

Matthew frowned and said, "Go on."

"We found hidden cameras all over Lindy's home. It appears someone has been watching her for some time now."

"Aww man! What else?"

"The dog was killed sometime this morning, and whoever let themselves in left no prints or sign of forced entry."

Matthew asked, "Was the lock picked?"

Don answered, "I think the person had a key and then went straight over to the security system and punched in the correct code. The cameras were top end and could easily be zoomed in to watch Lindy type in a few button each day."

"Unbelievable!" Matthew paused and then asked, "Anything else?"

"Yeah, got the warrant and ready to roll whenever you give the green light to visit Dr. Ashley."

"The doctor wants to keep her overnight. The soonest we can get the files would be tomorrow after she is released. Unless…"

Don asked, "Unless what?"

"Unless Dr. Ashley gives us permission to take Erin. Remember, she's the sister and secretary."

"Yeah, well, the sooner we get the files, the better. I really think this's connected somehow to the Night Killer."

Matthew ran a hand through his hair and said, "I know. I think you're right. Look, anything else on the four guys that dated all the girls?"

Don answered, "Nothing suspicious enough to move on. Still keeping them all under some surveillance just to be cautious."

"Good. I'll talk to the sister—she's here—and let you know when we can move."

Pamela piped in and said, "Matthew, a cleaning lady remembers seeing Professor Dobbs at his office on the night in question, so I think it's safe to move past him."

"Did she sign a statement?"

"Yep, all done, boss."

"Good. All right, with Steve gone for the night, Pamela, I want you for backup."

"Sure, already cleared my weekend."

"Thanks, Pamela. Keep me posted, guys, and I'll let you know when we can move on the office."

Matthew hung up the phone and cussed silently. *How the hell am I gonna break the news to Lindy that her every move has been watched. Filmed even, damn!*

Chapter 43

Melody Montgomery's body was carefully placed in the trunk. Clay Barry looked around once more just to make sure no one was watching. There wasn't anyone out here in the woods spying on him. The cabin was well hidden from any road, and not another house was within five miles. Satisfied the deed was done right, he slammed the trunk closed and smiled.

Clay carefully drove his dark SUV back onto the freeway and kept a close watch on the speedometer. Getting a speeding ticket would surely ruin this perfectly well laid plan, and he had no intention of that happening. Another five miles passed, and he correctly signaled and changed lanes and took the exit toward the campus of Central University. Clay didn't have to drive around randomly in search of the right location; he already had the spot marked out for Melody's body a day ago.

Going through two more intersections, he turned right onto Jefferson Drive. There wasn't a whole lot of traffic on a Saturday afternoon. Most students were chilling out in plans of another big Saturday night on campus. It also helped that the football team had an away game today in Mississippi that was in the third quarter and live on ESPN. So far the team was undefeated, and most students would be sitting in front of their TV right now about half-drunk, not out driving around.

Finally, Clay rolled the SUV to a complete stop, turned off the ignition, and got out of the vehicle. Casually he looked around and saw no one lurking nearby. There wouldn't be, especially behind a building that held no Saturday classes and was generally locked up for the weekend. To be on the safe side, he had backed the SUV into the wooded patch directly opposite the back of the building. Quickly he opened the trunk and threw Melody Montgomery's body into the small bushes and brush directly behind the SUV. Melody's head lay in a crooked position as it lodged against a small tree branch. Somehow her body still looked exquisite even in death.

Originally Clay was going to use the same knife as the one used on the others but just hadn't been able to bring himself to mutilate such a perfect body, so he had killed her with an overdose. Lying there naked, she still gave the appearance of sleeping, but he knew differently. After getting a last look at Melody, he turned away and closed the trunk. Looking around once more, he made his way back to the driver seat unnoticed and started the engine.

Matthew was making small talk with the officer on duty when Erin opened up Lindy's door and poked her head out. "Matthew, Lindy would like to see you now."

"Thanks. I would like for you to join us, if that's okay."

Erin smiled. "I wasn't planning on leaving."

Matthew smiled back and then turned to the officer. "Thanks. Let me know if you need me."

Officer Murphy said, "Sure will, Agent Blake."

Matthew followed Erin inside and saw Lindy reclined back once again with her eyes closed. Hearing them approach, she opened her blue eyes and slightly smiled. Matthew instantly went to her side and brushed her hair back and then kissed her on the forehead. "You look so tired."

Lindy half smiled. "It's the medicine. Doc wants me to sleep."

Matthew had a worried look on his face, and Lindy suddenly realized it was more than just her health on his mind. "What is it? Go ahead, I can take it."

Matthew looked down at Lindy's angelic face and then closed his eyes and took a deep breath. He glanced over at Erin, who was standing in the corner trying to give them some privacy. "Erin, come join us. You're gonna want to hear this as well."

Lindy's eyes narrowed, and once again she became protective of her sister. "How does this involve her?"

Matthew sat beside Lindy on the edge of the bed and held her hand. Erin walked around the bed and moved the chair closer to Matthew and Lindy and then sat down. "There's no easy way to say this. When the officers searched your home, they found video cameras set up." Squeezing her hand, he continued, "They're all over the townhouse, including the bedrooms and baths."

Lindy's complexion turned white, and Erin jumped up and ran to the bathroom and closed the door.

"I'm sorry. I didn't want to tell you, but you had a right to know."

Tears began to flow down Lindy's face as she asked, "For how long? Why, Matthew, why is someone doing this to me?"

Matthew released her hand and gently touched her face, wiping away her tears. Slowly he leaned down and pulled her into his arms and hugged her tightly against him. As Lindy cried, Matthew whispered in her ear and tried his best to console her.

Several minutes had passed as Matthew held on to Lindy not wanting to let her go. Over the last week, he had slowly started to fall in love with her, and now he could feel his heart tearing apart as she lay helpless in his arms, broken and full of pain and sorrow. When her sobs subsided, Matthew lowered Lindy back down and then leaned over and grabbed the tissue box and handed it to her. "I'm gonna check on Erin."

Lindy nodded, and Matthew stood up and knocked on the bathroom door. "Erin, come out and talk to us, please."

A moment passed and then the door opened to reveal a teary-eyed Erin. Matthew stepped forward and embraced her. "I know," he said. "I'm so sorry that ya'll are going through this. But believe me, I will get this sick bastard."

Erin released him and looked straight into his eyes and said, "You damn well better, because if I have a chance, I'll kill him."

Matthew didn't respond. It wouldn't do any good anyway. Gently he took her elbow and guided her back over to Lindy. He watched as the sisters embraced and then decided to give them a few moments of privacy. "I'm going to step outside. I'll be back soon."

No acknowledgement was made by either of them as he turned and headed out the door.

Clay Barry stopped the SUV outside his small, white two-bedroom home. Using the key, he opened the front door and then quickly made his way to the master bath, where he stripped down and took a shower. The warm water felt great as he washed away the dirt and grime from the day. As he washed, flashes of Melody entered his mind. She was so perfect in every way. He didn't enjoy the kill but knew it was necessary for his plan. She never knew death was taking over as she was slowly pulled back under for another deep sleep. This one, though, she would not awake from.

Getting out of the shower, he opened the bag he brought with him and pulled out Melody's underwear. He knew he should have left the articles with the body, but couldn't resist the urge. Walking over to the closet with only a towel wrapped around his waist, he knelt down and placed her underwear inside a pair of boots. Then he quickly got dressed and took his soiled clothing into the laundry room. There inside the washing machine was a load of clothes ready to be washed. He lifted a few items off the top and then threw his clothes in and covered them up.

Looking at his watch, he knew he needed to get back to the warehouse before someone noticed the SUV was missing. Picking up the bag, he left out the front door, locked the dead bolt behind him, and rolled away in the SUV unnoticed by any of his neighbors.

Chapter 44

Matthew and Erin drove away from the hospital in his shiny Camaro. He didn't want to leave Lindy but knew the sooner they got their hands on her files, the closer they would be to solving the puzzle. Erin had requested to drive, and Matthew had surprisingly agreed. Now sitting in the passenger seat, he was beginning to second-guess his decision. No female had ever driven his car, and he now couldn't believe he had agreed.

Matthew looked over at Erin and watched as she pushed down the clutch and shifted into fifth with such ease. The speedometer was climbing and fast. He wasn't too worried since they were on the interstate and Erin looked at ease behind the wheel. Several miles passed by, and Erin never said a word. Finally Matthew said, "When we get there, my team will be waiting with the warrant."

Remaining silent, Erin glanced over at Matthew. She then sped up but not for long. Their exit was just up ahead. She gracefully downshifted and took the sharp exit onto Kennedy Street, which led to Lindy's office. Another five minutes passed without mishap, and Erin pulled into the parking garage and was instantly greeted by a Matthew's team. Finding her usual parking spot, she parked his car and then turned off the ignition and handed him the keys.
"Thanks for letting me drive. I sure needed to blow off some steam."

"No problem. You ready?"

"More than ready. I want this bastard, and I want him to pay dearly."

Matthew nodded and opened the passenger door. As they got out of the car, Don and Pamela walked over with the warrant in hand. Matthew saw the quizzical look Pamela gave Don but ignored it. They were not accustomed to someone else driving his car. *Hell, I'm not either*, he thought.

Matthew introduced Erin to Don and Pamela. Quickly hands were shaken, and then the warrant was presented. Erin glanced over it and said, "Follow me."

Don waved bye to Davey, the security officer, and then said to Matthew, "Nothing new or suspicious here."

Not much was said on the way up to the fourth floor. Matthew took the keys to Lindy's office from Erin and said, "Wait out here with Pamela. Don and I are going to check it out first."

Erin did as she was told and then took a good look at Pamela for the first time. Pamela was cute—tall with golden brown hair. To Erin, she appeared to be in her thirties. Erin asked, "How long have you worked with Matthew?"

Pamela smiled and said, "About a year. I only moved up here last summer from Miami."

Erin thought back to one of her modeling shoots on South Beach when she was younger. "I love Miami."

Pamela said, "Yeah, well, unfortunately I saw too much of the dark side. I really miss the beaches and coastal canals though. They sure are pretty."

All chatter stopped when Don appeared at the door and said, "Clear, come on in."

Erin passed Don and walked straight back to Lindy's office where Matthew was waiting on her. Erin said, "The file cabinet holds all charts on every patient."

Matthew nodded. "First, I want you to pull male patients age fourteen to seventy who are current patients for the last six months. Next, I want you to make another stack of past male patients, same age. Last, female patients that are from age eighteen to fifty."

Erin nodded. "Okay."

As Erin pulled the files on current male patients, the team quickly read and made notes with names and addresses. An entire hour had gone by when Erin was finally finished with her three stacks. She closed the file drawer and turned to face the agents. "I'm going to make some coffee. Does anyone need any?"

All immediately said, "Yes," and Erin left them to work.

Erin put the coffee on and then went down the hall to her desk and took a seat. Erin reached into her purse that was resting on the desk and pulled out her cell phone. There were two missed calls and one voice message. Hitting a few keys, her mailbox made a beep and then Charlie's voice was heard. Erin smiled as she listened to the message and then immediately called him back.

"Hi, Charlie."

"Hi, Erin."

"Thanks for fixing that leaky faucet."

"No problem. I'm gonna head over to the market down the street. I was thinking steaks and some vegetables to grill tonight. Got any idea what time you're coming back?"

Erin thought about the question and then responded, "It's almost six now. I'll be back by seven."

"Sounds good. I'll probably have it all on the grill by then, so let's plan around seven-thirty to eat."

Erin smiled. "Perfect."

"I'll see you soon then," replied Charlie.

"Thanks, Charlie."

"Sure thing. I'm looking forward to this evening."

"Yes, so am I." Erin hung up the phone and placed it back into her purse before heading to the kitchen to grab the coffee. As she prepared the coffee Erin couldn't believe how great Charlie was toward her. *Fixed my faucet too! Boy, I sure hope I don't screw this up.*

Matthew saw her arrive with the tray of coffee cups and got up to help her. "Thanks, Erin," he said and then took a cup. After having a sip, he continued, "I know that you only have limited contact with Lindy's patients, but is there anyone who sticks out to you as one that might be dangerous?"

Erin laughed for a second and then took the last coffee and sat down. Matthew decided to restate his question. "In the last two weeks, have you been frightened by anyone in the office enough to want to call security or maybe just second-guess your safety?"

Erin said, "Yes, two patients have made me feel really uncomfortable this week alone—Clay Barry and Rhett Dobby."

Matthew pulled the files and quickly scanned back over them. Don pointed to a few things, and Matthew nodded.

Erin watched as glances were exchanged and more notes taken, and thought, *No one is going to divulge anything to me due to confidentiality. Besides, I don't want to know. God, I don't know how Lindy does this shit!*

After another five minutes of this, Erin finally said, "How much longer am I needed?"

Matthew looked up from a file and saw Erin's tired expression. Realizing her discomfort, he asked, "Where do you want to go?"

"Home. Charlie is cooking me dinner, and I told him I would be there by seven. If you need me to stay I will, but I really want to distance myself from all of this. It…it's just too painful and uncomfortable."

Matthew remembered Lindy telling him about this new guy, Charlie, and he seemed to be really good for her—the complete opposite from Leroy. Matthew looked at his watch. "No problem. Give us twenty more minutes and we should have everything for now. Did the contact list finish printing?"

"I'm sure it has. I'll go get it."

When Erin left the room, Matthew looked over to Don and Pamela. "Let's try to make it fifteen. She's been through enough today." Both agents nodded but never looked up and made eye contact as they feverishly read and made notes.

Erin came back in with papers and gave them to Matthew. "I'm going to wash up the cups and turn off the coffee machine."

Matthew nodded and then continued working as she left the room once more. Ten more minutes passed and Erin returned. Matthew stood up and said, "I think we have enough for tonight. We can go now."

Erin looked around the room at all the folders. "Should we just leave everything as it is for tomorrow?"

Matthew looked at Lindy's office and the mess that they had created. "Yes, sorry about all of this."

"Don't be. Let's just get out of here."

Matthew picked up his notebook and the papers Erin gave him and walked over to the door; Don and Pamela did the same. Matthew looked around one more time and then turned off the light and shut the door. In another five minutes, everything was locked up tight, and Matthew said to his team, "I'll come straight over after I drop Erin off."

Don spoke, "I'll get Janet to order us some dinner, and we'll meet you in the conference room."

Everyone stepped out of the elevator and went their separate ways. Matthew walked over to his car, and this time Erin went straight to the passenger door. He smiled as he thought, *Thank you, God! She doesn't want to drive again.*

Luke rang the doorbell and waited for his good friend to open the door. Hearing some noise from inside and seeing Bart's Tahoe in the parking lot, Luke knew his buddy was at home. Soon the door opened and Bart appeared. "Hey, Luke, what's up, man? Good to see you. Come on in."

Luke entered and followed Bart down the hallway to a messy kitchen.

"Want a beer?"

Luke said, "Hell yes, I could use a case," and then Luke lifted up his bag and pulled out two six-packs of Coors Light.

Bart smiled and put them both in the refrigerator and then pulled out two Bud Lights that were already good and cold. Luke took the offered beer and then headed over to the couch. Bart followed and sat in a chair. "You got plans tonight?"

"Nope, just to get smashed," Luke said. "How 'bout you?"

Bart smiled and leaned close to Luke. "Jamie's in the back," he whispered.

Luke stood up. "Aww, man, I'm sorry. I should've called first."

Bart tugged at Luke's arm. "Sit down, she's wasted and sleeping anyway."

Luke asked, "Already?"

Bart laughed. "I came home, and she'd been laying out by the pool drinking margaritas with the girl who lives next door."

Luke grinned. "Did she move in?"

Bart shook his head. "No, she's just staying the weekend. She'll go back to her place tomorrow night. Jamie and I are just good friends who like to enjoy each other, that's all. Nothing serious."

Luke nodded his head. "Hey, do you want to go get a bite to eat first before we drink all this beer?"

Bart stood up. "Yeah, that sounds good. Let me just check on her first."

Luke watched as Bart left the room and went down a small hallway. Two minutes later he came back. "She didn't even move. Remind me to pick up a burger for her on the way back."

"No problem." Luke walked over and grabbed two more beers from the refrigerator for the road.

Bart grabbed his car keys from the side table, and Luke offered, "Dude, I'll drive."

Bart shrugged. "Okay," as he threw the keys back down and followed Luke out the front door.

Chapter 45

Clay Barry was standing in the stairwell holding a vase of roses when he saw the perfect opportunity to make his move. The officer guarding Lindy's door had gotten up to help a nurse with an older patient who had fallen while trying to get out of his wheelchair.

Quickly, Clay opened the stairwell door and eased it shut behind him. It only took seven steps to get to room 302, Lindy's room. Taking one last look at the officer, Clay opened the door and slipped inside. He took a few steps toward Lindy and immediately saw that she was sleeping. Carefully he placed the vase of flowers on the rolling cart and then resisted the urge to touch her as her chest rose and fell with each breath. Knowing his time was limited, he quietly turned around and left. Opening the door just a crack, he peeked outside and saw that the officer still had his back to him. Easing into the hallway, Clay made it to the stairwell and never looked back.

Officer Murphy heard something from behind him, and he quickly turned around only to find a door closing on the stairwell. Turning back toward the nurse, he said, "I'm sorry, hold on. I'll be right back."

The officer had been on guard for several hours and had not left his post until now. Somehow he had a sickening feeling that he had just missed something. Sprinting toward the stairwell, he opened the door and looked inside, but saw no one. Turning around, he ran to Lindy's room and quietly pushed the door open. There, sitting on the rolling cart in front of Lindy's bed, was a vase of yellow roses, twelve in total. Mumbling under his breath, Officer Murphy stepped closer to Lindy and could tell she was still sleeping. He gently placed a hand on her arm. "Dr. Ashley?"

Lindy opened her sleepy blue eyes and looked up at the officer. "I'm sorry to wake you. Um, I had to make sure you were okay."

The roses caught her eye. "Roses? Who sent them?"

Officer Murphy looked down at his feet for a moment and then looked back up to face Lindy. "I turned my back for one moment to help a patient, and the next thing I knew, I heard the door to the stairwell shut behind me."

"There's a card. See what it says."

The officer put some gloves on and gently pulled the card off the holder. The envelope was pink with Lindy's name correctly and neatly written on the outside. There was no florist address given on the back of the envelope. Officer Murphy opened the envelope and pulled out the simple white cardstock. The message was written in the same handwriting and simply said:

> *Lindy,*
> *I'm sorry if I scared you. I hope you get well soon.*
>
> *Your future husband*

Lindy watched Officer Murphy intently as he read the message aloud. Instantly she felt sick. The same man who had been in her home and killed Parker had been here just a few moments ago while she was sleeping, just a few feet away from her.

Officer Murphy pressed the nurse's call button. "Dr. Ashley, I'll call Agent Blake. Someone had to have seen something." He stepped away and pulled out his phone just as a nurse came in, and he spoke to her briefly in passing. The nurse nodded and then walked over to Lindy and checked her IV and bag. "Hi, Lindy, I'm Rebecca, and I'll be with you tonight. Let's change this bag out just to be on the safe side."

Lindy could only nod as the nurse took down the bag and disconnected it from the IV strapped to her wrist. Then Rebecca said, "First, I want to check your vitals, and then I'll go get another bag of this juice."

Lindy nodded again and did as she was told while the nurse completed her tasks. When the nurse was finished, she said, "Your blood pressure is good, and you don't have a fever." She smiled. "Those are good things." Then the nurse left the room, and Lindy was alone once again.

Jamie rolled over onto her back and looked at the clock on the night-stand. It was quarter after eight. With an aching head, she slowly raised herself up on her elbows and looked around the dark room. Once her eyes adjusted to the darkness, she concluded that she was alone. Getting out of bed, Jamie picked up a T-shirt and pulled it on over her head. Next she found her underwear and shorts and pulled them on. Without turn-ing on a light, Jamie stumbled into the bathroom and used the facilities. Standing up, she found the same aspirin bottle from earlier and took out three tablets and then washed them down with some water from the faucet.

Flipping the light on, she looked at herself in the mirror. "Ugh!"

Jamie found the brush and pulled it through her red hair until the tan-gled mess looked somewhat decent. Next, she found a tube of toothpaste and brushed her teeth with her finger. After she was done with this task, she instantly felt better. As Jamie left the bathroom, she heard the TV in the living room. She continued down the hall and called out, "Bart?"

No answer came back, and Jamie stopped in front of the TV. It was still on the sports channel that had carried the game earlier today. Jamie spot-ted a couple of empty beer bottles on the coffee table and then walked over to the kitchen and opened up the refrigerator. "Okay, Bart," she said aloud, "there's beer in the house, so where are you?"

Jamie walked around the small kitchen and didn't find any notes left behind. Slowly she made her way toward the front door but stopped when she saw Bart's keys sitting on the side table. She continued forward and opened the unlocked apartment door. There parked in his usual spot was Bart's Tahoe. Jamie scanned the parking lot and then closed the door and locked it. She thought to herself, *How weird! Last night he puts a chair in front of the locked door, and today he leaves me sleeping alone with the door wide open for anyone to come waltzing in.*

Turning around, Jamie went in search of her cell phone.
After five minutes of searching, Jamie finally found her phone on the bedroom floor. She picked it up and dialed Bart's number. On the third ring, he answered. "Hello?"

"Hi, handsome. You know this is the second time I've woken up to an empty bed today. Any normal gal would get insecure."

Bart laughed. "We both know you aren't normal or insecure!"

Jamie smiled. "So where are you?"

"Luke stopped by. You know Luke. He's in my fantasy football league."

Jamie searched her memory until finally Luke's good-looking face entered her mind. "Oh yeah, I remember Luke."

"We're at Joe's Bar and Grill shooting pool. Do you want to join us, or do you want me to bring back a burger?"

Jamie scanned the bedroom floor and thought about her clothing options. "Sure, I'll drive your Tahoe."

"Great, babe. I'll see you soon."

Jamie replied, "Bye now."

"Oh, Jamie, wait!"

"Yeah?"

"Do you have a friend you can call for Luke?"

Jamie thought for a moment. "Sure, I'll go next door and see what Elizabeth's doing. Can't promise you anything though. She had more to drink than me."

"Great, I'll see you when you get here." After Bart hung up the phone, he looked over at Luke and smiled. "She might have company."

Luke cheered. "Sweet! Your shot, cowboy."

Thirty minutes later, Jamie unlocked the Tahoe and climbed behind the wheel. Elizabeth opened the passenger door, jumped in, and said, "Shit! What's that smell?"

Jamie fired up the engine and then rolled all the windows down and turned around to find an empty backseat. On the floorboard she saw some muddy boots, and that was it. "I have no idea. He must've been sweaty from working out when he rode in here last. Knowing him, there's probably a couple of workout towels in the trunk."

Elizabeth made a face. "Gross!"

Jamie smiled. "We're only going three miles. We can make it."

The drive took about five minutes due to the traffic lights on campus. As Jamie parked the Tahoe and rolled the windows up, Elizabeth said, "If Luke is as cute as you claim, I'm riding back with him."

Jamie watched as Elizabeth got out of the vehicle in her miniskirt, tank, and cowboy boots. Elizabeth had long black hair and dark green eyes. She was a little shorter than Jamie, and her white tank showed off a very dark natural tan. Jamie reassured her. "You'll like him. He's a hunk!"

Both girls entered the bar, and instantly all eyes were on them. Spotting the guys, Jamie walked over in her white cutoff jean shorts and a green tank she borrowed from Elizabeth. Bart grinned. "You look fantastic!"

and then picked her up and gave her a kiss on the lips. Putting her down, he gently slapped her ass and addressed her friend. "Hi, Elizabeth. This here is Luke."

Luke smiled his boyish grin. "Hi, Elizabeth. Nice to meet you." Turning toward Jamie, he said, "Jamie, it's been awhile. How are you?"

Jamie walked over and gave Luke a peck on the cheek and then turned toward Bart. "I'm starving!"

Luke looked at Elizabeth and motioned toward their table, while Bart asked for two more glasses for their pitcher of beer. When Luke had his back turned, Elizabeth looked at Jamie with big eyes. Jamie winked and mouthed, "Told you," and followed Luke over and slid into the booth. Soon, Bart slid in beside Jamie, set the two glasses down, and kissed Jamie once again while Luke poured the girls a beer.

Burgers and fries came thirty minutes later, and then, after eating, the foursome decided to play a game of pool. After the third game, Bart looked at Jamie and winked. Jamie winked back and nodded.

Bart set his pool stick down and then grabbed Jamie by the waist and escorted her toward the door. Jamie turned her head and looked over her shoulder. "See you guys later!"

Luke smiled back at Bart and Jamie and then looked at Elizabeth. She was holding her pool stick and trying to concentrate on making her next shot. Making a terrible shot once more, she stood back up and looked at the exit. "Looks like it's just us now," she said.

Luke set his stick on the table and then took hers out of her hands and placed it beside his. Slowly he slid both hands around her waist and pulled her close. Elizabeth waited as Luke timidly lowered his head for a kiss. She smiled back and then wrapped her arms around his neck and pulled him closer.

A couple behind them asked, "Are ya'll done with the table?"

Elizabeth turned her head to face them and replied, "Yep, sure are." Then, Elizabeth grabbed Luke's hand and pulled him toward the exit. "My place?" she whispered.

Luke just nodded and followed Elizabeth out the door and then led her over to his vehicle. The two quickly climbed in and sped away into the dark night.

Chapter 46

Matthew finally arrived at the hospital at nine-thirty. Easing Lindy's door open, he found her wide awake. He climbed in bed with her and placed his arms around her, and Lindy snuggled up to his chest without a word spoken.

Several minutes passed and Matthew said, "I've got people asking the hospital staff questions and looking at the security tapes."

Lindy lifted her head off his chest and replied, "We need a lead and soon. He's delusional!"

Matthew raked a hand through her jet-black hair and looked into her soft blue eyes. "We'll find him."

Lindy asked, "Where's Erin?"

"I dropped her off at her house. I met Charlie."

"Oh."

"Yeah, you were right. He seems like a good guy. Can you believe he made some repairs on her house today and cooked her dinner?"

Lindy smiled. "Huh, and she met him at a bar?"

Matthew smiled back. "I never met Leroy, but Charlie has to be a major improvement."

"We'll see. How did it go at the office?"

"The team is working on it now. They're pulling vehicle registration information as well."

"Do you think we'll get that lucky?"

Matthew touched a strand of her hair and pushed it back behind her ear. "Maybe. I think whoever we're looking for is smart, but with his warped sense of reality, he'll make a mistake."

"I hope so. Did you see how he signed my card?"

Matthew nodded.

She continued, "How scary is that? He sees himself married to me."

Matthew was about to respond when he heard some chatter outside her room. He slowly got off the bed. "I'll be right back."

Lindy watched him walk toward the door and then smiled as she said, "I'm counting on that."

Matthew quickly turned back and kissed her on her lips. "Good, I'll hold you to it." Then he disappeared into the hallway.

Lindy could hear voices outside her door but couldn't make out what was being said. She didn't have to wait long to find out what was going on. Within less than a minute, her door opened back up, and in walked Matthew with George.

Lindy closed her eyes and laid her head back and thought, *Great, this is going to be fun.*

George moved passed Matthew and made his way over to Lindy's bedside. "Hi, Lindy."

Lindy opened her eyes and faced him. "Hello, George."

"A nurse called me earlier today when you were admitted. I guess I'm still listed as your next of kin."

Lindy asked, "I thought you were out of town."

George looked at Matthew and then back to Lindy. "I was, but I was summoned back because one of my patients went missing."

"Yeah, I know. Matthew, has there been any word?"

Matthew looked at both of them and just shook his head. Lindy didn't press for more. "Well, thank you, George, for coming. I'm going to be fine, and I'll be released tomorrow."

George took a step closer to Lindy. "Marc told me about Parker. I'm so sorry, Lindy. He was such a good dog."

Lindy fought back the tears and just nodded.

George continued, "Well, I was thinking, why don't you stay with me until all of this mess is over and they catch whoever's doing these horrible things. I can stay with you tonight and then bring you home tomorrow."

Lindy was a little taken aback by George's idea and had to close her mouth. Finally she was able to pull herself together. "I appreciate the gesture, George, but I have Matthew." Lindy looked over at Matthew standing by the door. George turned as well and looked over his way. Lindy continued, "Matthew will stay with me. I won't be alone."

George looked back at Lindy with sad eyes. "I see. Well, I'll leave you now." Walking toward the door, George turned back. "Lindy, don't ever hesitate to call if you ever need anything."

A million thoughts were going through Lindy's mind. She wondered, *What would Amber, the little uptight girlfriend, think about your generous gesture, George?* Lindy didn't say anything, and Matthew stepped to the side as George left the room and closed the door behind him. Matthew turned toward Lindy and smiled. Lindy felt herself blush when she asked, "Matthew, can I come home with you tomorrow?"

Matthew grinned. "Absolutely."

Luke pulled into the apartment complex with Elizabeth practically sitting on his lap. He parked his vehicle beside Bart's Tahoe and got out with Elizabeth right behind him. He looked at Bart's closed apartment door and smiled as Elizabeth pulled him toward her apartment, a few steps away. Producing a key from the pocket of her miniskirt, Elizabeth opened the door to apartment 15. Once they were inside, she quickly bolted the lock and set the door chain. Elizabeth gestured toward the living room, "Make yourself comfortable. I'll be right back."

Luke just nodded.

After Elizabeth disappeared down a short hallway, he took a few steps into the living room and began to look around. Elizabeth's apartment was set up just like Bart's next door, except her furniture was nicer and the place looked cleaner. Luke picked up a photo album from the coffee table and sat down to look through it. On the fourth page was Jennifer Bailey, sitting on a blanket with four other girls. They were all smiling, wearing Central University tees and holding up bottles of beer. It appeared they were out on the grassy lawn on the campus quad before a football game. She looked so happy in this photo. Luke looked for a date but couldn't find one.

Hearing the bathroom door open down the hall, Luke closed the album and stood up as Elizabeth entered the room wearing nothing but a grin. Luke tossed the photo album down and walked toward Elizabeth. Slowly he picked her up and carried her back to the bedroom, closing the door on all memories of Jennifer Bailey.

Chapter 47

When the nurse came in with Lindy's breakfast, Matthew stood up from the recliner and stretched. He watched as she placed the food on the rolling cart and took Lindy's vitals. Within two minutes, the nurse had finished up and was gone. Lindy appeared to have already been awake while Matthew was sleeping away. Matthew walked over and pushed the cart toward her. "Good morning. How long have you been up?"

"Not too long. You were sleeping so peacefully, I didn't want to wake you. Besides, today will be busy for you, and it was good to see you sleep some."

As Matthew inspected the food. "Yeah, I'm sure today will be wide open. Hey, do you want me to sneak a McDonald's biscuit in?"

Lindy smiled. "No, I'm good with this. Now come here and kiss me good morning."

Matthew placed the fork down and carefully walked around the cart. Kneeling in closer, he whispered, "Good morning, beautiful," and then kissed her softly on the lips.
Lindy's eyes appeared smoky blue as she gazed back at Matthew with a big grin on her face. Matthew raised back up and said, "How do you feel, rested?"

"Actually, I do."

"Good. I need to make some calls. You eat, and I'll check back in on you later. Okay?"

"I'll be right here."

Matthew touched her cheek and then squeezed her hand. Slowly he pulled away and walked out the door. Outside, Officer Murphy was once again on guard. The night patrolman had already left his shift. Matthew walked over and greeted him. "Good morning. I have a little business to take care of, but I'll be back soon."

The officer acknowledged, and Matthew walked on down the hall before pulling out his cell phone. Don answered on the second ring. "This is Don."

"Hi, it's Matthew. Got anything new this morning?"

"The team has made a list of six male patients that have a dark SUV registered to their name."

"Good. How about the videos from the hospital? Anything yet?"

"They should be getting back to me in the next hour. They think they found an SUV matching the description around the same time the flowers were delivered. But the image isn't good, and they're still working on the tag numbers."

"Well, I'll have a look at it when I come in and see if it looks like the one following us yesterday."

"I think we're getting close, Matthew. I can just feel it."

"Let's hope you're right. Anything at all on Melody?"

"No, nothing. But we sure have a lot of nutcases out there that enjoy calling in."

Matthew frowned. "Yeah, follow up on them anyway."

"Oh, we are. It just takes time and manpower."

Matthew asked, "Heard from Steve yet?"

"No, but he should be landing soon. I think the flights leave at six each morning. I used to do that commute to see my old girlfriend."

Matthew looked at his watch and saw that it was ten till seven. "Okay, I should be there in about an hour or less. Call me if anything comes up before then."

"Will do. Oh, Matthew?"

"Yeah, I'm still here."

"Did Dr. Ashley ever say anything negative about her ex, George? I mean, anything about him having a violent side?"

Matthew thought for a moment and then said, "No, nothing like that. Why do you ask?"

"I don't know. Pamela was the one who interviewed him last night, and she sure didn't like him. She just said she had a bad feeling about him, that's all."

"I'll keep that in mind. I think we have both learned never to underestimate Pamela's intuition. I'll ask Lindy about it."

"Okay, good. See you soon."

Matthew closed his phone and placed it on his hip and then headed back down the hall to Lindy's room. Officer Murphy stopped him. "The doctor has a visitor, her sister."

Matthew nodded and gently pushed the door open a little. "Lindy?"

Erin said, "Come on in, Matthew. How are you this morning?"

"I'm good. You're here early."

"Yes, Charlie and I are going to have breakfast together, and then he has to head out."

Lindy looked toward the door. "Where is he now?"

"He's downstairs waiting. I asked, but he said he didn't want to come up."

Lindy smiled. "Sounds like a true gentleman."

"Well, I just wanted to check on you this morning. I'll stop by later, okay, sis?"

"Thanks, but call first. Hopefully I'll be released."

"Oh that's great! Well okay, um, I'll see you soon, bye now." Erin leaned down and gave Lindy a quick hug and waved to Matthew as she left.

Once she was gone, Matthew moved closer. "If you're released today, where are you going to go if I have work, which I will?"

Lindy thought for a moment. "Well, I could go to Erin's house. Or better yet, George did make an offer."

Matthew laughed. "Someone has a sense of humor this morning."

Lindy smiled back and then her face turned more serious. "That part of my life is over. I didn't feel anything when he stopped by last night."

Matthew walked over and sat beside Lindy on the bed. "I'm glad to hear that, but I do have to ask you a question about him."

"Okay, what's the question?"

"Did George ever hit you or threaten you in any way during the course of your relationship?"

Lindy hesitated and then looked away.

"I'm sorry I have to ask. We just want to cover everything with this investigation."

Lindy finally looked back at Matthew and simply said, "No. George just couldn't keep his pants up around beautiful women. That's all."

Matthew could clearly see the hurt in her eyes. *That man was an idiot!* "I'm sorry. No more about George, okay?"

Lindy half smiled. "Go to work. I'll be fine here. Erin will pick me up when I'm released."

Matthew knew he couldn't make any promises. Don was right, they were getting close. "Call me later this afternoon if you don't hear from me first."

"I will," Lindy said.

Matthew gave Lindy a gentle kiss. "Get some more sleep. I'll see you later." Slowly Matthew pulled away never breaking eye contact.

"I'll try. Bye."

After Matthew was gone, Lindy rolled over to her side and tried to push the thoughts of George out of her mind. Matthew was right, she needed sleep. She had been up since four tossing and turning. Images of Parker, George, Erin, and Matthew kept popping up in her mind, followed by all her patients who possibly could have done this—Luke, Clay, Rhett, Jerry, Henry, and several others.

Lindy heard the door open and flipped back over to see who it was. When she saw that it was the nurse, she smiled. Earlier Lindy had requested something for sleep, and now her wish had been granted.

Luke woke up to unfamiliar surroundings. He rolled over to his left side and saw a naked female lying with her back toward him. Luke immediately thought of Jennifer but realized right away the hair length was all wrong. As Luke reached out to her, memories of the previous night came flooding back, and he smiled.

"Hey, gorgeous. Good morning."

Elizabeth rolled over onto her back and smiled up at Luke, who had eased up on top of her. "Hi yourself."

"Do you have eggs? I'll go make us breakfast."

Elizabeth grinned. "Yes, but breakfast is gonna have to wait a little bit longer."

Luke responded to her touch and allowed himself to enjoy the moment even though his heart and mind were still thinking of Jennifer.

On the opposite side of the wall, Bart was just slowly waking up. He reached out for Jamie but found only empty space. Bart turned over to look. She was gone. Leaning his head back on the pillow, he tried to remember last night. Through the fog, he finally remembered Jamie getting a phone call around two o'clock in the morning and then leaving. Bart closed his eyes and turned back over. His head hurt, and he just wanted to go back to sleep. Jamie could wait. He would call her later.

Chapter 48

A little after eight o'clock, Steve Toowey walked into room A150 with a bag of biscuits. Cheers went up as everyone made their way over to grab one and give Steve a high five. "Sorry about last night, guys. What did I miss?"

Before anyone could answer, Matthew walked in the room and shouted, "Got a match! Clay Barry, age forty-seven, six foot two, has a black Ford Explorer with the plate number ZUP 459L. The tape from the hospital only showed the first two letters, ZU, but that's all we need for our warrant."

Pamela screamed out, "Address is 98 Pine Drive, Arlington!"

"That's only two miles from campus," Don said.

Janet walked in and started passing out photos of Clay Barry as Matthew said, "Okay, team, be careful. Barry is around two hundred thirty-five pounds, and he's a carpenter by trade. Treat him as armed and dangerous. We leave in five. Any questions?"

Questions were fired away and quickly answered as Don brought up a satellite image of the house at 98 Pine Drive on a projector for all to see. Matthew walked over and pointed at a few places and gave commands to where they would set up and enter. Like clockwork, all agents were out the door in precisely five minutes.

Matthew was behind the wheel of his Camaro, and Steve was sitting next to him checking his weapons. Matthew looked over. "How did last night go?"

"Very well. The girls were amazing. I just hate the timing, that's all."

Matthew shifted gears as a light turned red. "Yeah, well, it will always be something. I'm glad you went."

"Karen looked great, and she had this look like, wow, he showed?" Steve laughed. "She was genuinely surprised."

Matthew laughed too. "I bet she was."

"She's dating a guy named Dylan. He's a dentist and younger by five years."

"Oh, well, no problem with that. Just make sure your new wife is younger by ten. That should help even that out."

Steve didn't laugh. Instead his mind thought of the image of Clay Barry. "I hope this goes well with no bloodshed."

Matthew glanced over at Steve sitting there in his khakis and green knit polo shirt holding his weapon in his lap. "It will. We're ready and prepared, and Clay has no idea we're coming, so that gives us the advantage."

Neither man said anything else the remaining few miles, as they both thought about the job ahead. Twenty-six minutes had passed since the team left FBI headquarters. Now they were pulling onto Pine Drive, and all agents stopped their vehicles in front of house number 90, five houses down from where Barry lived.

Matthew gave a few commands and then pulled back out onto the street with one other car behind him. They rolled passed house number 98, but no car was visible. Matthew parked in front of house number 99, and he and Steve stepped out of his Camaro. Don, Pamela, Gary, and Doug emerged from the vehicle behind them. They quietly checked their surroundings and then quickly made the remaining steps up the driveway and to the front door. Don, Pamela, and Gary then continued on around back to cover any other exits.

The white house was small, only twelve to thirteen hundred square feet. There was no garage to hide a vehicle, and it appeared the place was empty. Matthew knocked on the door and waited. After no answer, Matthew knocked again, this time yelling, "FBI, open up!"

When no sound came back, Matthew gave the nod, and Doug barged through the flimsy wooden door breaking the lock. Matthew yelled, "FBI, we have a warrant for Clay Barry!"

Still no answer came back as the team quickly scanned each of the house's rooms. Pamela emerged from the back and shouted, "All clear out back. No sign of anyone."

Matthew lowered his gun. "Okay, team, split up, and don't leave anything uncovered. Yell if you got something."

Three minutes later, Matthew's cell rang, and he stopped what he was doing and answered, "Matthew."

"It's Copeland. Central University PD just called in. They found a body that matches the description of Melody Montgomery."

Matthew closed his eyes. "Damn it!"

"Tell me you found him, Matthew."

Matthew felt his face flush with anger. "No one's home. He isn't here, and there's no Explorer in the driveway."

"Got something!" shouted Don from the back room.

Matthew glanced to his right and began walking toward him. He spoke in his phone, "Hold on, we found something."

Matthew stepped into what appeared to be Clay's bedroom and saw Don bent down near the closet holding a boot. With his other gloved hand, he reached in and pulled out a bra and a matching pair of underwear. Pamela leaned in and read the bra size. "It would fit Melody."

Matthew talked into his phone and asked Copeland, "Was the body naked?" Matthew closed his eyes and hung his head at Copeland's confirmation. Matthew balled his fist and struck the air instead of the wall that he so desperately wanted to punch. Finally he found his words. "Where's the body?"

"On campus behind the Gordon Building, on Trinity Lane. Leave the team there, and come with Toowey."

Matthew replied, "Yes, sir. I'll be there in five."

Matthew closed the phone and looked at his team. "They found a body on campus that resembles Melody Montgomery. Toowey and I will go. Ya'll stay here and keep looking. Pamela, go ahead and bag those and send them to the ME. I want a match and fast."

Pamela carefully placed the items in a bag. "Understood. I'm on it."

Matthew watched Pamela walk out and then looked back at his team again. "Set up a perimeter of the neighborhood. I want this guy."

Don nodded, and Matthew walked out of the small house followed by Steve. Both looked around, but there was no sign of Clay Barry or his Ford Explorer. Matthew quickly unlocked the Camaro, and they jumped in and peeled off toward campus, only a few miles away.

Steve threw his hands up. "This doesn't add up. The ME said the killer was around five ten, and Clay Barry is around six two according to his license."

"I know, but that bra wouldn't fit Dr. Ashley."

"What about her sister, Erin?"

Matthew looked at Steve. "Shit, I don't know. We'll know soon though if they're Melody's."

Matthew found the Gordon Building and pulled up along the nearest vacant curb. Already, the building and surrounding area had been roped off. Matthew emerged from his car flashing his badge and was quickly waved through by Arlington Police. Matthew and Steve both were handed gloves and footies, and they quickly put them on. Matthew spotted the ME and walked straight over to her. "Is it her?"

Dr. Candy Johnson led them over to the body and then her assistant Kimberly gently pulled the white sheet down. Candy frowned. "Yes. It appears she may have been drugged. She isn't cut up like the others. But, there's a knife wound on her shoulder that appears to be a few days old. That would explain her blood being found beside her boyfriend, Andrew Mitt."

Matthew looked away from the lifeless body and quickly rubbed his face. "We found a set of matching underwear and bra, and Pamela is taking it to the lab as we speak. How fast will we know if they belonged to her?"

In a tired voice she responded, "Soon with a hair sample, later with DNA."

Matthew nodded. "I want any results ASAP. We want to go public with our suspect as soon as we can."

Candy reached out and touched Matthew's hand. "My team will work fast. You did good, Matthew."

"Well, there's one big inconsistency."

"What?"

"Our suspect is six two."

"Oh, I see. I'll get you that lab report soon," Candy replied and then walked away pulling out her phone.

Out of the corner of his eye, Matthew saw Steve talking to Central University police chief Jacob Knight, and he made his way over toward them. "Knight."

Jacob Knight turned toward Matthew. "So you have a suspect?"

"Nothing's confirmed, but damn! I sure hope so." Matthew heard a commotion behind him. He quickly turned toward Trinity Lane and saw the media. "That didn't take long. Shit, I gotta get out of here, can't do this now." Matthew walked away and was soon bombarded by questions, as Channel Nine's Stacy Bryan was looking toward him waving her hands in the air to get his attention. Matthew mumbled under his breath and slowly made his way over to her. When Matthew was a few feet away, other reporters started running toward him in hopes of a comment on the Night Killer striking again. Matthew held up his hands to everyone to back off. "No comment now. Soon. But not now."

Matthew saw Steve and motioned to him, and they both jogged away from the chaos of the media to his Camaro and sped away once again.

Chapter 49

Erin greeted Lindy as she was released from the hospital. "Hi, sis!"

Lindy closed her purse and placed it beside her on the bed and then stood up. "Hi, Erin. Thanks for coming."

Erin walked over and gave her a hug. "An FBI agent called earlier and said your house could be cleaned. I called Judy, and she's on her way over now. She's going to pick up some new bedding as well."

"Thanks. Did you hear the news about Melody?"

Erin looked away and blinked back tears. "Yes, it's all over the news. It's horrible! Have you heard anything from Matthew?"

Lindy shook her head. "I'm sure he's knee-deep with this investigation. I really don't expect to hear from him anytime soon."

Erin nodded. "Come on, let's get out of here. Charlie marinated some pork chops earlier in a special sauce. We can fire up the grill when we get home."

"So Charlie left?"

"Yes, a few hours ago. I already miss him terribly."

Erin noticed the look Lindy gave her. "I know, when I fall, I fall hard. At least this guy appears to be genuine."

Lindy smiled. "I hope so. Let's go."

As soon as they walked out the door, they were greeted by Officer Murphy. "Let me escort you downstairs. There's a patrol car ready and waiting."

Erin asked, "Has Lindy been given police protection?"

Officer Murphy nodded. "Yes, Agent Matthew Blake requested it until the case is closed."

Lindy and Erin exchanged looks and then followed the officer toward the elevator. Once outside, Lindy was introduced to two officers. "I'm not going home," she told them. "I'm going home with Erin, my sister."

The younger officer looked down at his notepad. "No problem. We have her address. When we arrive, we'll check out the property and then stay outside."

Lindy touched his arm lightly. "Thanks, I really appreciate it."

The officers nodded and then climbed into their patrol car and waited for Erin and Lindy to lead the way. Once Erin was behind the wheel she looked over at Lindy. "Okay, this is really weird. Do I need to pay attention now to my speed?"

Lindy smiled. "Probably a good idea."

Matthew, Steve, and Don were sitting at a table outlining a timeline on Clay Barry when Pamela interrupted. "Medical Examiner's on line two." Matthew got up to take the call. "Hi, Dr. Johnson. What do you have?"

"It's good news, Matthew. The hair samples taken from the underwear are a one hundred percent match for Melody Montgomery. Also, I have ordered a rush for a DNA sample as well."

Matthew closed his eyes and took a deep breath. "Thank you, Dr. Johnson. That's good news."

"There's something else."

"Go ahead." Matthew waited.

"Remember that hair sample from Dr. Ashley's office that you wanted tested?"

"Yes."

"It's strange, but some of the hair was Melody's, but not all of it."

"What are you saying?"

"The test shows hair belonging to two different females. One is Melody Montgomery."

"Wait! That would mean her hair was collected before she went missing and was murdered."

"I'm afraid so."

Matthew paused for a moment. "Wow, okay, thanks. Keep me posted if there's anything else."

"Will do."

Matthew hung up the phone and informed the team of the latest discovery. Don got up and began to mark places on the campus map where Barry had worked over the last two weeks. Loudly he stated, "According to the university, Barry was hired a year ago to complete maintenance and repair work on various buildings. As you can see here, Barry was hired to install carpet in the second-floor lecture hall at the Dunn Building."

Matthew ran a hand through his hair. "Amazing. He was probably the guy they called to replace that light bulb."

"What?" asked Pamela.

Matthew shook his head. "I just reported a broken light outside the Dunn Building. It wouldn't surprise me if he was the one who took it out so he could hide out better. Now it appears he was called to replace his own damn handiwork."

Fred Copeland walked in and announced, "Media is scheduled at two o'clock. Tell me we have enough to go live with Clay Barry."

Don answered, "As of five minutes ago, yeah, we got a match. Underwear belonged to Melody Montgomery."

Copeland looked at Matthew. "Can Dr. Ashley come in and give us more insight on Barry?"

Matthew looked at his watch. "She was being released from the hospital at one. I can call and ask her to come in."

Copeland commented, "Yeah, we just need more. I don't get it. Here's a guy in love with the doctor. He stalks her, kills her dog and Melody Montgomery. But why the murder of the male students?"

Pamela suggested, "To scare her or get her attention?"

"Possibly," answered Copeland.

Matthew said, "I know what you mean. What about the height difference? Barry is six foot two. The only connection we have with Barry is Melody, and she was stabbed in Andrew Mitt's apartment. We have nothing that connects him with Robby or Jaycee. He does not fit the ME's description of a killer standing five ten."

Copeland shook his head. "Call Dr. Ashley and keep digging. We've got to find that connection."

Matthew nodded as Copeland left the room and then he picked up his cell phone and dialed Lindy's number. Lindy answered on the third ring. "Hello?"

"Hi, Lindy. We have a lead and need your help. May the officers bring you to my office?"

Lindy looked over at Erin behind the wheel. They were just a few miles from Erin's house, and the officers were following close behind. Looking down, Lindy examined her clothing. She was still wearing the same jeans and white T from yesterday. Finally she answered, "Yeah, I'll come right over."

"Thanks, I'll be waiting." Matthew ended the call.

Erin heard the one-sided conversation. "Lindy, what is it?"

"Matthew needs me to come in. They have a lead. Just pull over at the next shopping center, and I'll get in with the officers and they'll take me."

Erin asked in a concern voice, "Are you sure? I mean, do you feel up for that?"

"Considering the lives lost, I really don't think I have a choice."

Erin nodded and then pulled into a drugstore parking lot. Parking the car, she said, "Do you want me to go with you? I can you know. I have nothing planned."

As one of the officers walked up to Lindy's door, she said, "No, I'll be fine, but thanks."

"Okay, but call me later. I can come get you."

Lindy opened the door, just as the officer said, "We got the call. It'll only take about twenty minutes to get there."

"Can you give me just a second?" Lindy asked.

"Sure." The officer walked back to his patrol car and got in.

Lindy turned toward Erin. "Baby sister, will you please trade tops with me?"

At one-thirty Lindy was escorted into room A150 wearing day-old faded jeans and Erin's red silk V-neck blouse. Her hair was pulled back, and she was wearing very little makeup. She was stunning, and almost everyone in the room did a double take.

Matthew immediately walked over to greet Lindy. "Thanks for coming. Here, take a seat."

Lindy looked around the room and stopped when her eyes found the bulletin board with Clay Barry's photo pinned on it. "Clay Barry?" she asked loudly.

Matthew followed her eyes to the photo. "Yes, he's our prime suspect in the murder of Melody Montgomery. His vehicle also fits the description of the one that followed you and me yesterday. And, part of his tag matches the hospital security tapes."

Lindy looked at Matthew dumbfounded. "I'm treating him for OCD, but you already know that."

Matthew motioned again for Lindy to have a seat. "That's why I brought you in. We need more."

Lindy took a seat at the large table while the others gathered around it with pens and papers. She looked at their faces and then back to Matthew. "Okay, I've been seeing Clay Barry for the last two years. He has a disorder known as OCD. When he's stressed, he repeats things in order to feel a sense of normalcy. He can get fixated on the smallest detail and will continue to seek out that detail until his brain has determined enough is enough."

Matthew asked, "How has his behavior been the last few sessions?"

"Anxiety has been higher. In fact, he stormed in my office unannounced last Monday afternoon. I was able to quickly defuse the situation and didn't need security."

Matthew looked at Lindy with a concerned look. "How many times have you seen him since Monday?"

Lindy thought for a moment and then said, "On Monday I was in a hurry because I had to get to the university, so I set up an appointment for Tuesday morning."

"Did he show?"

"Yes, and then I saw him again for a longer session on Wednesday, which was the last day I saw him."

"Okay, did he seem different in anyway with your last session."

Lindy closed her eyes and tried to concentrate on her hour-long session with Clay. "I saw him early that afternoon, I can't recall the time, but it was before the box showed up at Erin's desk."

Don got up and made some marks on the bulletin board, and someone else started making a phone call in the far corner.

"Clay seemed dependent on me those last few sessions. He had a strong desire to see me and wouldn't have settled on a later appointment if I would have suggested it." Lindy shook her head. "Now that this has happened, it fits his behavior. I should've seen this coming or known something wasn't right."

Pamela was the first to respond. "Dr. Ashley, it's always easier to look back and reflect instead of predicting the future."

Matthew said, "Pamela's right. This ball was already set in motion. He's been planning this for some time."

Lindy set back in her chair. "What are you saying? How long has he been spying on me?"

The room got quiet and no one answered. Finally Matthew spoke. "Clay was first employed by Central University a year ago. He started making repairs to the Dunn Building around the time you began to lecture."

"Are you suggesting that he's fixated on me and then started killing students on campus the nights I lectured?" Raising her voice, she continued, "To what? Get my attention or scare me?"

Pamela answered, "Dr. Ashley, try to look at this professionally for a moment. Is it possible he could expand his fantasy to murder?"

Lindy smoothed back a few strands of hair that had come loose from her ponytail and then rested her hands on her neck. She looked tired and scared. Matthew handed her a bottled water, and she thanked him and then took a few sips. Patiently everyone waited for Lindy to continue. A few more minutes passed, and then she finally spoke.

"You need to find Clay and soon. There's a clear pattern here as well as evidence of infatuation that has crossed the line between reality and fantasy. He can no longer see the difference. His obsessive-compulsive behaviors will increase, and he'll become even more violent, if that's even possible."

Matthew nodded at Lindy. "Thanks. I know this is difficult."

A man entered and yelled out as he walked over to the bulletin board, "We have confirmation from work logs that Clay Barry was at the Dunn Building on the evenings of Wednesday, September twenty-second, and Monday, September twenty-seventh."

Don jumped up first and walked over to the bulletin board to read the times from the sheet. "The night Robby Singleton was killed, he logged in at five o'clock, but there's no log out time."

"And Monday the twenty-seventh?" asked Matthew.

"Barry logged in that evening at six o'clock, and logged out at seven."

Matthew said, "Pamela, call Copeland and tell him, and I'll see him in the media room in..."

Pamela answered for him. "Five minutes. It's one fifty now."

Matthew leaned toward Lindy. "Would you wait for me in my office? I have a news conference at two. We're going live with Clay Barry as our person of interest."

Lindy nodded and got up. Matthew said, "Janet, at the desk just outside, will show you to my office. Again, thanks."

Lindy smiled and grabbed Matthew's hand. "Good luck. I'll see you soon."

After Lindy walked out, Matthew turned to Steve. "You were quiet. What are you thinking?"

Steve shook his head. "I don't know, but we're missing something."

Matthew frowned. "I know, I have the same feeling."

Chapter 50

Erin opened her front door and then closed and locked it behind her. Slowly she peeled off her tennis shoes and then went straight to the living room to stretch. Each day, she went for a two-mile run and then came home and practiced yoga for thirty minutes. In no time, Erin's thirty-minute routine was complete.

Erin looked at the clock. Charlie had already landed back in Houston and was sure to be home by now. Fighting the urge to call him, she made her way to the master bedroom and began stripping down for a shower. After removing the last article of clothing, she heard a voice behind her say, "Hi, babe. Miss me?"

Erin screamed and wrapped her arms around her chest. Instinctively she tried to run, but Leroy stepped in front of her and caught her. Smelling of whiskey, he clutched her tightly and held one hand over her mouth to keep her from screaming again. As Erin struggled to break free, Leroy pulled her toward the bed and then fell onto her, pushing her hard against the mattress.

Leroy slurred his words. "I don't understand how you can just move on so quickly. Don't…don't you know how much I love you? I need you in my life."

Erin wasn't able to respond since he still had his large hand over her mouth. She was struggling to breathe because he was partially covering her nose, and she was scared out of her mind. Leroy saw her eyes bulging and her discomfort. "Erin, baby, I'm gonna remove my hand now. Don't scream!"

Slowly Leroy moved his hand, and Erin gasped for air and coughed madly. When she caught her breath, she yelled, "What the hell are you doing, Leroy? I want you off of me now and out of my house! Now!"

Leroy grabbed both of her wrists with one hand and stretched her arms up over her head. With his other hand, he touched her face gently and then lowered his mouth to hers. Erin squirmed beneath him and then bit his lip. Leroy raised up and slapped her hard across the face. "You bitch, I'm bleeding!"

Erin started kicking and screaming. "Let me go, you filthy animal!"

Leroy started laughing loudly. "You've got a lot of guts, Erin, I'll give you that. Now shut the hell up before the neighbors hear you!"

Erin didn't give up. She thought, *If I stay quiet, he'll kill me. Screaming is my only chance. I might as well die fighting.* Erin screamed out once again, "Help!" and Leroy punched her in the nose. The room was spinning around her. She tasted blood and could feel it pouring down her face and filling up one of her ears. Leroy shook her and then flipped her over and shoved her head down into the pillows.

Erin couldn't breathe, and her world was slowly fading. Just when she thought she was going to die, she heard a deafening noise. Leroy's body slammed into the back of hers and then rolled off her and hit the floor. She could now move, as nothing was holding her face-down anymore. Slowly she turned her head to the side and, with blurry vision, saw Clay Barry standing in the doorway holding a shotgun.

Erin opened her mouth to speak, but no words emerged. Her eyes left Clay in search of Leroy and found him covered in blood with half his face gone. Erin lifted her shaking hand up toward her face and saw that it was covered in Leroy's blood and brain matter. Erin's world stopped spinning as she fainted face-down into her once yellow pillow.

Lindy patiently waited for Matthew in his office. After a few minutes, she stood up and wandered over to his desk and then took a seat in his over-sized leather chair. Looking around, she found no pictures of loved ones or a house or a ranch with horses. The only items on the walls were maps of downtown Dallas, Ft. Worth, and Arlington. No sports memorabilia or college diplomas, nothing personal that would give a hint as to who the person was that sat at this desk. Lindy was a little confused by all of this. *Why not a picture of a horse, or even one of the Dallas Cowboy's new stadium?* She thought.

Lindy looked at the door. Once she was sure it was still closed, she opened the bottom right drawer of his desk and peered inside. She was not disappointed. There she found a signed baseball, a box of Hershey's chocolate bars, protein shake mixes, and one upside-down picture frame.
Looking up once more to make sure she was alone, she reached in the drawer and touched the frame. As soon as she barely lifted it, her phone rang in her purse, and she jumped, hitting her knee under the desktop.

Lindy quickly closed the drawer and then hurried back over to the couch to retrieve her cell phone from her purse. It took a few moments to find it, as it was well buried, but she was able to open it in time to see Erin's name and number before hastily answering. "Hi, Erin."

A male voice answered, "It's not Erin."

A cold shiver ran down Lindy's spine as her mind worked to figure out the voice. Feeling unsteady, she sat down on the couch. "Who is this?"

"I saved her just for you. She's safe because of me."

"What? I don't understand?"

"Come to Erin's house right away. She needs you."

"Who is this? Clay is that you?"

The only response Lindy received was the sound of the call ending. Quickly, she hit send hoping desperately that Erin would answer. She didn't. No one did. Lindy jumped up from the couch and bolted for the door with her phone and purse, and ran smack into Matthew. Matthew took one look at Lindy's pale face. "What happened? What's wrong?"

Lindy was frantic. "I just got a call from Erin's phone, but it wasn't Erin. It was a strange man who said for me to go to Erin's house, that she needed me."

Matthew held out his hand for her phone, and she gave it to him. Opening it up, he hit send from the last call and waited.

"I already tried. No one answered."

Matthew nodded but remained quiet, silently willing Erin to answer the phone, but she didn't. Matthew walked out of his office and shouted to a man across the room. "I need a unit at—" He turned toward Lindy, and she stated the address loud enough for the man to hear. The man picked up a phone and began speaking into it without taking his eyes off Lindy or Matthew.

Hearing the commotion, Steve walked over and asked, "Whose house?"

Matthew said, "Her sister Erin's. I think it's a trap. Let's go. I'll fill you in on the way."

Lindy didn't ask, she just started jogging toward the exit without an invitation. She felt lost without a vehicle, and there was no way they were leaving her behind! Matthew caught up with her at the elevator. "Lindy, it might be best for you to stay here and wait."

The elevator door opened and Lindy stepped in without answering Matthew. Hesitating only a second, Matthew walked in and quickly pressed the parking garage button. Lindy stared at him but said nothing as he quickly filled Steve in on the phone conversation.

It took thirty-two minutes to get to Erin's house in Arlington. Ten minutes ago they received a call from Pamela stating that Erin was alive, but an unidentified dead man was in the house. When they rounded the last corner, they encountered a street filled with police cars. At the sight of two ambulances, Lindy felt her heart tighten. Her oxygen supply felt squeezed as each breath required concentration and extra strength.

Matthew parked the Camaro and then turned around to face Lindy. "Lindy, I think I should—"

Lindy opened the door and jumped out onto the lawn. Without answering Matthew, she started jogging toward Erin's perfect little three-bedroom home in her perfect little safe neighborhood. Gazing around, she saw people gathered around talking. *Probably neighbors wondering what has happened to shatter their perfect little world*, she thought.

"Lindy, wait!"

Matthew ran and caught up with her and carefully placed his hand on her elbow. Lindy stopped dead in her tracks when a stretcher with a blood-soaked sheet covering a body was carried out the front door. Matthew looked at Lindy and saw her shaking and tried to comfort her. "She's safe, that's not her."

Steve passed by both of them and went over to an officer and flashed his badge. After a brief conversation, the officer pointed toward the house. Steve walked back over to Matthew, who was still standing by Lindy's side.

"They found a wallet. It's her ex, Leroy."

Lindy pushed forward and said to the officer up ahead, "Where's Erin? She's my sister, and I want to see her."

Matthew flashed his badge and nodded to the officer. The officer guarding the door said, "She's with the paramedics in the living room."

Lindy didn't wait for more. She moved on by him and entered the house and quickly scanned the room until she found her sister. Erin was sitting on the couch with a blanket wrapped around her while someone was checking her blood pressure and making notes. Erin's eyes met Lindy's, and she began to cry and shake. "Lindy!"

Chapter 51

"It was Clay Barry, I'm positive. He was holding a shotgun!"

Lindy caressed Erin's shoulder and then held her tight as she continued.

"It was horrible. I...I...it was all so fast, and it seemed like it was happening far away. But it did, and Leroy's blood and brains are everywhere. I can't get it off of me! It won't come off of me!"

Lindy took the washcloth and continued to wipe Erin's face and hair. She responded in a voice that didn't sound like her own, "It will. Let's get you in the shower."

Lindy looked toward Matthew and waited for some indication that he had a plan to help. Matthew looked at the female officer who was standing nearby and asked, "Has the bathroom on this side of the house been cleared?"

The officer looked at where he was pointing and said, "Yes."

A paramedic responded with, "I would like to take her to the hospital. She can wash up there and have a doctor take another look at her nose."

Matthew bent down and looked into Erin's eyes. "He's right. We need to take you in. Lindy and I will stay with you."

Erin just stared back with glassy eyes. Another paramedic came around the couch with a stretcher and lowered it for Erin. Without another word spoken by Erin, she was helped onto the small mattress and then carefully taken out the front door. Lindy never left her side and only let go of her hand when they had to lift her into the back of the ambulance. Lindy turned toward Matthew. "I'm going to ride with her, okay?"

Matthew walked over and touched Lindy's cheek. "I'll be there soon. And don't go anywhere alone, and stay in the presence of an officer. Promise?"

Lindy nodded, and then Matthew helped her get inside with Erin. As the ambulance pulled away, Steve said, "This just gets weirder by the hour. Why would Clay Barry save Erin?"

Matthew looked at his trusted partner with a scowl. "I have no idea, but we got to figure this shit out and soon."

Clay Barry was riding around in his black SUV in shock as the radio announced the news of a manhunt for a person of interest—him!—in the recent murders of the college students. Clay banged on the steering wheel and tried to think. "No, no! This is all wrong! What must Lindy be thinking? No, if I can't have her then no one will."

Chapter 52

Jamie was soaking in a hot tub surrounded by lush palms and pink azaleas. She took another sip of her wine and then heard her phone ringing again in her purse a few feet away.

"Do you want me to get that for you?"

Jamie had checked earlier when he was in the house and saw that the three missed calls were all from Bart. She owed him some sort of explanation but just didn't care at the moment to come up with one. "No, there's no place I would rather be than here with you."

He smiled and then stretched out his hand and pulled her close to him. "Good, 'cause I'm not letting you go tonight."

Jamie allowed herself to be pulled close but fought a nagging twinge of guilt for leaving Bart alone with no explanation. She quickly pushed the thoughts away and leaned in for another kiss.

Bart laid his cell phone down and said to Luke, "No answer. For some odd reason, she isn't answering or calling me back."

Luke offered, "That is odd. She couldn't keep her hands off of you last night."

Bart shrugged. "I knew what I was getting into when we hooked up. Jamie doesn't answer to nobody. She flies by the seat of her pants and thinks of no one but herself."

"And you like those fine qualities?"

Bart laughed. "She's fun, and she makes me feel untouchable when I'm with her. But I'm not stupid. I don't mix that up with love."

Luke walked over from the kitchen counter with two beers and extended one to Bart. "So, how are my players doing today?"

Bart huffed a little. "Better than mine. My quarterback threw three interceptions today."

"Ouch! How bad's that going to set you back?"

"Well, if my running back has a good game here, not much."

Luke took a swig of his beer. His players had done exceptionally well, and if he kept this up, he was going to get a big payout from his fantasy football league. The game continued on as the guys drank and ate nachos. Then, a couple of minutes into halftime, there was a knock at the door. Luke looked at Bart. "Do you want me to get that?"

"Nah, they'll go away."

Luke nodded and sat back on the sofa. *For a guy that didn't care about Jamie, Bart sure had a funny way of showing it,* he thought.

It was ten o'clock when Lindy and Matthew pulled up at his ranch. The place was incredible even at night. There seemed to be no lights, only stars, like nothing else existed and they were in the middle of nowhere. Lindy looked through the window and saw white fences outlining what appeared to be a barn and an arena for his horses. Slowly Lindy stepped out of the Camaro and looked around in the dark. Up ahead, there was the faint glow of a porch light coming from what appeared to be Matthew's home.

"Come on, I'll show you the house, and then I need to go out and check on Ethel and Fred."

Lindy looked toward the barn. "The house can wait. I would like to meet your horses."

Matthew smiled. "Sure, but I'm going to warn you. They aren't happy with me for leaving them so long."

Lindy faced Matthew. "Animals are forgiving creatures. Come on, they'll still love you."

As Matthew held Lindy's hand and led her to the stables, he saw tears in her eyes. There was no doubt in his mind that she was thinking of Parker. *Damn, when is this going to end?* He thought. Matthew held the barn door open for Lindy and then followed her in. Finding the switch, he turned on the main lights. Fred and Ethel glanced at them and then looked away immediately. "I told you, they aren't happy with me!"

Despite the dull pain in Lindy's chest, she started laughing. Stepping forward, she asked, "Which one is Fred?"

Matthew pointed toward the right. "The brown one. Ethel is the white and black one."

Lindy smiled and touched each of them gently with her hands. "Hi, Fred, Ethel, it's nice to finally meet you."

Ethel nickered softly.

Matthew grabbed some carrots and handed two to Lindy. "Here, they'll love you forever if you feed them."

Smiling again, Lindy began to feed both of them at the same time. Matthew just watched. There was something gentle about her touch that the horses could feel, that much he could easily see. She grabbed more carrots and fed them again, and Matthew didn't have the heart to tell her no more, not to spoil them. When they were done, Lindy turned to Matthew and smiled. "Thank you for bringing me here. It's very soothing."

Matthew nodded. "Would you like to go for a ride? It's almost a full moon, plenty enough light to see."

Lindy answered immediately. "Yes, I would like that very much."

"We'll take Fred. He knows every inch of this ranch, daylight or dark."

"What about Ethel? Won't she be upset that she has to stay behind?"

Matthew smirked. "Probably. Have you ridden before?"

She shook her head. "Not really. Been on a horse once a long time ago."

"I tell you what we'll do. We'll tie her behind us so she can go too."

Lindy's eyes were shining. "That sounds better."

Matthew picked up a saddle that was hanging on a hook nearby and began to buckle it around Fred. Next he took another rope and made a special knot and attached it to Ethel's halter. After a few more minutes, Matthew asked, "Ready?"

Nodding yes, Lindy walked forward and allowed Matthew to help pull her up on the saddle behind him. Lindy shifted her weight some. He asked, "All good?"

"Yes, now take me for a ride, cowboy."

"Yes, ma'am!"

For the next ten minutes, they rode in silence. The only sounds they heard were coming from the horses and the crickets. Lindy had both arms wrapped around Matthew, and her hands were resting on his chest. Her face was turned, and she rested her left cheek up against his back. With each step the horse made, she could feel Matthew's heart beating. Was it her imagination, or was his heart pounding just as fast as hers? Several more moments passed, and then they began to climb a hill. When they were at the top, Matthew said, "Let's stop here. I want to show you something."

With such grace, Matthew slid off the horse, and he guided Fred and Ethel over to a tree and tied them up. Next, he turned toward Lindy and extended his hand to help her dismount. Lindy let go of the saddle and touched his hand. Placing her hand in his, she felt a jolt of electricity as he placed his other hand on top of hers. Steadying herself, she swung her other leg over and then slid down Fred into Matthew's waiting arms. Time seemed to stop as Matthew looked down into Lindy's blue eyes and held onto her. Finally he broke the spell. "Come, follow me."

Lindy held onto Matthew's hand and followed him a few steps until he stopped. She looked away from Matthew and gazed up at the night sky. Far, far away, down below the hill, the city lights were shining. "Wow, this is quite a view. It's incredible!"

Lindy turned toward Matthew and was immediately swept up in his muscular arms. Matthew lowered his face and placed his lips gently on hers and held her tight. Lindy was trembling beneath his touch, and he slowly pulled back. "You're shaking."

Lindy spoke so softly Matthew barely heard her. "I am, but in a good way."

So many thoughts were going through Matthew's mind. He wanted to hold on to her and never let go. The setting was beautiful, except he knew what lay on the other side of the hill. Pushing all other thoughts away, he said, "Take my hand. I want to show you something along this path."

Lindy took his hand and then looked down. She could barely see the trampled ground that resembled an old path. Trusting him, she followed. Walking side by side for about another fifty yards, Lindy could now make out what was up ahead. There, a few feet in front of her, was a small area enclosed by a white fence. Several small markers jutted from the ground inside.

"I had them bury Parker here today, beside my horses and dogs. If you want to move him somewhere else later, you can, or you can come and visit whenever you like."

Lindy was so touched by the gesture that she was speechless.

"I'll wait here and give you some time to say good-bye."

Lindy looked at Matthew and squeezed his hand and then turned and walked inside the gate. She took small, slow steps toward the fresh pile of dirt that was Parker's grave and knelt down. Matthew watched from afar as Lindy spent the next five minutes alone. When he saw her stand up, he made his way over and took her hand and led her back to the horses. No words were exchanged as they untied the horses and mounted once again for the ride back to the stables.

Lindy was content with listening to the night sounds and taking in the beauty and peacefulness that surrounded her. She didn't pursue a conversation nor did Matthew. With each gentle sway of the horse's back, she felt all the nightmares move a little farther away. Matthew finally broke the silence when they arrived at the stable door. "It won't take me long here, and then we can go up to the house."

Matthew carefully dismounted and then helped Lindy down once more. When her feet hit the ground, she looked up into Matthew's tender eyes. "Thank you, for everything."

Matthew pulled her close and kissed her on the forehead and then picked up her hands and kissed them. Slowly Lindy pulled away and said, "Let me help." She walked over to Ethel and began to untie her rope while Matthew unsaddled Fred. It didn't take long to get the horses settled, and then they closed the stable doors behind them and headed back to the Camaro to grab Matthew's backpack.

When Matthew shut the door, they heard a noise come from behind in the trees that bordered the driveway. Instinct took over, and Matthew pulled his gun and spun around in front of Lindy to shield her. Matthew carefully continued to scan the area with his eyes until he saw the source of the noise. Walking along the grassy area that edged the trees was a fox. Spotting the couple, it took off back toward the woods, its eyes shining low to the ground.

Matthew holstered his gun and turned back to face Lindy. "Lots of wild-life out here. Sorry, didn't mean to frighten you."

Lindy tried to smile to hide her frayed nerves, but it didn't work well thanks to a bottom lip that trembled slightly. Matthew grabbed her hand and quickly led her to the front porch. Within a matter of seconds, he had the front door opened and the alarm reset and the place locked up and secure.

"Let me show you around. Do you need anything? Are you hungry?"

Lindy shook her head. "No. I just want a hot shower and a nice bed."

Matthew nodded and then gestured toward the hallway, and Lindy followed. Opening a door, Matthew said, "Here's the guest room, and it has its own bath." He went in and turned on the lights and then opened the door to the bathroom. "There's fresh towels in the closet and anything else you might need."

"Thanks."

Matthew walked toward the bedroom door and then turned back around. "I'll bring in a fresh T-shirt and some sweats."

"That would be lovely. Just put them on the bed." Lindy broke eye contact and went into the bathroom, closing the door behind her.

Matthew headed into the kitchen and grabbed a beer. He really wanted something stronger but decided against it considering Clay Barry was still out there and hadn't been captured yet. Until then, he needed to be on his toes. He thought, *How the hell am I gonna be able to sleep tonight with just one wall separating us?* Pushing back his thoughts, he dug out his phone and checked his messages. Nothing. With beer in hand, he left the kitchen in search of a clean T-shirt and some sweatpants with a drawstring. After rummaging through his dresser for a minute, he found what he was looking for and placed the items on the bed in the guest room. Hearing the water running, Matthew walked over and placed his hand on the closed bathroom door and stood there a moment. He thought, *She's safe and that's all that matters right now.* He removed his hand and then left, closing the bedroom door behind him.

Lindy opened the door with a towel wrapped around her body and saw the clothes on the bed. She was a little disappointed to find the room empty. She thought, *Oh, Lindy, what were you expecting? Him to be standing here waiting on you? You're a basket case right now! I'm sure that's attractive!"*

Lindy removed her towel and picked up his clothes to get dressed. Instead of slipping them on, though, she brought them to her face and inhaled deeply, trying to catch his scent. Nothing. Shrugging her shoulders, she thought, *They're clean, silly girl. Of course they wouldn't smell like him.* She pulled them onto her naked body.

Walking back in the bathroom, she found a brush and then brushed out her long jet-black hair and then found a new toothbrush and toothpaste and brushed her teeth. Leaving the bathroom, she walked over to the bed and pulled back the covers to settle in. With the flip of a switch beside her bed, the room went dark, and Lindy lay her head back onto the pillow and closed her eyes. Immediately thoughts of Matthew flashed through her mind. She opened her eyes and stared at the white ceiling above, wishing for sleep to come quickly.

Matthew set his beer down by the computer and checked his e-mail. Next he logged onto his bank account and paid a bill. Picking his beer back up, he took the last sip and then decided to call it a night. Pressing the shutdown button, Matthew got up and rechecked the doors and then headed for his bedroom.

When he walked by Lindy's door, he paused to listen. Nothing. Slowly he continued down the hallway and entered his bedroom. A hot shower sounded good, so he began stripping down. Looking back at the bedroom door, he decided to keep it open, just in case an emergency arose. Smiling to himself, he thought, *Yeah, just keep telling yourself that's why you're leaving the door open.*

Adjusting the water to the desired temperature, Matthew finally stepped in. He made the shower a quick one. Within no time, he was back in his bedroom with a towel wrapped around his waist. Opening his dresser, he found some boxers and pulled them on, and then he went back into the bathroom and brushed his teeth. Grabbing his gun, he flipped the light switch off in the bathroom and made his way over to his bed, still alone. Gently he laid his gun on the table and then plugged in his cell phone. Looking at the empty doorway once more, he contemplated his next move. With a sigh, he turned toward his bed, pulled back the covers, and got in. As soon as he reached over and flipped the light off, he heard a voice.

"Matthew?"

Matthew flipped the switch back on and quickly sat up in bed. Lindy was walking toward him. Matthew could feel his heart pounding faster with each step she took. He was sure she could hear it.

Lindy stopped when she made it to his bed and spoke softly. "I can't sleep. Um, do you mind if I just stay in here with you tonight. Um, just to sleep." She looked down at her bare feet and then back up with a slightly embarrassed look on her face. "I know that sounds so inappropriate and—"

Matthew immediately pulled the covers down and slid over to the other side of the bed and then patted the empty warm space. Lindy considered again what she had just requested and then hastily got in bed and pulled the covers over her. When she reached out and flipped the light switch, Matthew finally broke the awkward silence. "Come here and let me hold you. I promise to be good."

Lindy thought to herself, *I don't know if I want you to be good or not.* She allowed Matthew to slide over and place his muscular arms around her. Immediately Lindy felt warm and secure as she snuggled against his body. She was about to speak, but he stopped her. "Don't say anything. Just close your eyes and let me hold you while you sleep. We can talk tomorrow."

For the first time in a long time, Lindy felt safe and began to relax and close her eyes. Soon sleep came and took her away.

Chapter 53

Monday morning

Lindy woke up to an alarm clock that was not her own. Slowly she turned toward the never-ending noise and cracked her eyes open. Matthew was leaning over and hitting a button, and after he silenced the beeping, he fell back on his pillow. She watched him quietly as he rubbed his eyes and then closed them once more. A minute passed by, and then Matthew turned his head toward Lindy. "Good morning, how did you sleep?"

A smile crept across her face. "Peacefully. What time is it?"

Matthew reached out and swirled a strand of Lindy's hair around his finger. "Five o'clock."

With a frown, she said, "I need to get going. My first appointment's around eight-thirty, and we have to go back to my place first so I can get some clothes."

Matthew looked at Lindy funny. "You're gonna try to work today?"

Lindy sat up. "Of course. It's Monday, and the world is still turning despite our every hope and desire to stop it."

Matthew pulled Lindy back down and then leaned in close and whispered, "Can I have ten minutes to try and stop t?"

Lindy pondered his request. Slowly she reached out and touched his bare chest with trembling hands. "Ten minutes I have, but it won't be long enough."

Matthew let his head fall back against the pillow. "I'll go make breakfast."

Lindy watched him leave and then got out of bed and walked into the bathroom. Finding a brush, she brushed out her hair and then went in search of Matthew to help in the kitchen. Looking around for the first time and really noticing things, she immediately fell in love with his warm, masculine ranch house. Lots of dark wood with nice rustic oak floors flowed throughout the house. Someone had done a magnificent job decorating it, and Lindy couldn't help but feel jealous at the thought that it might have been a past girlfriend. Stepping into the kitchen, Lindy found Matthew scrambling eggs and then pouring them in a hot skillet. She offered, "I'll make toast and pour us some coffee. How do you like yours?"

"Black."

Lindy said, "Easy enough."

Soon the toast was ready, and Lindy got out two plates for Matthew to scoop the eggs onto. "This smells so good."

"My real specialty is omelets. I hope one day soon to make them for you."

Lindy turned toward Matthew without any thought and coyly responded. "An hour in bed with me and you'll be starving." Lindy quickly took the plates over to the table and thought, *Oh shit, I just said that out loud!*

Matthew walked up behind her and turned her back around to face him. "Why, Doctor, is that a proposition?" His grin was sexy as he continued, "If so, I'll have to stop by the store. I just used up all the eggs."

Lindy's heart was pounding in her chest as his lips moved closer to hers. She was speechless. Her eyes left his lips and then found his eyes, and she noticed how green and intense they looked. Soon his lips were on hers and his body was pressed against hers and pushing her backward toward the kitchen wall. Matthew's hands were all over her: her hair, her throat, her chest, and her hips. His passion was so intense that she almost couldn't breathe. Finally, she wrapped her arms around his neck and, in a short panting voice, said, "Okay, thirty...thirty minutes!"

Swiftly Matthew picked her up and carried her to the wide leather couch in the living room and took her—heart, soul, and mind—right there.

Forty-five minutes later, Lindy was lying on top of Matthew in the bedroom with tangled sheets all around them. She rolled over and looked at the clock. It was now six o'clock. Matthew saw the time too. "Oops, thirty minutes just wasn't enough time."

Lindy smiled. "I'm going to take a shower."

Matthew sat up. "I'll help."

Lindy shook her head and laughed. "No, I'm going to the guest bathroom. I saw how big your shower is."

"I designed it for two."

"I saw that. We jump in there and we'll never leave."

Matthew touched her exposed nipple and rubbed gently. As he lowered his mouth he mumbled, "That's the plan."

Lindy just shook her head and pushed him away in a playful gesture.

Matthew pulled back. "All right. I'm going out to feed the horses. I'll be back soon."

Lindy watched him get dressed. After he pulled on his boots, he walked over and gave her a kiss on the forehead and then slid his hand down her cheek. "You make me so happy, Lindy."

She smiled at his admission and replied, "I'm glad, 'cause you make me feel the same way." Matthew winked and then left the bedroom.

Fifteen minutes had passed, and Lindy was now out of the shower and dressed. Brushing out her hair, she decided to let it dry naturally since time was not on her side. Walking out of the bathroom, she made her way

over to the guest bed and made it up. When she walked out and heard
the shower running in Matthew's bathroom, temptation almost pulled
her back in, but she was finally able to move past his bedroom door and
on down the hallway. Soon she arrived in the living room, and that was
worse; there she saw the couch where it all began.

Lindy peeled her eyes off the couch and focused her attention on the large
windows that covered the back wall of the living room. Walking toward
them she saw the back patio. The place looked nice and was designed well
for outdoor living and entertaining. Past the grill she spotted the stable,
and soon her thoughts went to Fred and Ethel. Deciding to go and see
them again, Lindy put on her flip-flops and went out the back door.

The barn wasn't too far away, and Lindy could still see the back porch
clearly when she opened the barn door. Instantly, she could hear the
horses. Lindy walked over and said, "Good morning, guys. Did you sleep
well?"

Ethel swung her head toward Lindy, and she began to stroke the horse's
face. Fred moved closer, and Lindy extended her other hand. "Good thing
I can multitask. Looks like you want some attention, too!"

Several minutes went by, and Lindy was having a good time talking
to and petting the cute couple until the barn door slammed, startling
both her and the horses. Lindy turned around fast and found only empty
space behind her. As the horses nervously moved away, Lindy yelled out,
"Matthew!"

When no sound emerged, Lindy began to look around in the barn and
found a wall with tools hanging on it. She began to tremble when she saw
the pitchfork swinging. "Matthew!" Lindy yelled again. Turning around
quickly, she ran smack into his chest.

"Lindy, what's wrong?"

Lindy looked around and then said, "The door slammed behind me, and
the horses got spooked. Look at the pitchfork. It's swinging!"

They both looked over at the pitchfork, but it was no longer moving. "Matthew, I swear, it was swaying side to side," she said in a frantic voice.

Matthew placed an arm around her. "Okay, it was probably from the door. Look, I'll show you."

Matthew walked over and slammed the door, and both watched as the tools shook and rattled. Lindy looked away toward the horses and then back to Matthew. "Why did the door slam?"

Matthew walked over to the door and opened it back up. He stood there a few moments until the wind picked back up and began to move the door once more. This time Matthew caught the door so it wouldn't scare the animals. "It's six-thirty. Are you ready?"

Lindy looked back over at Fred and Ethel. "Bye guys, see you soon."

Matthew held the door for Lindy and then stepped out behind her and closed the door. Without letting on, Matthew scanned the area and placed his hand on the weapon that was under his waistband. Another five minutes passed as Lindy grabbed her clothing from yesterday and Matthew locked up. Soon they were back in his Camaro and on their way.

The ride over to Lindy's place was too quiet, and Matthew finally broke the silence. "I hope you have no regrets."

Lindy shook her head side to side. "None. I'm just thinking about Clay Barry and how badly I want all of this to be over with."

With a serious face, Matthew said, "It will be. The media has been talking of nothing else, and with Barry's face plastered on every newspaper stand and news station, he can't hide long."

"So why do you think he showed up at Erin's house?"

"Looking for you, I'm sorry to say."

"Yes, but he came with a shotgun and didn't hurt Erin. He saved her."

Matthew didn't answer, and Lindy continued. "You think he was planning on killing me?"

"Let's not jump to conclusions. You and your sister are safe, and we'll continue to watch both of you until he's found."

Lindy was about to say something else but stopped when Matthew's cell phone went off. "I have to take this." He opened up his phone. "Blake."

Lindy looked outside the window and watched as the world went by. People were dressed for the day's work ahead and concentrating on driving. Some were drinking coffee, and others were talking to someone else in the car. Lindy thought, *Do they have any idea the state of mind Clay Barry's in? Please, God, let us catch him soon before he kills again.* Lindy leaned her head back and closed her eyes and patiently waited to get to work.

Somehow Lindy had made it to her office in time for her eight-thirty appointment with Luke James. She was sitting at Erin's desk reviewing his file before their appointment, and the office was quiet—too quiet. Looking around, Lindy felt a little spooked, but she was instantly relieved when she saw the officer walk by her glass entrance. Officer Remini was on her detail until Clay Barry was apprehended. Lindy looked away and back down at the file, trying to concentrate. *I should have taken the day off to be with Erin,* she thought. Picking up her cell phone, Lindy dialed Erin's number and was happy to hear her sister's voice once more.

"Hi, Lindy. Is everything okay at the office?"

"Yes, the temp service is sending someone in at nine. But I'm worried about you. I think this was a bad idea for me to work today. I should be with you instead."

"Oh no! Don't even think about it. Rescheduling would be a nightmare when I return. Now that would be stressful!"

"I could keep the temp here, and she could reschedule for you."

"Lindy, stop it! I'm fine. Besides, you would be a third wheel in my room."

"What? Erin, you're not making any sense."

"Charlie is here. When we talked earlier this morning, he took off work and drove straight here to be with me."

"Oh, wow, I see."

"Sis, don't worry. They plan on releasing me this afternoon, and Charlie will stay with me. He's already arranged for my house to be cleaned."

Lindy thought, *How many times in the last few days have we needed our houses cleaned? When is this hell going to end?*

"Lindy?"

"Yes, I'm still here. I'll call you around lunch, okay? But don't hesitate to call me if you need me."

"I will. Love you, Lindy."

Lindy smiled into her cell phone. "I love you too, sis."

Just as Lindy closed her phone, Luke James strolled into her office.

"Hiya, Doc! Where's Erin?"

"Erin has the flu. Someone will be in shortly though to answer the phones. Are you ready to go back?"

"Sure, though I'm not real sure why you wanted to see me so soon after last week."

Lindy didn't comment and continued on toward her office with Luke a few steps behind her.

"You look nice today, Doc. Something's different."

Lindy glanced down at her yellow silk dress with tiny cap sleeves. The dress had a small fitted black belt that matched the mini floral design. She was wearing black strappy heels and had her hair back in a low pony-tail. Not a whole lot of time was spent this morning on her makeup or hair. She was only wearing mascara, blush, and a little lipstick. "Thank you, Luke. You look nice today as well."

Luke laughed. "I didn't have time for a shower, and I'm wearing the same clothes from yesterday."

Lindy looked him over. "Oh. Well, you still look nice."

Luke just shook his head and took a seat on the couch while Lindy settled in her chair with his file on her lap. Luke looked around the room and saw the mess. "What's with the files? You moving your office?"

Lindy glanced at the stack of files on the floor and answered, "Not exactly. Just reorganizing."

Neither spoke for a few moments as Lindy thought of the FBI agents in her office going through everyone's files. Finally, she broke the silence and asked, "So why are you wearing the same clothing from yesterday?"

"I was at a friend's house on campus."

Lindy smiled. "Yeah? Tell me about your friend."

"Bart's in my fantasy football league. He and I hung out this weekend, and he hooked me up with a cute chick."

"Oh, no plans with Jennifer?"

"No, I did see her though, and I told her some personal things about me. You would be proud."

"Luke, that's good. How did she respond?"

"She was supportive, but she basically said she needed some time to think, and we both know what that means."

"Maybe not, Luke."

"Anyway, I hooked up with another chick and had a really good time."

Lindy tilted her head. "How many times did you think of Jennifer when you were with this other girl?"

Luke frowned. "Too many times."

Lindy decided to take the conversation elsewhere. "How did you sleep this weekend?"

Luke's face turned a little pink, and then he bashfully said, "Very nicely."

"Oh, so no dreams that kept you up?"

"I partied a little hard this weekend. Trust me, I slept like a baby."

Lindy was about to ask another question, but Luke interrupted. "Look, Doc, I don't mean any disrespect, but I don't think I needed to come in today. I had a great weekend and really cut loose, which was a good feeling."

Lindy placed her pen down. "Okay, Luke. I just wanted to touch base with you after the weekend." Leaning forward some, Lindy said, "I have seen a lot of progress, and I didn't want you to backslide because of your breakup with Jennifer."

Luke sat up and looked closely at Lindy. "What breakup?"

Lindy treaded carefully. "Jennifer wanted some space and time to think."

Luke genuinely looked confused. "Jennifer and I are fine. I plan to see her later tonight after class."

Lindy asked timidly, "Tell me about your last visit with Jennifer."

"We hung out by the pool at her apartment and had a great time."

"Do you plan on sharing some personal information with her anytime soon?"

"I'm not ready yet, but soon."

Lindy tried her best to smile as to not show her worry. "Good. You'll know when the time is right."

Luke jumped up quickly and rubbed his hands down his jeans. "Thanks, Lindy, but I really need to go. I have some schoolwork to do."

Lindy followed his lead and stood as well. She stretched out her hand. "Okay, Luke, but let's stay in touch."

Luke shook her hand and then smiled. "I will come in next week. I'll call with a day that works best for me. I'm thinking about going on some job interviews."

"Well then, I'll wait for your call."

Luke smiled his boyish grin as they walked out of her office. She watched as Luke left out the exit door across the hall. Lindy literally felt she was standing in some kind of time warp. The front door chimed, and Lindy looked at her watch. It was fifteen minutes till nine, a little too early for the temp service. They usually didn't arrive early or stay late. Lindy tried to push Luke out of her mind and headed toward the front to see who was there. Rounding the last corner, she saw a man she had never met before.

"Hello, I'm Dr. Lindy Ashley. May I help you?"

"Yes, my name is Dwayne Moore. I'm a colleague of Joshua Dobbs."

A warm smile spread across Lindy's face. "Of course, he's mentioned your name before."

"Good. Well, the reason I'm here is Joshua's not going to make class tonight. I think his mother won't make it another twelve hours."

"I see. Did he cancel class tonight, or does he want to continue?"

"Well, that's what I wanted to talk with you about. I thought we could step in and manage the class tonight since he will obviously have to cancel a future one."

"That's a good idea. I'm sure the university understands, but, at the same time, fewer class cancellations will be better for everyone involved."

"Exactly. Joshua gave me access to his roll and plans, so I will start class off and then allow you some time to lecture, and then I'll finish up the class afterward."

"That sounds wonderful."

"I assume you guys are still on topic."

"Yes, I did talk about the characteristics of a serial killer last week since it was on everyone's mind."

"Good. What better time to bring that in, unfortunately."

The door opened behind Dwayne, and the chime sounded. Both turned their attention to the young woman walking in. Lindy smiled to the woman. "I'll be with you in a moment," and then motioned for Dwayne to walk with her down the hall toward the back exit door. Opening the door, Lindy said, "I'll do my best to be there by five forty-five."

"Thanks, Dr. Ashley. I'll see you tonight."

Lindy closed the door behind him and then walked back into the reception area. "Hello, Maureen. How are you this morning?"

Maureen spoke quietly. "Not bad."

"Good. Come on back."

Bart heard his phone ring in his pocket, and, with one hand on the wheel, he pulled it out with his other hand. "Hello?"

"Hi, Bart. It's Jamie."

"Oh, Jamie, hi. Um, I'm on my way to class."

"Okay, I'll be quick. I'm sorry about running out in the middle of the night. It was one of my girlfriends, and she had just caught her finance in their bed with someone else."

"Wow, sounds intense."

"It was. I should've called you back, though, but I was trying to be a good friend. I'm sorry. Am I forgiven?"

Bart reached for his turn signal and then gently rolled his Tahoe into the campus parking lot. Finally, after an awkward moment, he said, "Look, Jamie, no apology needed. We're just good friends anyway, right?"

After a short pause, she responded, "Sure, you're right."

Bart turned off the Tahoe's engine and opened his door. He then opened the door to the backseat and grabbed his backpack while still trying to listen to Jamie on the other end. "Jamie, I'm at class now. Can I get back with you later?"

"Yeah. If you don't mind, I'm going to drop by later tonight and get some of my stuff that I left."

"No problem. See you later." With that, he hung up and placed his phone back into his pocket and jogged the rest of the way to class.

Chapter 54

Lindy went through the day with lightning speed and was surprised when she looked up at the clock and it was already four-thirty. The door chime sounded, and she stood up from her desk to go see who was there. Timidly she walked down the hall remembering she was alone since the temp girl left thirty minutes ago.

When she rounded the corner, she was instantly relieved to see Matthew standing by his partner, Steve Toowey. When Lindy's eyes met Matthew's, she immediately blushed. Matthew took a step toward her and, with a grin, said, "Hi, Lindy, how was your day?"

Lindy looked over at Steve's face and tried to read his expression. *Can he tell a difference today?* "Hello, Agent Toowey, Matthew. Everything's been fine today. Extremely busy though, which is expected on a Monday."

Matthew eyes locked with Lindy's. "Any more patients today?"

"No, just finished up with my last one a couple of minutes ago."

Steve asked, "Are you still up for tonight?"

All day long Lindy had been asking herself the same question. Yesterday at the hospital with Erin, the decision was made to continue with tonight's class as planned. There would be several FBI agents staked out all over campus waiting for Clay Barry to show. Everyone thought the chances were slim except Lindy. She had stated her professional opinion that Clay had crossed the line between reality and fantasy and he would show. Matthew had agreed with Lindy, and so, the plan was designed.

Matthew instructed, "There's a car downstairs that's ready whenever you are. It's a white Lincoln Navigator, and it'll stay two to five car lengths behind you. Once you get within three miles of the campus, another SUV, also white, will pick up the detail and follow you in."

"All right. I have a few more things to finish up here, and then I'll be leaving a little after five."

Matthew stepped forward and placed a hand on Lindy's arm and spoke softly. "Be careful. I'll see you tonight, and hopefully all of this will be behind us."

Lindy nodded. "Bye, gentlemen. I'll see you later, and you both be careful as well."

Matthew relaxed as Steve spoke, "We will, ma'am." And then both turned and walked out of Lindy's office.

Once Lindy sat behind her desk, she could no longer concentrate. Picking up one file after another, her mind barely registered what she was reading. After another five minutes, Lindy decided it just wasn't working, and she stacked up all the files and neatly placed them on the corner of her desk. Deciding there were some things to do that didn't require thinking, she hit a few keys on her computer keypad and printed off a schedule of tomorrow's patients. Looking over the list, she decided it was going to be a fairly easy day. Lindy pushed back in her chair and walked barefooted over to her file cabinet with her list and started pulling files. When she got to the last name, Rhett Dobby, she decided not to pull the file. The chances of him showing with his new wife weren't good. *Piece of shit, you will probably not call or will wait till the last thirty minutes to cancel,* she thought.

Closing the file cabinet, Lindy jumped and whirled around when she heard her phone ringing. She hurried over and pulled out her phone, which was in the top drawer, and saw that the number was Erin's. "Hi, baby sis. How's it going?"

"Oh, Lindy, I'm wonderful. I'm standing on a balcony overlooking Ft. Worth at the Ritz Carlton."

"Ritz? What are you doing there?"

"Well, Charlie decided to get us a suite for the night. He said it was too soon for me to go back home."

"Charlie's probably right. In fact, you don't have to. You can come and stay at my place and then look into selling and finding something else."

"No offense, Lindy, but I don't think I'm ready to go back to your place either."

Lindy didn't respond.

"I'm sorry, Lindy. Look, we're going to be fine!"

Lindy glanced up at the time and saw that it was five fifteen. "Erin, I'm going to campus tonight, to class."

"What? You didn't tell me about this. Why?"

Lindy took a deep breath and tried to explain quickly. "An officer will follow me there, and then I will be surrounded by officers all night, and then Matthew will stay with me again tonight."

"Well, that all sounds good, but isn't it still too risky? I mean, it almost sounds as if they're using you as bait."

"No, Erin. I'm doing this for Joshua. His mom might not make it through the night, and he has no one to cover for him."

"Lindy, are you sure? Can they really keep you safe?"

"I trust Matthew, so I'm going."

"Okay, but please call me after class when you're safely out of harm's way and with Matthew."

"I promise. Bye now. I love you, Erin."

Erin replied, "I love you too. Bye."

Quickly Lindy picked up her small purse and briefcase and then walked out of her office and locked up behind her. Officer Remini was already waiting for her at the end of the hallway by the elevator. "Hello, Dr. Ashley. You all set?"

"Yes, I'm ready."

The officer pressed the down button, and they were on their way.

Clay Barry was sitting on a two-by-four high above the lecture hall where Lindy was scheduled to speak tonight. Carefully holding on with one hand, he reached over and found the string with his other hand and pulled on it slightly to check the resistance. Seeing that everything was still in place, he climbed back down and onto another narrow walkway that led back to the attic door.

Once he was standing and had his full balance, Clay smiled as he looked at his handiwork. With his eyes, Clay continued to follow the string as it wrapped around another beam and then led to a small clasp. Earlier, the small metal clasp had been rigged to cause a slight accident when the string was cut. Looking down below, the second podium was standing directly below a dark metal light beam that weighed around fifty pounds. Clay figured that with the height and the weight of the beam, there was sure to be significant damage when the string was finally cut.

After a while Clay stopped smiling, and a tear rolled down his cheek. Carefully Clay took a seat on the small platform and waited. Looking at his watch, he had about another two hours to go.

Chapter 55

Lindy arrived at campus around five forty and carefully dodged all the students on foot and found a parking space close to the Dunn Building. Lindy turned off the engine and pulled the mirror down on her visor. Reaching in her purse, she found some lipstick and a brush. Quickly Lindy removed her ponytail and brushed her hair and then pulled it back up again into a low ponytail. Next she carefully applied her lipstick and noticed her hands were shaking. Pushing the bad thoughts out of her mind, she placed her keys and other items back into her purse and then grabbed her briefcase and got out.

Lindy noticed right away that the outside temperature was starting to change. It was now October, and the nights were starting to get a little cooler. Lindy looked around and recognized some familiar faces among the students walking to the Dunn Building. Some called out to her, and others just waved, but no one walked over and engaged in a conversation.

When Lindy was about twenty yards away she saw Matthew, and her heart skipped a beat. He was dressed in jeans, a Central University T-shirt, and a Texas Rangers baseball hat, which he wore backward. Matthew continued to walk past Lindy without even a glance her way. She watched as he slowly walked away carrying a backpack, and she tried to remain casual. He and several others were undercover, and the last thing she needed to do was to ruin their hard work.

Lindy walked up the last remaining steps and then made her way to Joshua's classroom. The man she had met earlier was already down front talking with a few students. Lindy walked down the aisle of seats and then up the five stairs to the platform that held two podiums. She smiled at Dwayne Moore and then set down her briefcase and pulled out her notes.

Several more minutes passed, and Lindy tried to act and remain calm. Dwayne looked her way and said, "Everything set and ready?"

"Yes, thank you. I'm ready when you are."

He called the class to order and then passed around the attendance sheet. After introductions were made, it was time for Lindy to start. Taking a deep breath, she picked up her notes and began. As she started talking, she felt her lips slightly trembling, but she finally was able to work through the anxiety and settle down. Looking around the room, Lindy looked for familiar faces and then found an empty chair to use as the focal point that would help her relax.

Another ten minutes passed, and Lindy was confidently walking around some and making eye contact with her audience. Every now and then, she would stop and walk back to her podium and glance at her notes. It didn't take long for Lindy to find agents Steve Toowey and Matthew Blake scattered among the students and dressed to blend in. It wasn't unusual to see older students on campus. Like most campuses around the country, the general consensus was that one was never too old to go back to school.

Matthew made eye contact with Lindy and smiled. Soon, she broke away and looked elsewhere as she continued lecturing. He continued to scan the area as she talked. After a while everything looked good and was running smoothly, and Matthew was finally able to relax a little. It was so hard for him to stay focused. Once Lindy relaxed, she was just as captivating as the last time he heard her speak. It was hard not to get drawn into her discussion and forget everything else around him.

Matthew continued to watch intently as Lindy walked around. As she stepped behind her podium, her hair glimmered under the light. He thought, *She is truly stunning.* It was at this moment that Matthew looked up toward the lighting that gave Lindy such a remarkable glow. Matthew found the two single light beams hanging from the ceiling. Each light was designed to shine upon one podium and its speaker.

When Matthew followed the second beam, he noticed a shadow and it moved.

Glancing at her watch, Lindy saw that it was six thirty-five. She needed to wrap this up in about another five minutes. Taking another look over her notes, she had about two more small topics to cover with three examples. Taking another step sideways, Lindy noticed someone standing up in the audience and looked up to see who it was. Instantly she heard a shout, "Move, Lindy, now! Move! Move!"

Lindy saw Matthew running toward her down the aisle, and she tried her best to register what he was saying. Instinct took over, and Lindy stepped toward Matthew, and then a loud popping noise sounded. Suddenly she was hit by an object that propelled her forward. As she landed face-first on the stage, she was barely able to brace herself with one hand before her face slammed into the hardwood floor.

Lindy looked up to a scene of mass chaos, as students were getting up from their seats and running around yelling. She slowly turned her head to see where the loud bang and broken glass sound had come from. Lying beside her ankle was a large black light beam, and she was surrounded by shattered glass. She heard a man's voice and turned back to see Matthew crouching down in front of her.

"Lindy, don't move! There's glass everywhere."

Lindy didn't respond as Matthew gently began to run his hand over her back and legs.

"Where did it hit you?"

"My back."

Matthew began to touch her lower back and then upper back. "Can you feel my hand? Does anything hurt?"

"Yes, my upper back, but I think I can get up. Just help me."

Gently Matthew placed both hands under her arms and helped her stand. As Matthew and Lindy shuffled their feet, they could hear glass breaking underneath. "Can you walk? We need to move off this stage, now."

Lindy nodded and started walking slowly as Matthew guided her down a few steps and into a small corner. He gently pressed her into the wall and then stood with his back facing her. His hand was on his gun, and, like a switch, Lindy was now able to hear everything else going on in the room. Students were screaming and officers and FBI agents were all running about and moving the students out of the lecture hall. Lindy looked up at the stage and saw what had happened. If she had moved a second or two later, she would probably be dead. Lindy began to sway side to side, and she thought, *Don't let me faint. Please God, don't let me faint.*

Matthew was speaking into a small microphone that Lindy hadn't noticed him wearing earlier. He was continually looking up and shouting. And then a shot was fired, and Lindy watched in horror as Agent Steve Toowey fell to the ground. In slow motion, she watched as more officers and agents ducked as shots rang out from above. Everyone was looking up.

Suddenly, Matthew broke away from Lindy, ran a couple of steps, and then turned around and fired several times. A piercing scream traveled through the lecture hall, and a large object fell from above and landed awkwardly on the seats below. Several law enforcement officers ran forward with guns raised, and one officer knelt down to check the man's vitals. As guns were slowly lowered, several people then ran toward Agent Toowey. Lindy heard several shouts of, "Agent down, repeat, Agent down."

Matthew turned back toward Lindy. "Are you okay?"

Lindy tried to speak but couldn't form the words. She desperately wanted to say, *Is that Clay? Is Steve okay?* She tried once more but stopped when Matthew grabbed her and pulled her close.

"Shh now. Clay's dead." Matthew looked into her eyes and spoke softly. "Stay here. I need to check on Steve. Nod if you understand."

Lindy nodded, and Matthew yelled out at someone. Immediately an officer came running and stayed with Lindy. She heard the female officer saying words, but nothing sounded like anything she had ever heard before. She continued to watch as Matthew kneeled down at his partner's body with his back to her. There were too many people, and Lindy couldn't see Agent Toowey.

Time began to stand still as people came and went from the lecture hall. Finally paramedics arrived with a stretcher, and they carefully lifted Steve Toowey and placed him on the small cot. Once the medical team had him securely locked in and had stopped the bleeding, they left quickly out of the building. Lindy looked for Matthew but couldn't find him. Somehow she had lost him in the commotion and sea of people. Suddenly something touched her from the right. It was Matthew, and he wore a very solemn face.

"I'm going to the hospital, and I want you to ride with me."

Lindy nodded. The female officer handed Matthew Lindy's briefcase and purse, and they started walking slowly. Matthew said, "Don't look at Clay, just keep moving."

Lindy heard but didn't listen. She stopped in front of Clay Barry's lifeless body, which hadn't been covered by a sheet yet. Blood oozed from his nose and mouth, and there was a gunshot wound to his chest. Beside him, photographers were taking pictures from every angle. Lindy continued to stare and watch. She thought, *This is the man who killed Melody and the young men. He spied on me for weeks and then killed Parker.* Lindy took a step closer but was stopped by Matthew's hand on her arm.

"Lindy, come on. He's dead."

Slowly Lindy peeled her eyes away from Clay and looked at Matthew. His eyes looked worried and tired. Reluctantly she began moving again, and they left the building in the direction of the hospital.

Jamie showed up at Bart's house wearing a nice dress with flip-flops. Bart opened the door for her to come in. "You look nice, Jamie."

"Thanks. We had doctors and nurses that came to our class today."

"Do you know what hospital you'll work at in January?"

"No, we get our assignments in November. What about you? Do you have some job prospects after you graduate in December?"

"Yeah, a few."

Jamie walked closer to Bart and placed her hand gently on his chest. "I missed you, and I'm sorry for running out like that."

Bart touched her hand and then pulled away and walked toward the kitchen. "It's no big deal."

Jamie continued to watch his back as he grabbed a beer out of the refrigerator. "Do you want one?" he asked.

Looking at her watch, she said, "Sure, it's only seven, but I have some work to do later tonight. How about you?"

"Nah, I'm finished. This semester really isn't that hard."

Jamie took a long swig of her beer. Bart did the same. When the two finally made eye contact, Jamie smiled. Bart grinned slightly and then took a step forward, placing his free hand on her bare shoulder. Jamie took another long sip and then set her beer down. Bart did the same, and then, with his other hand, he reached up and untied the strap at the base of Jamie's neck. Jamie let out a small gasp as Bart's hands began to move toward her neck and then down her exposed chest. In one swift move, Bart picked Jamie up and carried her to the couch.

"You're gonna be the death of me, Jamie."

Jamie only responded with kisses.

Chapter 56

Lindy paced around in the hospital waiting room. Once she and Matthew had arrived, Matthew left her in the hands of FBI Agent Pamela Meadows, and then she was whisked away to a room to be thoroughly checked out. Everyone around her continued to say things like, "You're so lucky," or "Just one more inch..."

Lindy was tired, and she had given her statement several times to many different FBI agents now, including Matthew's boss, Fred Copeland. She looked at her watch; it was ten o'clock. No word had been given yet about Agent Steve Toowey. Supposedly, he was still in surgery and they would all know something soon.

The room was full of agents and officers. Apparently, someone else was injured as well. Professor Dwayne Moore had also come to the hospital and stayed a little while. He had already spoken to Joshua Dobbs and didn't have the heart to tell him about tonight because Joshua had just lost his mom an hour earlier. Lindy agreed to call Joshua tomorrow and tell him of the events.

The media had shown up, and Lindy saw Stacy Bryan from Channel Nine news waiting patiently with her small crew in the corner of the waiting room. It didn't take long for the public to catch wind that Clay Barry had been killed on campus during a night lecture class. The media was in a feeding frenzy with all the juicy details flying around. Lindy watched as Stacy Bryan jumped up with her crew and then looked over at the double swinging doors as Matthew walked out with a doctor and a nurse.

The doctor and Matthew were quickly swarmed by agents, officers, and news crews. Matthew held up his hand toward Stacy and gave a hard stare, and she didn't shout out or ask any questions. Instead, she waited silently like everyone else while the doctor spoke.

"Steve Toowey made it through surgery and is listed still in critical condition. I will update his status tomorrow morning." He paused and looked toward Matthew and then back to his audience, and continued solemnly, "I'm sorry to report that Officer Glen Wright was pronounced dead at nine forty-five on the operating table. I'm sorry. We did all that we could do."

A young woman who was standing by several officers broke down and cried. Lindy had learned earlier that it was her fiancé who had been injured; they were to be married later on this year in December. A tear slowly slid down Lindy's face as she turned toward Matthew and met his gaze. Matthew turned to the doctor and thanked him and then walked over and led Lindy to a vacant sofa.

"I need to finish up some things, but I won't be long. Do you mind waiting on me a little longer?"

Lindy touched his hand. "No, of course not. I'll be right here."

Matthew saw Stacy Bryan walking their way and whispered, "Don't talk to the media."

Lindy nodded and then watched Matthew walk toward Stacy and exchange a few words. Stacy glanced over at Lindy with a frown but then agreed to walk away. Matthew turned back toward Lindy. "I'll be right back."

Lindy took a seat on the couch and attempted to read a magazine. As she flipped through the pages, a few minutes turned into thirty minutes until Matthew finally walked back over. He said, "Sorry. Are you ready?"

Lindy nodded and then stood as Matthew placed his hand on her arm and escorted her out to the parking lot. Getting into his Camaro and firing it up, Matthew asked, "Where to?"

Without looking at Matthew, she spoke quietly, "My house."

Matthew nodded and then turned out of the parking lot and headed toward The Palms. They drove in silence. Earlier the radio was announcing that the Night Killer was dead and began explaining the night's events. It was Matthew who reached up and pushed the button, turning it off. Pulling into Lindy's driveway, he asked, "Are you sure you want to stay here tonight?"

Lindy looked over at Matthew and found his soft, gentle eyes showing his concern. "Only if you stay with me."

Matthew turned off the engine and then leaned over and kissed her softly on the lips. The feel of his lips against hers set a fire that burned through her body, and she kissed him back deeply. Slowly she pulled away, and they both stepped from the car. Matthew reached for her hand, and they walked up the driveway holding hands. They entered to find an empty living room and a dark house. The furniture had been removed but not replaced. In a matter of a few short moments, Matthew had the place lit up and the security system set.

Lindy said, "I'm going to take a hot bath. There's a bottle of wine in the kitchen. Do you mind?"

"No, I was about to ask if you had any."

Lindy smirked. "Always. I try never to run out."

"Would you like for me to bring a glass back to you?"

Lindy nodded and then turned around and headed for her bathroom. When Lindy reached her bedroom, memories came flooding back of Parker jumping on the bed and wagging his tail. She closed her eyes briefly and then took another step and turned on the light to an empty bed with a new comforter and pillows. The room smelled clean, and it saddened her that she couldn't smell Parker's scent anymore.

Making her way into the bathroom, Lindy turned on another light switch and then sat down on the edge of the garden tub and looked around. The mirrors had been replaced, and there was no sign of broken glass anywhere. Slowly she turned on the water and adjusted the temperature.

She looked back up to find Matthew standing there with two glasses of wine and the wine bottle under his arm. She stood and walked forward. "Thanks."

Matthew placed the bottle of wine on the floor beside the tub and then sat on the edge and felt of the water. "Feels good."

Without thinking anymore, Lindy began to unzip the side of her dress with her free hand. Matthew stood up. "I'll give you some privacy. Yell if you need anything."

Lindy shook her head. "Stay. Take a bath with me."

Matthew wanted to ask if she was sure but was afraid she would reconsider, so he quickly agreed. Matthew placed his wine glass on the edge and then took hers from her and placed it beside his. They continued to look into each other's eyes for several moments, and then Lindy bent forward slightly and picked up the hem of her dress. She then lifted it up and over her head. Matthew watched and took a quick, ragged breath. Following suit, he removed his T-shirt and then unzipped his jeans and quickly pulled them off.

When he threw them to the side, Lindy took a step toward him and felt his hard chest. She ran her hand up and down slowly and watched as his chest rose with each breath. She stopped and took her hand away and then, with one swift movement, removed her bra and then her matching pink underwear. Matthew continued watching her as she then lifted her leg up and stepped into the garden tub. She eased down into the water without saying anything. Once she was submerged in the water from her chest down, she carefully picked up her wine glass. "Don't be shy. I won't bite."

Matthew smiled and lowered his boxers and then joined her in the tub. He decided to move to the opposite side to face her. With a slight tremble, Matthew picked up his wine glass and then eased his back down onto the side of the tub. Lindy took a sip of her wine and then lifted her leg and touched his chest with her toes. With a serious look on her face, she said, "Wash me, Matthew. Wash away everything until I can no longer feel or see pain."

Matthew placed his wine glass on the floor and then held her tightly in his arms. Slowly he pulled away and then grabbed the bar of soap and began to rub it several times in his hand to form a good lather. Finally satisfied, he placed the soap down onto the holder and gently placed his hands on her shoulders and began rubbing.

Matthew's hands gently moved up and down her arms, and then he moved them up to her neck. As Matthew continued to rub, Lindy tilted her head back and slightly moaned. Moving forward more, Matthew's hands ran down her neck, and Lindy let out a small gasp. Matthew moved closer and kissed her. He tasted salt on her lips and quickly realized she was crying. Gently Matthew reached behind her and lifted her to him. He placed her on his lap and began to stroke her back. "Shh, Lindy, don't cry."

Lindy raised her head off his shoulder and faced him. "Love me, Matthew, just love me." And Matthew did, again and again.

Jamie rolled over in Bart's bed when she heard her cell phone ring. Bart yawned and rubbed his face. In a sleepy voice he suggested, "It's eleven. Let it go to voice mail."

"I'm sorry, Bart, it might be my friend."

Bart rolled over and watched a naked Jamie get up and walk out of the bedroom. He wanted to act like he really didn't care, but he couldn't help himself. Getting up and out of the bed, he threw on some boxers that were lying on the floor. Making his way into the living room, he could hear Jamie talking.

"What? Why? I don't understand."

Bart watched her and could tell she was irritated and upset by whoever was on the other end. Bart eased his body up against the door frame and watched as Jamie continued talking and pacing around absolutely naked in his living room. A smile crept across his face as he watched her. Jamie turned toward him and mouthed, "What?"

Bart just motioned with his hands at her naked body. Jamie rolled her eyes and shrugged but continued talking into the phone. "Do you want me to leave now?"

Jamie turned away from Bart so she wouldn't have to see his disappointment. She listened as the man on the other end continued. Suddenly Jamie felt her phone being snatched away, and she turned toward Bart, who had already stuck the phone to his ear and was listening to the man speaking on the other end.

Jamie shook her head and said, "Don't."

Bart walked away toward his bedroom and then slammed the door and locked it, leaving Jamie in the living room yelling at him. In a deep, strong voice, Bart said, "Hello, this's Bart. Whoever this is, you're interrupting some very valuable fucking time for Jamie and me!"

"Who the hell are you?" an angry male voice responded.

"I said I'm Bart. Who the hell are you?"

Bart didn't wait for a response; he looked at the phone to see whose name was displayed. "George Williams, do you know how late it is? Leave Jamie alone tonight. She's all mine tonight, and I don't intend on letting her go. In fact, I don't ever intend on letting her go!"

The man on the other end said, "I see. Just give our little Jamie a message for me, would you do that?"

Jamie was still cussing up a storm on the other side of the door when Bart replied, "Sure, George, I can give her a message."

"Tell her to forget the internship."

Bart frowned. "Internship? What the hell? Did you-" the phone went dead. Angrily, Bart threw down the phone and opened the door to a still very naked Jamie, who was now pounding on his chest. Grabbing her wrist with one hand, and with his other arm scooping her up, he carried her back to his bed. Jamie was talking on and on, but Bart wasn't listening. Instead, he placed his mouth to hers and began kissing her. Finally Jamie stopped fighting him and put her arms around him and kissed him back.

Bart leaned up just long enough to say, "You're mine, do you hear me, Jamie? You're mine. I think I love you, you crazy girl!"

Jamie looked into his eyes and then whispered, "Oh, Bart, how can you love me? I'm damaged."

Bart shook his head. "No you're not. Stupid for getting involved with a doctor, but other than that, you're perfect," and then he leaned down and began to show her just how much he loved her.

Chapter 57

Tuesday morning

Lindy opened her eyes at six o'clock the next morning. She looked at the nightstand and wasn't surprised at the time. No matter the circumstances of the day or night before, her body just wouldn't let her sleep any later on a weekday. Lindy closed her eyes and thought about the night before. She remembered Matthew's soft touches and gentleness with her. *It was beautiful and wonderful*, she thought. Slowly she rolled over to face the man she was falling in love with—her dear Matthew.

Rolling over, she opened her eyes and was startled. The other side of the bed was empty. Leaning up on her elbows, she looked around and stopped when she found a note folded on the nightstand on his side of the bed. Slowly she leaned forward to a sitting position and closed her eyes. She thought happy thoughts and tried to block out her insecurities, and then finally she opened her eyes and grabbed the note.

Rearranging the pillows, Lindy leaned back and pulled the sheets up over her naked body and opened the note to read.

Lindy,

Good morning, sunshine. Last night was too good to be true. I still feel like I dreamed it all as I write you this note. I got up at four and couldn't go back to sleep. Something about this case keeps nagging at my brain and won't give me peace. I made some breakfast for you, pancakes and cut-up fruit. I covered it up and left it on the stove. Please stay put until I return. I shouldn't be long. I'm just going to the office for a little while to check some things. I should return by nine o'clock at the latest. Let's plan on lunch, or better yet, takeout, and I can feed you in bed.

I'm all yours baby,
Matthew

Lindy smiled and reread the letter three more times. With a spring in her step, Lindy jumped out of bed and went into the bathroom. Wrapping her hair up, she took a shower without washing her hair. She thought about a bath but didn't dare jump in again anytime soon without Matthew.

Smiling, Lindy stepped under the hot water and began to wash. Several minutes passed, and she tore herself away from the hot water. The warmth had felt good to her back. It was a little sore this morning from the fall. Or was it from making love all night with Matthew? Either way, Lindy finally turned off the water and stepped out.

Drying off, she walked into her closet and looked around. There weren't as many clothes hanging as before, but that would change soon. She thought, *What to wear for Matthew?* Five more minutes passed as she finally settled on a navy knit dress with short sleeves and loose knit tie belt. The dress was casual, and it made Lindy feel comfortable as well as sexy.

Barefooted, Lindy went to the vanity and undid her hair clip. Carefully she brushed her long black hair until it was smooth and straight. Then she applied some light base makeup and mascara. She debated on the lipstick color and then finally chose a soft pink shade. Looking once again in the mirror, she felt it was just enough and all she needed. She smiled at her reflection and thought, *No need for blush, I'm glowing!*

With happy thoughts, Lindy left the bathroom and made her way toward the living room, but she stopped suddenly when she heard a noise. It wasn't Matthew or human. It sounded almost like a dog. Lindy began to tremble slightly, and she slowly walked over to the back french doors. She thought, *Is my mind playing tricks on me?* Closing her eyes, she reminded herself Parker was dead. Hearing the noise again, Lindy opened her eyes and found a Jack Russell sitting at the door and hitting the glass with his paw. She said in a soft, sad voice, "Parker?"

As Lindy started unlocking the door, she saw someone stand up from the corner of the porch and her throat tightened. Soon she was able to let out a deep breath when she recognized who it was, her ex, George. "Good morning Lindy. I got you a new dog—well, a puppy—one that looks just like Parker when he was a pup."

Lindy closed her eyes briefly and then opened them up and met his stare.

"Well, are you surprised Lindy?"

In a voice that sounded distant, she asked, "By which, you or the puppy?"

George smiled. "Both."

"Yes and yes."

George walked over and gently reached out and hugged Lindy. "I heard what happened, and I was able to get in touch with Erin. She told me all about Clay Barry, your patient."

Lindy tilted her head to the side. "She did?"

"Yes. Why didn't you tell me there was a mad, psycho patient after you? I could have protected you. You could have come back to my home and stayed with me. It's like a fortress."

Lindy looked at George's face and body language. She thought, *Is he for real? Didn't I see him at the hospital and tell him I had Matthew?* Lindy continued to think, and then George interrupted her thoughts and asked, "Well, what do you want to name the little fellow? Maybe Parker the second?"

Lindy tore her eyes away from George and looked down at the little puppy. He was jumping around at her feet and wagging his short tail.

"Never mind naming him now, let's eat! I got take away at your favorite coffee shop around the corner from the house."

Lindy looked at George's hand on top of hers and then glanced back down at the puppy. She thought, *Something's not right.* In a quiet voice, Lindy said, "Okay, George. The puppy can wait."

George smiled and then took her hand and stepped into the house. Thinking of the pancakes Matthew left for her she suggested, "Let's eat outside. It's a nice morning."

George shrugged his shoulders and walked over to the table and chairs and pulled a chair out for Lindy. Taking a seat she reached for the cup of coffee and took a sip. Placing the cup down on the table, she noticed she was shaking. Calmly, Lindy placed both hands in her lap and squeezed them together. *All this is too much. George showing up, a new puppy, like Parker can be replaced?* She thought.

Matthew was sitting at a desk in room A150 and reading over the files once again. He thought, *Why do I still think Clay Barry is not the killer of the university students?* He continued talking to himself, this time aloud, "Yes, Melody's clothing was in his home, and he clearly pulled the trigger on Steve and Officer Wright and had set the trap for Lindy. But why doesn't he seem right?"

Fred Copeland walked into the conference room. "I didn't plan on seeing you this early. I thought you were going to take the morning off and come in this afternoon?"

"Yeah, well, plans changed."

Fred sat down and looked at Matthew and noted the files he was reading. He was a good judge of character, and it didn't surprise Matthew when he asked, "What's wrong?"

"Clay Barry's not the right height for the stabbing of Jaycee."

Fred rubbed his face and pinched his nose. "Okay, so there is about what, two to three inches difference from Dr. Johnson's assessment?"

"Yes, but how many times has she been wrong since you've worked with her?"

Fred pondered. "Once, but it wasn't her fault. There was a dirty cop, and he fudged the test results."

"So, what now? We searched Clay's apartment, and there was nothing in there about Lindy or the three male students."

"Yes, but we found his computer in his vehicle. There's several videos of Lindy from her home and office. And don't forget her sister is also in them."

Matthew tapped a pen on the open file. "Okay, I'm not arguing whether he was obsessed with Lindy, but why cut up the three male students? According to Lindy, she didn't know them and had no personal contact with any of them."

"Are you suggesting he didn't act alone?"

Frustrated, he answered, "I don't know."

Fred changed the subject. "I talked to the doctor a few moments ago. Nothing has changed on Steve's condition."

"I talked to his wife, Karen, this morning. She should be at the hospital by now. She has both girls with her. I think she drove all night."

Fred Copeland stood up. "Keep working on it. Maybe something else will rear its ugly head. I'm going back to the hospital and I'll talk to Karen."

"What about the media? They keep reporting the Night Killer is dead."

"I know. Unofficially he is."

Matthew got his point. "Okay, how much time do I have?"

Fred looked at his watch. "I set up a news conference for two, so if you're going to find something, find it soon—with evidence to back it up. If not, we have evidence that is screaming Clay Barry. Oh, and Matthew..."

"What?"

"Don't forget there are over fifty eyewitnesses who saw Clay Barry pull the trigger on two lawmen."

"Yeah, don't remind me."

Fred put his hand on Matthew's shoulder. "Sometimes things continue to nag long after the crime has been solved. One thing is for sure, Clay Barry was a psychopath. Does it really have to make sense that he stabbed three male students that had no connection with Lindy? And, Melody was injured and abducted beside a dead Andrew Mitt. Last, we have evidence that Clay Barry killed her."

"Yeah, I know. Maybe he just wanted to scare Lindy and somehow in his twisted mind thought she would run to him for protection."

"Now you're getting somewhere. I'll see you at two."

"I'll be there."

Matthew glanced at his watch after Fred left. He only had six and a half hours before the news conference. Closing the file, he got up and headed out the door.

Jamie woke up to kisses on her neck. Looking at the time, she screamed, "Oh shit, I got class in thirty minutes. I gotta go!"

Bart released his hold on Jamie and watched as she jumped out of bed naked once again. As she entered the bathroom, he called out to her, "Jamie, when are you going to tell me who the hell George is?"

With a toothbrush in her mouth, she peeked around the corner and shook her head. "Not now, I can't be late."

Bart lay back onto the bed and sighed. Last night was wild. Neither of them left the apartment, and they ate leftover pizza and drank beer while listening to his iPod plugged into his sound system. After he heard the water shut off, he climbed out of bed and walked in the bathroom. "Look, baby, it's important. He seemed—"

"What?"

"I don't know, like he was threatening you."

"What did he say? No, never mind. I have to go, and it was a mistake for you to talk to him."

Bart was moved to the side, and Jamie squeezed by. She went to the closet and grabbed one of his T-shirts and slipped it over her head. Next she went in search of her underwear and found them lying under her dress. Pulling them on she said, "I thought I left some shorts over here."

Bart pointed to the dresser drawer. Jamie walked over and opened it up and found her shorts and pulled them on. Next she put on a flip-flop and looked around. "Where's my other one?"

"In the living room. I'll get it."

Jamie pulled her hair up in a ponytail and then grabbed the shoe in Bart's hand and slid her foot into it. "Thanks. I gotta go now. I'll come right back and then we'll talk. Okay?"

Bart shrugged. "I have class at ten. Meet me for lunch at the rec center."

Jamie ran back over and gave him a kiss on the lips and then turned around to leave. Bart grabbed her arm and pulled her back, kissing her back deeply. He slowly pulled back. "That's better. Go now before you're late. I'll see you at noon."

Jamie smiled and turned around, and Bart smacked her on her ass as she ran toward the door with her backpack.

Chapter 58

George looked at Lindy slowly picking away at her food. He asked curiously. "Are you okay? You look pale, Lindy."

"Oh, no, I'm fine," she lied. "I'm just a little worn down with everything that's been going on."

"Are you taking your medicine?"

"Yes."

Picking up his fork, he asked, "Getting enough sleep?"

Lindy felt her face flush and then quickly picked up her fork and took a bite. After chewing, she said, "This is good. Thank you."

"You welcome! I'm just sorry we didn't do this more often when we were married."

"Oh, George. We shouldn't reflect back on what we should and shouldn't have done."

George put down his fork. "Why not?"

Shaking her head she blurted out, "Why are you here?"

George stared back at her dumbfounded. "Because I'm worried about you. You could've been killed last night."

In an exasperated voice she said, "George! I have moved on. You have moved on, oh and by the way, I met Amber, is she a nurse as well?"

"Amber? She's nothing! When did you meet her?"

"Oh never mind, it doesn't matter!" Quickly she stood up and pushed her chair back as the little puppy ran toward her and began jumping at her feet. Slowly Lindy bent down and picked him up and began petting him gently. Soon she continued, "George, I think it's best if you left. We need to move forward without each other from here on out."

George slowly stood up. "Are you sure this is what you want?"

Lindy met his eyes with confidence. "Yes. This is what I want."

George looked hard into her eyes and saw nothing. Next he laid down his napkin on the table and frowned. Lindy turned around and opened the french doors and walked straight toward the front door with George following in behind. When she opened the door, she saw Matthew's shiny Camaro pulling into her driveway and she smiled.

George stepped outside and watched as Matthew exited his vehicle. He paused for a moment and then turned around and faced Lindy one last time. He opened his mouth to comment but decided at the last moment to keep his thoughts to himself.

Matthew walked up the driveway and stopped in front of George. "A little early for a visit don't you think?"

"I'm just leaving" and he turned around and walked down the driveway without looking back.

Epilogue

Christmas Morning

Lindy hurried in the house with Berkley right on her heels. He was barking and sliding on the wood floor trying to get traction as he ran past Lindy to his dog bowl. Lindy smiled as he finished lapping up his water and looked at her with dark, imploring eyes when he spotted no food. "Oh no, you already ate. Besides, I'm sure you'll get lots of scraps today."

Lindy grabbed Berkley up and headed toward the living room in search of Matthew. She found him placing a gift under the tree. "Ha! I caught you! I thought you weren't going to snoop."

With a guilty face, Matthew rushed over and took her in his arms. "I lied. So when are we going to open presents?"

"When Steve and the girls and Charlie and Erin get here, which should be in the next five minutes. Now come and help me." Lindy swatted Matthew on the rump, and he slowly released her.

"You don't need my help. The kitchen looks perfect, everything's ready. I just need to fire up the grill."

"So go and fire it up, will you?"

Matthew smiled. "Just for you."

Lindy froze and her face drained of color. Matthew realized instantly what he had said. "Oh, Lindy, I'm sorry. Come here."

Allowing him to embrace her, she closed her eyes and then quickly opened them. She pulled away and smiled back at him. "Quit getting me sidetracked. Go light that grill."

"Yes, ma'am!"

The doorbell rang, and Lindy and Berkley hurried to the front door to let their guest in. Opening the door, Lindy was taken aback when she saw a delivery man holding yellow roses.

"Dr. Lindy Ashley?"

"Yes, that's me."

"The flowers are for you. I'll need you to sign first."

Lindy took the electronic notepad and signed her name. "I didn't realize you guys worked today."

He took the notepad back. "Oh yeah, three hundred sixty-five days a year."

Lindy tried to form a smile. "Well, have a Merry Christmas."

"You have a Merry Christmas as well, thanks."

Lindy watched him leave and then closed the door back. She looked at Berkley. "Berkley, why don't you bark at strangers?"

No answer.

Lindy walked in the living room and placed the roses on the coffee table and then picked up the card. Suddenly she noticed her hands were trembling. She thought, *Don't be silly. Clay Barry is dead. He couldn't have possibly sent them.*

More memories came flooding back. *What happened to that box on the back porch? Whose hair was in the box along with Melody's that was left at her office?*

She pushed the thoughts out of her mind. Slowly she opened the note and read the handwritten message:

Doc Lindy,

I just wanted to say thank you for all of your help. Have a Merry Christmas and Happy New Year.

Sincerely,
Luke James

Lindy reread the message, and a smile slowly formed on her face. Luke had made such progress over the last few months and she was more determined than ever to help him overcome his multiple personality disorder.

"Who was at the door?"

Lindy looked up and handed Matthew the note. After reading it, he said, "That was awfully nice. But how did he know to send them here to the ranch?"

Lindy looked at Matthew. "Good question. I don't know. But I'll see him in January, and I'll be sure to ask him."

Matthew put down the card and pulled Lindy toward him. "I can't wait any longer! Open my present."

Lindy was about to say yes but the doorbell sounded, and Matthew groaned. Lindy smiled at him as she heard Erin's voice call out, "Hello," after letting herself and Charlie in.
Matthew pulled Lindy to him for a quick kiss and then let go so she could hug Erin and Charlie.

Under the tree, Berkley was poking his head around among the presents, and Matthew bent down and spoke softly so no one else would hear, "If you eat that ring, I'll send you to the pound."

Berkley looked up and licked Matthew in the face. Lindy yelled out, "Oh, I think he's starting to like you."

Matthew looked back at Lindy. "It's a good thing."

Jamie was in her bedroom lying on her bed when Becky came in. "When you leaving to go to Bart's house?"

"Soon. I was just thinking, why don't you come with me? It'll be fun."

Becky shrugged. "Who'll be there?"

"His family, his friend Luke, and Luke's girlfriend, Jennifer."

"I don't know. I would feel like a fifth wheel around you guys."

Jamie swung her legs off the bed and stood up. "Becky, you already lied to your parents and told them you were spending the day at Robby's parents' house. I don't know why you did that."

"I just didn't want to be around my family today and have them look at me with sad eyes and pity."

"Okay, but I don't want you here all alone. Please come."

Becky shrugged again. "I'm going to get a shower and I'll think about it."

"Well, let me know soon. I'm going to be leaving in thirty minutes."

After Becky disappeared into the bathroom, Jamie sat down on the bed and gazed at her open closet. She had debated on what to wear now for a good hour. Scanning the hanging items, something shiny caught her eye. She stood and walked over.

Kneeling down in the closet, Jamie moved a pair of old flip-flops that were lying in the back corner. Picking up the second one, Jamie saw the knife. Immediately she frowned and shook her head. "I don't plan on using you anymore!" Slowly a smile spread across her face as she thought about Bart and knew down deep in her heart that he was the one.

Becky approached from behind. "Who are you talking to?"

Startled, Jamie threw the flip-flop back over the knife and spun around. "No one, just to myself. I have no idea what I'm gonna wear today."

Becky frowned. "I forgot my house shoes. I hate stepping out of the hot shower onto the cold floor." Becky walked toward her looking for her shoes. "And I don't know what you're fussing about. You could wear a brown paper bag and look wonderful. You always have and always will."

Jamie quickly handed Becky a pair of her house shoes. "Here, wear these."

"Thanks," Becky answered and turned to walk away.

Jamie asked once more, "Please go with me today."

Becky turned back around and faced her best friend. Nodding her head, she smiled. "Okay. Just for you."

Here is a sneak preview…

Breathless

Chapter 1

Early Sunday Morning 3am
October 2010
Gatlinburg, Tennessee

Melissa slowly opened her eyes and looked around a strange room. Blue curtains were hanging down from a circular silver rod and she instantly knew she was in a hospital. Slowly she leaned upward and looked over her body. She was covered with a blanket except for her arms and hands lying on top. Noticing tape, she studied her hand and noticed she was hooked up to an IV. Melissa followed the line from her hand and saw that it was attached to a bag of clear liquid hanging on a metal stand. Leaning forward more she felt sudden pain exploding in her head so she stopped and gently laid back down on a pillow.

Closing her eyes she tried to concentrate on what happened that landed her in this condition. Suddenly a memory flashed before her eyes and she remembered driving her husband's Mercedes and sliding down a steep hill and hitting a tree head on. She was alive, but what about her husband of three years, Quinton Pierson?

Melissa fought through the pain and forced herself to sit up in the bed. Carefully with her other free hand she stretched over her chest and pressed the nurse's call button and patiently waited. Looking over her body, nothing looked broken. Next she moved her toes and then felt her head for damage. On the left side of her head she found bandages and her hair felt gritty. Looking downward and pulling on her long blond hair, she was finally able to look at her once golden locks. Now they were spotted with brown matted crust. She thought, *Is that blood? Did I cut myself?* She once again felt around her head and the bandaged area was sore. Just then a hand touched the curtains and then pulled them back and revealed an older woman who was dressed as a nurse.

"Oh sweetie, don't touch your head. Here, you need to lie back down."

The nurse took another step and gently pushed Melissa back onto the pillow. She stated, "I'm Shea, you're in a hospital. Do you know who you are?"

"Yes, Melissa Pierson, but that's not important now, where's my husband? Why isn't he here with me?"

Shea looked away slightly and then stated, "Let me get the doctor."

As the nurse turned around, Melissa yelled out, "Wait... is he okay?"

Shea turned back around with pleading eyes and said, "The doctor will be in shortly and he can answer all your questions."

Melissa opened her mouth to respond but couldn't form the words and the nurse left.

A tear rolled down Melissa face as she closed her eyes and prayed, "Dear God, oh please, please let him be dead."

Chapter 2

Seven Years Earlier
Friday Night
October 2003

Melissa Brock Mason was sitting on a couch eating popcorn and surrounded by her two best friends, Alison Roeske and Amanda Fields. They were watching Julia Roberts' movie 'Sleeping with the Enemy' for the first time. Even though the movie came out in the 90's none of the girls had seen the film before, until now. Tonight was unusually quiet for the campus of Ole Miss. The Rebels were playing an away football game on Saturday at Auburn, a college in Alabama. Most students had left for the weekend for the big game and only few remained.

The movie ended and Alison was the first to comment, "You have got to be joking! Why didn't she kill that SOB the first time he hit her."

Melissa threw popcorn at Alison. "If they did that, dummy, it wouldn't be a movie!"

Amanda chimed in, "Yeah, the movie would've been over after five minutes."

"Guys I know, but I'm just saying, she's the stupid one for not killing him to begin with."

Melissa thought about the statement and then said, "You're right. She should have planned his murder and then taken all his money."

Alison smiled, "Exactly! Did you see that house on the coast? What a house!"

"I would have drugged him and then when the other guy wasn't looking, pushed him overboard into the water. He wasn't wearing a lifejacket" stated Amanda.

Melissa added, "Yep, then she would have remarried and they would have lived happily ever after in his house."

All the girls giggled.

"So what's the next movie?" asked Amanda.

Melissa answered, "'Pretty Woman', it's an all night marathon starring Julia Roberts."

Amanda exclaimed, "Yes! I love that movie!"

"You would and you-" but Melissa stopped in mid sentence when the doorbell rang.

Everyone got real quiet and looked around. Suddenly Melissa burst out laughing, "What? It's a crazy man at the door?"

Melissa got up off the couch and made her way over to the front door of their home, Phi Delta. Turning around once she could see how the girls were slowly following her but at the same time smoothing down their hair and checking out their outfits. Melissa rolled her eyes and thought, *that didn't last long, Mr. Killer just turned into a hopeful date.*

Melissa reached out and twisted the antique door knob just as the doorbell rang again. Pulling open the door she was immediately greeted by a stranger, who happened to be Mr. Tall, Dark and Handsome. Opening the door wider for her girlfriends to see, Melissa asked, "Can I help you?"

The six feet two, sandy brown haired, brown eyed gentleman replied, "Yes. I'm looking for Melissa Mason."

Melissa quickly stated, "She isn't here. Can I take a message?"

The tall stranger looked into her blue eyes and stated, "That won't be necessary Melissa."

Taking a step back she said, "Excuse me?"

The stranger looked past her and over toward the other college girls and said loudly for all to hear. "Is she normally like this? Because if so, I'm gonna have to call her grandma back and say 'thanks, but no thanks.'"

Melissa's face turned a shade red and she blurted out, "What has Nana gone and done now?"

For the first time the stranger smiled and then he held up a picture of a beautiful blond haired blue eyed girl wearing a designer dark green dress standing in front of a spiral staircase of a house built in the mid 1800s in Jackson, Mississippi. Amanda and Alison quickly made their way over and Alison grabbed the picture, "Pretty! Melissa, I haven't seen this one before."

Quinton Robert Pierson met Melissa's gaze and smiled.